The
Sacred
Stone

Emma Batten

First published in the UK by Emma Batten

ISBN 978-1-9995820-9-8

Printed and bound in the UK.

A catalogue record of this book can be found in the British Library.

Edited by Maud Matley

Further editing and proofreading by Rosemary Bartholomew

Cover painting by Lisa Jane Castle/Hunter

With love to my son Zac, whose antics once inspired me to write a novel!

With thanks to Lisa Jane who fully embraced the Saxon theme when she researched flowers for the era while creating this fantastic cover painting.

Thank you to Anne Petrie and Maud Matley for advice on historical details, as well as valuable feedback.

About the Book

Thirteen years have passed since readers left Eadlyn on Romney Marsh, reunited with the golden cross. In my sequel to *The Pendant Cross,* I return to the story of her family, as well as introducing new characters.

Aldington now takes centre stage as the main location featured in the novel. The current village has evolved a short distance north-west of the church, and is famous for its connections with smugglers, but my tale takes you a thousand years before those times. My 7th-century settlement is entirely fictional and sited near the church we see today. Old maps show an Archbishop's Palace in this area during Saxon times, but this came later, so does not feature. Aldington appears to have been a wealthy area back then, with vast tracts of land across Romney Marsh.

Nearby Lympne features as a setting. In those times it was not a parish in its own right but was in the Manor of Aldington. For the sake of the story, it is ruled separately. Manor is an ancient name for an estate ruled under a lord. It would include a village and land.

Readers will also return to Lyminge briefly. As in *The Pendant Cross*, the village was established with a stone church (excavated in 2019) and a minster.

The remains of the Roman fort on the hillside below Lympne can still be viewed today. Did these ruins slip and fall during an earthquake? There is no evidence, but my inspiration came from a line in the book *Hythe Haven*, by Duncan Forbes.

This is my second novel written in the 2020/21 lockdown and I would like to thank my loyal readers who have given so much support during this time. With many sales opportunities lost, I would like to thank the team at Salts Farm, near Rye, and Frances Esdaile, from The Chocolate Deli in Hythe, for being amazing at selling books on my behalf.

Thank you to Maud Matley and Chris Dann for reading and editing my first drafts of the book, and Rosemary Bartholomew for further editing and proofreading. Also, thanks to Anne Petrie and Liz Hopkins for checks prior to printing.

The following websites have been valuable resources for learning about the Roman fort near Lympne and Aldington Knoll, a rise in the land overlooking Romney Marsh:
  www.historicengland.org.uk
  www.favonius.com/romans/lympne
  www.hythehistory.org
  For a less cluttered view of the landscape I like to look at maps from the late Victorian period on:
  www.maps.nls.uk

The Characters

The metalworkers of Aldington and their families:

Arlo Smith
Eadlyn – his wife
Clover & Cym – her children by Todd Leatherman
Alfrid & Hilda – the younger children in the family

Penton Smith– Arlo's older brother
Megan – Penton's wife
Eadric, Alfreda & Osric – their children

The Thane of Aldington and his family:

Thane Cenric
Otha – his wife
Edina – their daughter, the eldest of three girls

Godwin – brother to Cenric

Cate of Lympne – sister to Cenric and Godwin
Brice of Lympne – her husband

Father Theodore – close confidant of the thane

The main characters in Lyminge:

Alwin Leatherman
Bertana – his wife
Cedric – Alwin's older brother
Ora – Cedric's wife

Janna – Eadlyn's sister

Mildrithe – a wise woman living nearby

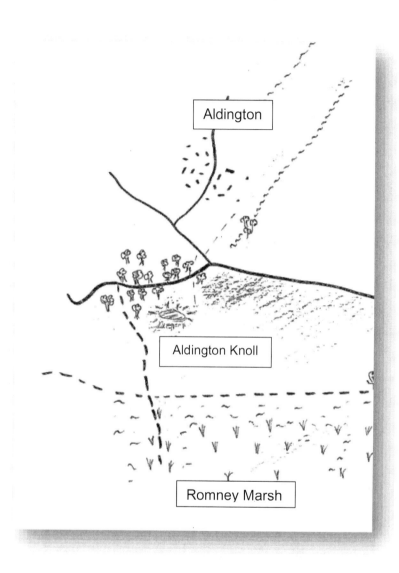

Aldington

Aldington Knoll

Romney Marsh

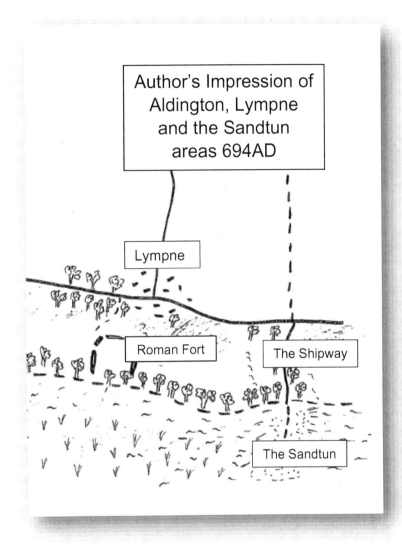

Author's Impression of Aldington, Lympne and the Sandtun areas 694AD

Lympne

Roman Fort

The Shipway

The Sandtun

Prologue
Circa 278 AD

"Who is that woman lurking in the trees by the shoreline?" the navarch, or squadron commander, asked his deputy. They were standing on a steep hillside overlooking a vast tract of tidal water. Behind them, great oak stakes loomed raw and unsightly, while blocks of reclaimed ragstone were beginning to form the foundations of a new fort.

"The woman?" the trierarch repeated. "She is nothing but an old Briton who comes from her hovel on the hilltop to gather shellfish."

"She rambles on about this or that, bothering my men as they work." The navarch stepped over a taut rope marking out the extent of the fort.

"In another week, the men will have exhausted the supply of stone they can retrieve from the flooded base," the trierarch replied. "It becomes harder every day to extract it. If she follows them to the new site, then I'll have her removed." He fell in step beside his commander as they strode with ease over the rough ground to approach the men labouring in the shallows.

"We have done well!" The satisfaction in the navarch's voice was clear. He tilted his aquiline nose towards the sun, nodding in appreciation at the clear sky. The weather in Britannia was notoriously temperamental. "The old shore fort has given us enough stone for our foundations, and I expect delivery of new ragstone any time."

His pleasure in the day was short-lived, for as they reached the band of trees between sea and hillside, the old woman stepped forward, stumbling in her eagerness to approach the stately Romans. Words flowed quickly, like water over rapids, becoming jumbled in her zeal to be heard.

"Lord, sir, captain... You must listen. Give me a moment, just a moment, of your time. I've been watching and listening, and it worries me to see the seabed unsettled in this way. I had a feeling – it came to me again and again – I had a feeling that something was amiss. It terrifies me. Now my fears have come to pass: there is a holy stone, from a time before our own Christian God was accepted. It must lie in peace with the sea creatures and the saltwater washing over it. If it is disturbed... taken from its place... then I dread what is to come."

"A stone, you say?" The commander's voice had a hint of laughter in it. "We are in need of stone, as you can see." He strode onwards, the old soothsayer now at his heels.

They passed through the trees to find the labourers revealed – at least a score of them, most up to their muscular calves in tidal water. Four of them were hauling a stone onto the shore, pulling seaweed, twigs and muddy sand with it.

"We've a fine piece here," one of them called. "At least seven palms in length. It would do nicely as a door plinth."

"A plinth?" The woman's wail flew along the coastline, and up the hillside to the foundations of the new fort. She snatched at the sleeve of the navarch. "This is the one! This is the one which must be returned to the sea! Take the others. Take them all. But if this stone is disturbed, it will bring sorrow to those who have been part of its removal."

The men who had finally dragged it free of the water faltered, looking to their superiors for guidance. The world was a dangerous place; none of them wanted to tempt fate.

Noting their hesitation, the wizened old woman spoke again: "It will bring troubles twice over: first for those who are a part of moving it now, and again when many centuries have passed. By that time, the fort will have fallen, and others will seek to use it for their own gain."

"Remove your hand from my clothes," the navarch snapped, seeing the filth under her nails, and smelling her sour breath. "Move aside or I will have you locked up for this impertinence." Turning to his men, he added, "Take no heed of this woman. If she bothers you again, do not hesitate to lash her with a leather."

Chapter One
The Sandtun, Romney Marsh, Kent
694 AD

The night was still. The sun had dipped below the horizon, with the last of its light still casting a mellow glow across the sky. Seabirds settled on the beach and on the low-lying scrubland near the lagoon. Insects no longer hovered above the marshland, filling the air with the click of their wings and the hum from their throats. Arlo shifted on the rough grass – a miserable mattress under a thin blanket of wool. Above him, a canopy stretched out from his cart. He pulled the blanket tight against his body and listened for the tide lapping on the beach, but it could not be heard. In his memories of the Sandtun, he had never known it to be so quiet: for there to be no breeze pressing on the reeds lining the ditches, and no ripples on the water in the lagoon.

Something was not right. Was it just that he missed the soft curves of his wife? Arlo allowed his thoughts to stray to Eadlyn in the main tent with the younger children and her daughter, Clover. It had been fourteen years since they had first met here at the seasonal trading settlement, and almost thirteen since he took her as his wife. They had been good years, he reflected.

He missed her and would like to be lying beside her now, but that was not what worried him.

Rolling onto his front, Arlo lifted his cover then crawled out from the low tent beside his cart. He stood, eyes roaming over the contents of the cart. His intricate metalwork had sold well over the past three days, but there were still plenty of valuable goods stored here. It was the usual habit for the craftsmen to sleep with their wares. Any number of desperate thieves might be lurking on the wooded hillside, ready to sneak down after dusk and raid the camp.

Arlo listened, his eyebrows knitted together in a frown. He heard the snores of his fellow traders in their tents, and the occasional grunt. But these were the sounds of humans. Where were those caused by nature, he wondered? He reached into the cart, feeling for his shoes, then slipped his feet into them. The ground he walked upon was sandy, with coarse grass and ragged weeds. On arrival at the Sandtun, he found driftwood and debris from high tides had been strewn upon it, but anything which could be burned was cleared away on the first evening when the area came to life. The moon was full, lighting his way to the beach, and before long Arlo stood with his back to the camp, gazing out over the lagoon.

There were three boats at anchor. They had journeyed from Francia, a land of men less skilled than those from the Kingdom of Kent. These men came to buy from the craftsmen on the Sandtun, returning with quality goods to keep or sell in their own country. All was well: the boats slumbered on the saltwater; the seabirds shifted as they sensed his arrival but decided to ignore him; the moon shone steadily on the land and the air was warm. Yet Arlo remained uneasy.

Again, the metalworker listened. Forty summers had passed since his birth. He had watched the elders of his village grow old and die; he had seen babies and children fail to survive into adulthood; he had held his own first wife as she faded and died in childbirth, taking the baby with her. Not much surprised him and little disturbed him. Arlo worked hard and was content with his second wife and family. When feeling uneasy, he waited, wondered, and considered what could be wrong.

Then it happened.

There was a sensation as if an excess of Cousin Fremund's mead had been consumed. Arlo's frame was sturdy and strong, yet his body seemed to sway, and his head swam. The ground moved beneath him, giving an odd feeling of being firm underfoot but resting on an area of soft, shifting earth. He turned to see the tents in the camp shudder, the horses rise on their hind legs, and the carts lurch.

The land was no longer silent.

The birds roosting in the trees, and within the undergrowth by the edge of the marsh, rose as one great squawking mass. The tent poles gave way, heavy material draping itself on those who were waking, causing shrieks and shouts, along with high-pitched wails from children and babies. Horses screamed their distress. Wolves lurking in the wooded hillside howled.

The movement of the earth did not come and go in a flash, such as forked lightning does; it rumbled on like thunder. At first, Arlo was rooted to the spot, if only for a few seconds. Then he ran, bounding up the beach and onto the rough ground. Just once he paused to look behind him, expecting to see the sea boiling up. The scene caused fear to rip through his body: a tidal wave was curling up, gathering water and strength, before moving forwards. It had already tossed the boats aside, as if they were nothing but dried leaves on the surface. Now it was seconds away from breaking on the beach.

He uttered a great guttural roar. "The sea! The sea!" Arlo bellowed. "Hold onto your children and the old people. Stay strong together."

The faces of the traders turned towards him, lit by the moonlight. "Stay strong," he repeated, while the ground still shuddered beneath his feet. "Hold on!"

Arlo was nearing Eadlyn and their children now. She clutched the young ones to her. With no time to flee the Sandtun for the hillside, he could only hope to reach them in time and daren't look back, for it would slow him down. As he launched himself towards his wife and children, the ground stopped moving. They came together in a mass of four bodies, seawater hitting Arlo's back then pouring past them. They swayed, falling to their knees as the water turned to wash past them again, but remained on their spot of the Sandtun.

Now the water was up to their hunched shoulders, and Arlo feared they could not stay firm if another wave came. He looked back. "It was the only one." The tension eased a little, but he knew this was just the beginning: horrors would be revealed in the aftermath of both earth tremor and the tidal wash.

Still clutching Alfrid and Hilda, Eadlyn began to pull herself to her feet. "But one was enough to flood the Sandtun. There will be no more trading this year." Her hair shone pale gold, threaded with silver, in the moonlight. It fell in a thick plait down her back. There were fine lines around her eyes, but at that moment she was still the young woman Arlo admired as first another man's wife, then as a widow.

"What happened?" Nine-year-old Hilda's voice was low. "The ground was… it was moving… shaking." She was drenched and beginning to shiver. Pushing aside her mother's grip on her, Hilda rubbed at her limbs. Her hair, the colour of summer wheat, lay in sodden waves down her back. The shape of her slender body could be seen under her light shift.

"I've known nothing like it before," her father answered. He glanced at Eadlyn.

"There are no stories passed down," she said, thinking of songs told at the fireside; it was their way of keeping the past alive.

"It was as if the earth trembled and settled in a different place," Alfrid reflected. He was serious beyond his eleven years. Healthy and muscular, the boy was almost as tall as Eadlyn and, like his sister, Alfrid was pushing aside his mother's arms.

In those seconds after the tidal wave, the family were bound together, thinking first of their own safety. The shock of the water hitting the Sandtun had silenced the screams coming from those around them, but now they became aware of the high-pitched wail of a child, the movement of bodies, and the calls from one person to another. They saw tents floating on the water or pulling at tethers. People were clutching at one another; some appeared to be fighting against the sheets of their shelters.

"There are people trapped within their tents," Eadlyn said, horror in her voice.

"They will soon be freed," Arlo replied. "Better a small child is caught for a moment than washed off the Sandtun onto the marsh. The creeks have filled beyond their usual limits and it will be dangerous to be there."

"But we will go there, if it is to save a life," Eadlyn observed.

All this was played out under silver moonlight reflecting on the water and highlighting the figures of about sixty people who traditionally came to the Sandtun during the longest days of the year. The great wave had passed, but the area of slightly raised land remained under water. Reaching to just below the knees of the adults, drifting back and forth with a gentle swell, it was enough to make movement awkward.

Alfrid was the first to step away from the family group, "We must go to the cart, Faeder. We may be able to save some of the metalwork. Nay – we *will* save it. I worked hard at it!" The cart was listing in the water, having been pushed from its usual spot. Now on the slope leading to the flooded marshland, it was in danger of slipping further from their reach. They saw it move a little, and Alfrid took more steps towards it. From the side of the cart, the tent under which Arlo had sheltered was swaying about on the water, like a sodden cape.

Arlo grinned, despite the horror unfolding around them. His son was both serious and hard-working. "We'll go to the cart, once I am certain your modor and sister are safe."

"We are safe," Eadlyn reassured him. "Just cold and shaken. If you can steady the cart, we'll gather what we can and put it in there."

"I doubt we'll be able to pull it through the water." Arlo started wading after Alfrid. "But we must try our best, and if we can calm the horse then her strength will be welcome."

"Modor," Hilda pulled at Eadlyn's arm. "I can't see Clover, I thought she was sitting with Eadric by the fire." They turned towards where the cooking area had been, scanning the area for Eadlyn's eldest daughter.

"She *was* with Eadric and Osric. I saw them after the wave," Eadlyn replied, referring to the sons of Arlo's brother. "I checked they were safe, and I saw the three of them…" But now only Eadric's younger brother was there, wrestling with the small tent. Eadlyn frowned, "I thought she was…"

"I haven't seen her," Hilda's voice was small. "I was looking and didn't see her… afterwards we fell over."

Eadlyn was wading towards where Arlo's nephews had set up their small tent. "Osric! Where are Clover and Eadric?"

He was only thirteen, too young to cope alone with what had happened. Osric glanced up from the tent, which was pulling away from him on the water. "I don't know," he responded, turning back to the tent in an attempt to haul it to their cart.

"I'll send Alfrid to help you," Eadlyn called. They were only boys but Alfrid was strong and together they could salvage something. Then she faced her younger daughter and said: "I don't know where your sister is. I was mistaken; Clover isn't here."

Before the words had left her lips, there came a new sound, causing everyone on the Sandtun to turn and face the hillside. It was a great rumble reverberating through the land.

21

Chapter Two

"What's this?" Eadric's hand strayed from the tempting curve of Clover's breasts to the heavy cross nestled between them. His forefinger felt the dome of a stone set in the centre of the pendant and moved across the decorative scrolls. He frowned, already knowing it to be something of value.

"It was a gift from my faeder," Clover told him. Her slim hand was tracing the lines of his muscular chest; she felt wiry hairs slip between her fingers. Her desire for him was strong, and before harvest time they would marry.

"Your faeder?" he queried. Todd of Lyminge had died not far from where they now lay on the hillside above the Sandtun. At the time Clover had been a child of six years.

"Aye, he had it with him when he passed away, and Modor kept it safe." Her hand moved down to his navel, tracing the line of fiery red hairs.

Eadric, a young man of twenty, had been labouring hard to provide a home for the woman he longed to marry and his yearning to be alone with her was as powerful as always. However, he was curious about the pendant, now secreted away under Clover's tunic. "Why do you keep it hidden?" he asked.

"Because of its value," she told him. "Even the thane's wife has nothing as impressive, and people would wonder where it came from." Clover loosened the leather lace and lifted the pendant over her head.

Assuming the cross to be made of bronze, Eadric was stunned to see a glint of gold. Frowning, he held it up to the evening light as best he could and turned it to catch the soft rays. The red of the stone shone. "Why wear it now?" he asked.

"We always bring it to the Sandtun," Clover told him. "It came from here, or at least we believe it did."

"Your faeder hadn't mentioned the cross before he died?"

"Nay. We knew nothing of it, but Modor says it came from here. She believes he found it."

"I would love to know its history," Eadric said, as he reached forward and placed the leather over Clover's head, then leaned in to kiss her.

Eadric of Aldington was the son of Arlo's brother. Having moved to Aldington with her mother and brother when she was seven years old, Clover became Arlo's stepdaughter. The two families lived and worked side by side, children running freely between the homes, and meals being taken together in the open air during the summer months. Yet the friendship between these two young people went beyond those years, as the families had journeyed to the Sandtun for generations, meeting on a yearly basis to camp by the lagoon and sell their wares.

That evening, before the sun set and the fires burned to glowing embers, Clover and Eadric had left the Sandtun for the steep hillside where the ruins of a Roman fort stood. Many of the grey stone walls rose far

23

more than twice the height of a man. In the shape of an irregular arc, they covered a vast area of the sloping hillside. Three sides of the fort were enclosed by these walls and the fourth was open to the tidal marshland, once a sheltered bay. The ruins, deserted three centuries earlier, still held many signs to show how they had appeared in their prime: circular bastions, doorways and windows were still in place, albeit with roofs long-gone and the tops of the walls now ragged. Inside there were clues to show how the Romans once lived: floor tiles, stone foundations, and holes where wooden posts had once supported internal walls.

Saxon man had no respect for the skills of the Romans. They reused the walls as shelter for their sheep and cattle, then stood before the blocks of cut stone, debating on whether it could be put to better use for a church at the top of the escarpment. They took wood and stone, once part of the buildings within the great walls, and the tiles used on the roofs. As the seventh century drew to an end, the fort remained weather-worn but, despite some stone and wood-gathering forays, it remained largely untouched.

Clover and Eadric had explored the fort many times in their youth. That evening, they had scrambled up the hillside, barely looking at the gateways, towers and slim lines of Roman bricks between the worked ragstone. Its grandeur was lost on them through familiarity. They used the fort as a place to find seclusion and had settled on a grassy knoll just above the walls. The ground was dry, and they lay close, comfortable in each other's company while admiring the far-reaching views across Romney Marsh. Vast areas of tidal creeks, marshland and fertile soil now blended together in a palate of soft green and purple, as the sun dropped behind the hills in the far distance. The sky, fast losing its richness, was streaked in pale yellow and grey.

Eadric let the pendant cross nestle against Clover's skin. His lips were on hers, and his fingers tangled in her long golden hair, when the ground beneath them began to shudder.

The vibrations shook the clay soil on the hillside, travelling through the ground and taking a grip on the foundations of the ancient fort. They shook up the ribbons of water, working their way through the earth to the numerous springs. The land was steep, with the tremors coming from the depths of the earth. Every block of stone, rounded flint and thin Roman brick, shuddered but stayed firm in its place.

"What's happening?" Clover whispered. She and Eadric were now sitting, their fingers entwined and knuckles white.

"I don't know; but it will pass. At least I hope so."

"It must..."

They had to believe it would end.

A gust of warm wind swept up the hillside, and they became aware of a great squawking in the air, as the roosting birds flew from the trees lining the base of the escarpment where hills met marshland. Amidst the panic from the birds, wolves howled from the wooded areas and, further away, the horses at the camp on the Sandtun screamed.

Then the ground began to slide.

For a moment, they were mesmerised by the great wall of the fort which appeared to be moving away from them. Seconds passed, and their instincts took over: moving in unison, Eadric and Clover turned to clamber up the hillside, knowing they needed to distance themselves from the fort and the might of its stone walls. Taking no heed of the streams, nettles or stones, they half-crawled, half-ran.

"It's stopped," Eadric gasped. "The shaking has stopped."

"I thank God for that," Clover replied. "But something has unsettled our land and the walls..."

She stopped speaking as a new sound ripped through the night. Centuries-old mortar started to crack, and parts of the fort began to topple. Stones fell, one after the other, as the ground beneath the walls shifted and twisted into new positions. Although the earth no longer quaked, it had been too much for the steep hillside with its layers of slick clay-earth. The ground continued to slowly slump, taking the fort with it. Down the escarpment it slipped, towards the flat marshland and, as it did so, the stone blocks fell.

"We have to keep moving away from the fort." Eadric pulled at Clover's arm. "The weight of the stone is more than we can imagine. If it slides further, it may pull us down."

But the summit of the hill was wooded, and Clover looked up to realise a new fear. "If the land falls from the top, it will take the trees with it."

"You're right." Eadric glanced to the east. "We must move towards the Shipway, so we are no longer above the fort. The land may be slipping there, but it will not be dragged along by great walls of stone. It will be safer."

They moved like crabs along the steep hillside towards the ancient Shipway – a track leading from the top of the hill to the Sandtun. Before long, they had put a fair distance between themselves and the toppled fort. With their arms wrapped around each other, Clover and Eadric stood to survey the scene. The ground beneath them was stable, and the stones of the fort still fell, not as an occasional thud, but a steady stream of movement.

The sky was light where the sun had set to the west, and above them the moon was full, but the creeks, bent willows and reedbeds of Romney Marsh were hard to decipher. Clover gazed towards the Sandtun. "Did it happen down there?" she wondered. "Do you think the ground shook?" She pulled at Eadric and continued with more urgency in her voice: "We must get back there." Now they were safe, her mind was on her family and his.

Eadric didn't reply, neither did he move with Clover. Instead, his eyes were fixed on the Sandtun area, and he frowned, trying to make sense of it all.

"What is it?" Clover felt the panic rise within her.

"I don't know. I can't understand it. The lagoon… it's changed. There's more water." Eadric studied the area, not wanting to say the words until he was sure of it. "I think… I think the Sandtun has flooded."

"Flooded? It can't have done." But Clover knew the sandy bank well. She understood it was vulnerable to the sea and only truly dried out over the summer months. If the ground had trembled there, as it had done by the fort, then of course the sea could have been stirred up, and the area overcome by the huge volume of water held within the lagoon. The sky was darkening rapidly, making it difficult to judge if the Sandtun had suffered from the tremor, or if the suggestion of flooding was nothing more than a trick of the light.

"We must return." Eadric began to move down the hillside, stumbling on the ridges and tussocks, while pulling Clover with him. "I left my brother!" His voice rose, as he pictured Osric, overcome by the tide, struggling to save the metalwork and tent on his own.

"They'll be looking for us... We didn't say... Didn't think of them..." Clover's reply was disjointed as the result of their actions swamped her. "We only thought of ourselves."

"We weren't to know," Eadric reasoned.

The terrain was difficult underfoot, with hillocks and streams. They splashed through muddy areas and followed narrow tracks formed by wild animals, before searching out the gap in the trees and entering an area of greater darkness. The Shipway was steep, the ground strewn with rubble and rivulets of water.

"We must slow down," Eadric cautioned, knowing that any injury to himself or Clover would only hinder the efforts of the traders to save their wares and flee the Sandtun. As he spoke, the ground gave a slight tremor and there came the long, low creaking sound of the earth giving up its hold on the roots of an ancient oak tree. Eadric gripped Clover's arm, pulling her backwards, up the Shipway track, and as he did so, there was an almighty splintering, crashing clamour as the oak smashed down on a beech tree to rest on its strong branches.

They paused, waiting for the tree to settle, hearing the smaller branches break and fall, and the leaves rustling. Neither of them spoke. The Shipway was the only track to the Sandtun, and it was best to be sure that the beech could hold the oak before they walked beneath it. After a few moments, it seemed as if all were quiet and the tree would stay as it was, perhaps until the winter storms caused further damage, or man chose to take the prized wood. Clover was about to pull on Eadric's arm when a movement caught her attention and she turned to look through a gap in the trees on the far side of the track. There was someone standing there, on a low hillock.

"Look," Clover whispered to Eadric. "Bertana!"

Chapter Three

Bertana of Lyminge stood on the lower reaches of the hillside, not far from the lagoon. She had finished with her lover at that moment when the earth began to shudder, and now watched as the Sandtun camp was deluged by a tidal wave. The air was filled with the roar of the sea; it was thick with the scent of salt and seaweed. Standing not far from the marshland and lagoon, yet free from danger, elation filled Bertana. She felt glorious. She *was* glorious! Nature was heralding a new beginning! Throwing her arms upwards, she wanted to bellow and shout – to pitch her voice against that of the sea.

Instead, Bertana turned her attention to the man who stood beside her. He was half a head shorter, his frame muscular and legs a little bowed. His nose was good and straight, lips full and he was blessed with a head of thick brown hair. It was these features she had noted when selecting him for her purpose. There were few men who could match her height; her husband was shorter than her and had a face like a rat.

He was a fisherman, this man who stood at her side, his muscles prominent from managing the nets and handling his boat. Only minutes beforehand, Bertana had thought him to be a fine specimen of a male, while he had believed himself to be a lucky man. His desires had just been sated for the third evening since the traders had arrived, and there was the promise of another two or three days ahead of them. The fisherman had no name, or none that was of any interest to her. He did not know that her fascination with him went no further than contriving that he planted his seed within her. It was when he had responded to her subtle probing and told of the seven children fathered by him, that his worth to her became apparent. Bertana did not want to dally with a man from her home village, nor anyone in the locality. Once this man had fulfilled her needs, there would be no reason for her to make the annual trek to the Sandtun. She would be at home tending her son.

Now he almost cowered at the side of the woman so often admired. The trembling of the earth had subsided, and the tidal wave passed, but the fisherman was struck with anxiety. His family lived in the village at the top of the hill, and he knew they would be terrified. The air filled with the gut-wrenching cracking sound of a tree falling in the region of the Shipway. It dropped, taking with it the branches of another.

Another tree fell, closer to hand this time. An odd sound rumbled in the distance and the fisherman frowned, turning towards it, although his view was obscured by both the darkness and the trees lining the Shipway. "It is Lympne – my home on the hill!" There was panic in his voice as the words tumbled out. "Do you hear it? Lympne is falling. A terrible thing has happened." The thunderous vibration continued. He began to sweat, fearing for the lives of his family.

"Go, go to your wife," Bertana barked at him. It was nothing to her if the settlement fell. She wished him no ill-fortune and intended to present him with some good leather shoes, or a jerkin crafted by her husband, but his home and family meant nothing to her. "Go now to your wife," she repeated. "She will be frightened."

"I cannot leave you…" The fisherman hesitated, feeling some need to take care of the magnificent woman who had just offered him such pleasure. He should have been racing up the hillside with no thought of this woman from Lyminge.

"Cannot leave me?" Her eyes flashed with scorn. "I am done. There is nothing more you can offer me now. No doubt my husband is fretting over his leatherwork, and with good reason. I must go."

Bertana took a step away from him. Despite her harsh words, he was torn between concern for his family and desire for the woman whose voluptuous breasts had him mesmerised. He reached out to touch her before the opportunity had passed, and she allowed his fingertips to trace her curves. It was the least she could do, when hoping and praying he had given her the child she had been waiting for since her marriage nearly fourteen years ago. But while allowing him this final delight, Bertana's attention was on the Sandtun, fully understanding the carnage awaiting her.

Nothing more passed between them. By the time he spoke again, she had moved further from him and his words of adoration went unheard. The fisherman turned his back on the Sandtun, the lagoon and the woman, then scampered up the hillside and onto the track.

It only took minutes for Bertana to cross the rugged hillside, before stepping through the gap in the trees to the Shipway. It seemed as if a spring had broken through the stony track; the ground was wet underfoot,

32

yet it had not rained for days. An uprooted tree was balancing on another and there was little choice but to pass underneath it. Bertana glanced upwards, seeing the risk but believing herself to be invincible. The ground gave a slight tremor and the tree shook, casting some twigs upon the woman's shoulders before the danger was passed.

Near the Sandtun, the sounds of the traders could be heard as they called to one another. The trees obscured her vision and, at this distance, the voices were disjointed – a word or two here, a shout, a cry. There was a wide bridge of strong planks spanning the tidal creek which flowed from the lagoon and inland along the base of the escarpment as far as the Roman fort. Even before she stepped on the planks, Bertana felt the cool seawater soaking through her shoes, then licking at her ankles. The bridge had stayed in place, for it was well-built, but water now flowed across its surface, reaching her strong calves. *It will be dangerous to guide the horses and carts over here at night. But we will be left with no choice – the Sandtun will have to be abandoned.*

On reaching the far side of the bridge, the results of the catastrophe were now displayed in front of her with the moon lighting the scene. Nothing was still: tent coverings swayed on the water; pans, half-burned firewood and wooden bowls knocked against one another on the gentle swell of the tide; men and women moved about as they secured their belongings and checked on the safety of loved ones. Amongst it all, millions of silvery water droplets cascaded from items lifted from the sea and shone atop the saltwater as it flowed around the objects in its path.

Taking a few steps forward, Bertana scanned the area, searching for her husband, Alwin. She hoped he was saving the leatherwork rather than concerning himself too much about her absence. A figure caught her attention – a woman moving away from the others and wading towards her. A moment passed and Bertana, realising it was Eadlyn, felt some of her feelings of glory slip away.

There were several reasons to dislike the woman approaching her – none of them fair. Elder-Modor, her husband's mother, had once mentioned amongst her ramblings that Eadlyn had been Alwin's first choice as a wife. It had been a matter of practicality, of course, as she was his brother's widow, and he felt a duty to care for her. Nonetheless, as a new wife, it had irritated her to have Eadlyn's presence nearby. Within a year of Bertana marrying Alwin and moving to his home in Lyminge, the woman who had spurned his offer to take care of her had found herself a new husband. Another year passed and news came that she had given birth to a healthy son. Two years later a daughter followed. In this time, Bertana's monthly bleed came without fail, and her stomach remained flat. The children grew up, and Eadlyn was once more at the Sandtun, with her family around her. A couple of times a year they visited Lyminge to see both her family and that of her first husband. Sometimes Arlo of Aldington came – a tall man, sturdy and good-natured, with clear skin and blond hair. If Bertana could have used him to father the much-wanted child, then she would have thought herself fortunate.

This wasn't the time to dwell on all that Eadlyn was blessed with. Bertana spotted the grey horse belonging to her husband, with Alwin at her head, guiding the frightened beast towards their cart. She moved on again, conscious of floating debris sliding past her lower legs, and intending to ignore the other woman.

"Bertana?" Eadlyn spoke, her voice clear but anxious. "Have you seen Clover? She's not here and we think she is with... I mean she must be with... Eadric."

"I took a walk on the hillside, to the east of the Shipway," Bertana replied. "I saw no one."

"So, you escaped the worst of it," Eadlyn remarked.

Bertana noticed that Eadlyn was wet through. Even her thick golden hair was nothing but a dark rat's tail, flat against her back. "I can only pray no one has been injured." Her words were kindly, but they were no more than that. She cared nothing for her fellow traders, and only for the silver coins collecting in the pouch hanging from her husband's belt. "Alwin needs my help," she said, taking a step forwards, as if to pass by.

At that moment, they both became aware of movement behind them. Someone else had crossed the bridge. "Modor! Is that you?" Clover's voice rang out.

Bertana turned to see Clover and Eadric, hand in hand, wading towards them.

"I thank you, God." Eadlyn raised a hand to her chest and looked up to the heavens. She took a step forward, then another, before reaching her daughter.

Bertana gave a sneer and continued on her way to her weasel-faced husband.

Chapter Four

On the Sandtun, the traders laboured with seawater washing about their calves. In salty depths it carried part-burned wood from the fires, shells and seaweed from the high-tide line and small items not yet salvaged. Most likely a leather pouch holding precious silver sceattas, the knife used to fillet the fish, and the pretty box inlaid with brass would be washed to the edge of the marshland to settle with a layer of sand and shells over them. By the time the following summer came, they would have been covered further with dry reeds, grass, and the sand swept over by winds coming off the sea. Nature would hide the effects of the tidal surge – which would become a story to be passed on through the generations.

Arlo kicked at a length of cloth which was intent on wrapping itself around his ankle. It released its grip and drifted away. All his attention was on soothing the horse before harnessing her to the cart. At this moment, his world was reduced to the wagon laden with their sodden tent, blankets and his metalwork, along with other items they had recovered. His daughter, Hilda, worked beside him. There was little chance to consider the fate of others on the Sandtun, and certainly no opportunity to offer any help.

Nearby, his son, Alfrid, toiled with Cousin Osric. Arlo would have liked to do more to assist his brother's son, but it had taken all his efforts to save their own belongings and coax the distressed horse back to the cart. The best he could do was to spare his son to help Osric. Every so often, Arlo glanced in the direction of the boys and was satisfied they were managing the best they could.

"Hilda, come closer and stroke her neck," Arlo beckoned. "If you comfort her with your voice, I pray she'll stay calm." He placed his hand on his daughter's shoulder, feeling the sodden wool of Hilda's shift as she stood beside him, and raised her slender arm to rest it on the dark-brown mane. *Poor child, she has not complained once, but is cold and wet through. The small children have suffered the most from the water and we have nothing dry to offer them.* He felt her shiver.

Taking his time, Arlo began to encourage the horse to back towards the cart. With Hilda remaining at the beast's head, he fastened the straps to the metal loops on the shafts. The horse remained steady, trusting her master, and he was thankful.

"Now you must coax her to walk," Arlo instructed the girl. She was too young to be responsible, but there was no one else. "I will have to push from the rear; the ground is soft, and the wheels will have sunk from the weight of our tent and metalwork."

"We can do it, Faeder," Hilda insisted. "Modor will be back to help soon, and Clover too."

"Your modor must take her time and tread carefully," Arlo reflected. Then he added, "She will, of course. She is sensible, and I'm sure Clover and Eadric are safe wherever they are." He clasped his daughter around her shoulders. "Try not to worry about them; there will be news soon."

"I'm not worried," Hilda answered, her voice pure and clear. "Clover wears the pendant cross. Her own faeder gave it to keep her safe – I am sure of it."

Arlo smiled to hear his daughter's faith in the golden cross. It had been with Todd of Lyminge when he was killed on the hillside above the Sandtun and was believed to be an item of religious decoration, most likely belonging to a person of high status within the church. The reason Todd had it on his person could have only been told by the dead man. His wife and family were none the wiser. For the women of the family – his wife, her daughter and Hilda – the cross with its red stone at the centre held a great deal of fascination and they trusted that it kept them safe. The men displayed a mild curiosity but endowed the pendant with none of the powers bestowed by the women.

Thoughts of Todd and their meeting at the Sandtun fourteen years beforehand remained in his mind as Arlo began to wade to the rear of the cart. His hand rested on the horse's flank and then on the wooden shafts. It was as he positioned himself to push that Hilda spoke again, her voice high as she called to him.

"Faeder! They are here! Modor has Clover, and I can see Eadric, but he's going to Osric."

Arlo felt some of the tension ease from his body. No one knew what dangers were on the escarpment or by the creek between the Sandtun and hill. It had been with some trepidation he had given Eadlyn his blessing to go to search for her daughter.

"They came from the Shipway," Eadlyn announced. "There are trees fallen."

She had voiced another of Arlo's fears and now he asked, "Will we be able to take the cart up there?" It was the only suitable track from the Sandtun to the hilltop.

"I don't know," Eadlyn replied. "The fallen tree they spoke of was on the lower reaches and held up by another. There could be more." She was moving along the side of the cart, knowing that it would take all their strength to help the horse pull it free from the soft ground.

"We'll have to trust in our luck." Arlo now turned his attention to his wife's daughter. "Clover, if you could stand with Hilda, the horse will need persuading to move on. She is frightened, as are we all."

"I'm sorry, Faeder." The young woman was subdued. "You needed me and, worse than that, Modor left you too."

Arlo shrugged, "You are safe. That is all that matters to us. Let's start moving and there will be time to talk when we are on the road to Aldington."

He began to push on the back of the cart. The horse, trusting them to do their best for her, strained against the harness, at first with no luck. Great wheels began to move out of the ruts, and they all surged forwards. Arlo and Eadlyn slipped, but pressed on, unable to ease the pressure for a moment, lest they should slide back and the cart become further embedded in the soft ground.

Not only was Arlo responsible for his own family, but his brother's sons were at the Sandtun to sell their own selection of metalwork. Eadric, who had stolen some time with Clover, was twenty years of age, sensible and hard-working. His brother was only thirteen – too young to be left to cope with the aftermath of the tidal wave, and only his younger cousin to help them. *Thank God, Eadric and Clover were found, and we can leave the Sandtun as one family.* The words of a short prayer ran through Arlo's mind*: I thank you, Lord, for keeping our family safe when our land was unsettled by things beyond our control. I pray that you look upon us with love and guide our feet across this swamped land, to the safety of the hillside. Amen.* As they approached the highest point of the Sandtun – a track leading from the Shipway towards areas of raised land amongst the marshes – Eadric could be seen with his cart and the two younger boys. He turned and raised his arm to acknowledge his uncle. Arlo lifted his own hand in response. "They are ready to leave with us," he said to Eadlyn.

"Aye. I thank God for that," she responded. "If their modor felt the tremors, she'll be fearing for their safety."

"I hadn't thought." There had been so much to do, and as quickly as possible. "I wonder…" But he was too busy pushing the cart, and thinking of the Shipway track, possibly blocked by fallen trees, to imagine the extent of the vibrations which shook the land.

"The fort has fallen," Eadlyn told him. "Clover was there."

"Of course." Arlo recalled the rumble from the hillside. It seemed like an age ago, but most likely little time had passed since he had stood on the beach and been the first to witness the tidal surge. "We heard it begin to fall, but I thought nothing of it." He considered the extent of the building: the height and width of the walls. "They were lucky to escape from it."

40

"They were," Eadlyn replied. She moved her hand slightly, so it touched against his on the rear of the cart. "I'm sure they'll tell us about it later."

Arlo nodded. They needed their wits about them and already his thoughts were on the creek separating the Sandtun from the Shipway. It would be full to the brim, there was no doubt about it. But his fear was that the bridge had not held firm. "When you found Clover, were you able to cross the creek?" he asked.

"Aye, although we had to feel our way over the bridge. The water was around our calves."

"I thank God for that. I would not take the horse through if the planks had been washed away." But the crossing would still take some care. With the bridge submerged and in the shadow of the trees, one wrong move would send the horse and cart toppling. It would mean certain death to the loyal animal.

They moved as part of a trail of skilled workers in leather, metal, wood and clay, who found the track at the highest point on this area of land before shifting into position. It would be foolish to rush, and no one could move any faster than the man in front. Arlo had been formulating a plan in his mind and, as they neared the bridge, he called out to the young woman leading their horse, "Clover, go to Eadric. The pair of you must stand on either side of the bridge, to ensure we guide the horses through the centre. The younger boys can lead their pony. Your sister and modor will take ours."

"I'll go now, Faeder," Clover said. He saw her give the horse a pat on her neck, then move away. She exchanged a few words with Eadric and the pair of them slipped ahead, separating before they reached the creek.

41

The bridge spanning the water was wide and solid, and their journey across proved to be uneventful. For those leaving the flooded Sandtun there was both a sense of relief for having saved so many of their belongings and escaping relatively unscathed, coupled with trepidation for what was to come. The steep track leading to the top of the hills bordering Romney Marsh was now rising ahead of those who had hastily abandoned their camp. Where the moon had previously lit their way, they were now plunged into darkness, beneath a canopy of lush leaves from overhanging trees. The progress was slower than before: The Shipway track was treacherous with loose stones, slippery clay earth and the prospect of fallen trees.

The upturned oak, which had fallen in front of Eadric and Clover, remained in the grip of the neighbouring beech tree. Beneath it, carts moved with the men and women urging the horses to pick up speed. The family of metalworkers continued with no knowledge of the dangers ahead; they could only listen for the call from those trudging up the Shipway before them. Luck was with them – the track was free of debris, save for a few small branches, easily cast aside, and soon they were coming out onto the open hilltop.

The Sandtun traders bade muted farewells at the Shipway crossroads as they moved away in various directions, returning to their home villages a couple of days earlier than expected. They would return next year, when it would, most likely, be as if the earth tremor had never happened. On the Roman road leading to the west, the brothers, Eadric and Osric, took the lead with their small cart. Alfrid returned to his immediate family, who followed behind.

"I thank you, son," Arlo clasped the boy around his shoulders. "You helped your cousin and together you saved many of their belongings."

"What happened?" The boy was weary and spoke with none of his usual vitality.

"I don't know. The earth trembled like I have never known it; perchance the elders of our village will recall such an event from the past."

"And the sea – will it return to its place?"

"I believe so. It is in the hands of God," Arlo declared. "Who knows what plans He has for Romney Marsh? It will be for your sons and grandsons to learn."

"Tomorrow, or whenever I can be spared, I will go to the knoll and see what has become of that land," Alfrid suggested.

His father smiled to hear some of the boy's enthusiasm return. "Aye. You'll see a lot from up there."

In time, the village of Lympne was behind them, and the trees thinned. They skirted the edge of the hillside, with Romney Marsh no more than a mysterious blackness below them to the south. Sometimes they paused, hopeful of the moonlight giving a clue to the extent of the flooding but the night was at its darkest, and the marsh too distant. Before long, they turned, putting their backs to the escarpment. The landscape was now one of rolling hills. In fields, cattle and sheep woke to turn their heads towards the sounds of human activity, then returned to their slumber. Alongside the pasture, almost-ripe heads of wheat, oats and barley swayed a little in the breeze, while nearby peas and beans sprawled along the furrowed earth.

The village of Aldington was situated on a rise in the heart of these fields, Winding streams passed nearby, and tracks led to neighbouring settlements. The wooden church stood at the summit of this gentle hill, and from it the land sloped away in all directions. Close to the settlement, there were copses of oak, ash and beech.

It was a pleasant location. People were spared the bad air of Romney Marsh, while landowners hoped to benefit from the fertile soil of the drained marshland and staked their claims on vast tracts of it. The Romans had once inhabited the area: one of the tracks passing nearby was known locally as the Roman road and, if it was not quite as straight as its counterparts, it bore the evidence of being created by them. The knoll which Alfrid spoke of was more than a natural prominence on the edge of the escarpment but known to be a burial mound from that era, or possibly from earlier times. Stories of when the Romans travelled between their fort near Lympne to Ashford – the place with a river and a grove of ash trees – were passed down through the Saxon families in the form of songs and stories told around the fire.

The family unit were almost upon the village before outlines of homes built in wood and thatch took shape. Placed in irregular groups, these stood alongside animal pens and huts where craftsmen laboured over items produced to trade or sell. Walking closer still, they saw chicken coops, bread ovens and open communal fires. When two horses approached, their own beasts pulling the carts raised their heads and whinnied a greeting. The horsemen, sensing no danger, kept their swords at their sides. "Is that you, Arlo Smith?" one of them called out, his voice low.

"Aye. It is me Arlo of Aldington, with my wife and family."

"Why do you travel by night?" one asked.

"We felt the earth tremble, not long after sunset – was it the same on the Sandtun? Or worse?" There was an urgency in the voice of the second watchman.

"It was worse, I believe. The Sandtun has flooded, and there will be no more trading," Arlo explained. "We saved what we could before leaving in haste. I will give the news to your cousin, Thane Cenric, when the new day dawns. He will want to hear of it."

One of the men dismounted. "Until then, let me settle the horses. I see your clothes are wet, and you must be weary. Rest, my friend; it will soon be dawn."

"I thank you," Arlo inclined his head. Behind him, his family murmured their appreciation.

With the events of the night still fresh in their minds, and their bodies clammy from the wet clothes, Arlo, Eadlyn, and the younger ones trudged the last few steps through the village. It was an almost silent world they moved through. Small sounds told a story of village life: the shuffle of an animal in its straw bed, the snore of an old man who had consumed too much ale, and the cry of a fretful baby. The homes of Arlo and his brother, both metalworkers, were to the west of the wooden church and the thane's hall. Once the carts were placed in the gap between the plank walls, it was with gratitude that the horses were handed over to the thane's cousins, who watched over Aldington that night.

"Hang the tents over the side of the carts," Arlo suggested. None of them wanted to do any more than sink into their beds, but to leave the material lying over the unsold items of metalwork could only lead to them rusting. He turned to Eadlyn, "Our daughter is shivering, and it won't take all of us to move the tents. Go inside and dry yourselves."

"I will. But when Hilda is settled, you may welcome my help."

The whispered words and movement woke the family members left behind. Eadlyn's son Cym was the first to surface. Then from Arlo's brother's home, there came Penton, dragging his twisted leg. His wife, Megan, and their daughter followed. The news was told, but in few words. "We will explain properly in the morning" or words to such effect were repeated over and over. They were not ready to relive it yet, and the rest of Aldington still slept.

They were all yearning for sleep, having laboured through the darkest hours to take the carts across the Sandtun and up the Shipway, then walking home without pausing to rest. Any excitement felt by the boys, Alfrid and Osric, had passed. Their limbs ached and their skin was irritated by wet clothes. Everyone prepared for their beds with few words exchanged; they had become too weary to form one sentence after the next. Linen shifts, worn in the camp when the waters came, were finally stripped off and replaced with clean dry ones. The nights were at their shortest, so as the metalworker and his family settled in their beds, the sky was already turning pink to the east. Sleep came quickly, and they were grateful for it. Before long, the birds would be announcing daybreak. The respite would be brief for those who had returned from the stricken Sandtun.

Chapter Five

"What news do you bring?" Thane Cenric of Aldington asked his cousins. "I pray there was no trouble in the night?" They were fortunate to live in peaceful times. It had been that way throughout his time as thane, and that of his father before him. He had lived his thirty-five years with few reasons to draw his sword in anger. Yet this morning, he saw in the faces of the other men that there had been a drama of some sort overnight.

"No concerns for us, but news nonetheless," one cousin replied. He nodded his thanks to Cenric's daughter as she handed him a beaker of mild ale.

"Arlo Smith has returned from the Sandtun," the other announced. He too accepted the ale and they both seated themselves on carved benches of oak outside the tall double doors leading to the thane's hall.

"If a man such as he has suffered difficulties from others, it is indeed a concern for me." The thane had high regard for both the quality of Arlo's metalwork and his steady character. "What caused him to leave by night?"

"It was nothing to do with trouble in the camp, nor from the men voyaging from Francia," the cousin started to explain.

"There was an earth tremor at night." The other was quick to jump in. "Then a great wave came from the lagoon, flooding the Sandtun. They say it was like nothing they had seen before."

"Was anyone injured? Or worse?" Thane Cenric frowned, as he pictured the vulnerable camp.

"Nay, at least not that we know of."

"Arlo and his family returned unharmed, but we cannot speak for the others."

"Most likely he could not know," Thane Cenric surmised. "It must have been dark, and they would have fled in haste, perhaps having lost some of their belongings."

The sun had not long risen over the treetops and gentle hills to the east. Aldington basked in a soft light. At this time of day all the colours were enhanced: the corn and wheat shone gold; the green of the grass was lush; the clods of earth were moist and rich. Birds stirred first, then the animals, and now villagers eased themselves from their straw mattresses laid on wooden pallets. Thane Cenric always rose at first light then, after ensuring all had been well overnight, he would go to the small wooden church to pray with Father Theodore. Rarely did he allow anything to interrupt his routines and, on this day, despite his urge to visit Arlo, Cenric's desire to pray beside his priest was as strong as ever.

Having left his cousins with their ale, the thane rose and walked towards the church. The building was of a simple design, yet it stood out from the scattered homes in the settlement due to being almost twice the height of a man. Oak plank walls were tall and straight – a contrast to other dwellings where the walls were short, and thatched roofs so low a child could touch their fringes. The reeds on the church's roof were fresh – free

48

from the ravages of weather or invasive plants. Below the eaves eight small openings let in light, four on each side.

Not far from this holy place, a humble dwelling settled low to the ground, and from it the priest emerged. No better than a shelter for pigs, it was here that Father Theodore rested at night. By day, he drifted amongst the villagers, a slim man with long fingers, a bony nose and thinning hair of dark brown. He ate at the thane's table, always protesting that the food was too fine and the comfort too much, yet the priest remained a constant presence at Cenric's side.

As Father Theodore approached, the gold of a plain cross on a leather lace glinted in the morning sun. The cross had been a gift from the thane on his return from Canterbury just a few months ago. It was a generous reward for all that the priest did: his devotion to the souls of the villagers; the hours spent ruminating on religious tales from the past with Cenric; his advice in all matters, many beyond his remit; his care of the church. Whereas most priests of his status wore a modest wooden cross, nothing seemed to be too good for this godly man.

"Father!" Thane Cenric voiced his pleasure. "I trust you slept well and the heat from the sun was not too stifling for you? If you would allow me to have some windows cut into your walls, I would ensure they were well shuttered, and you would not suffer for them in the wintertime."

"I thank you, but if my sleep is to be disturbed then I have all the more time to reflect on the good works of our Lord." He reached forward to clasp the other man's hands.

"You know best," the thane replied.

"There was an odd trembling in the night," the priest offered. "It was as if the ground quivered beneath me. Did you feel it?"

"I felt nothing, but my cousins have reports of this happening at the Sandtun. The land there has shifted. Word is that the Roman fort has fallen, and the Sandtun was overcome by the sea. Arlo Smith and his family had to flee for their lives."

Asking nothing about the plight of the other people from Aldington or further afield, the priest pondered on this for a moment. "I felt it was bringing a message for me. As yet I am unsure of the meaning, but I feel certain it will come to light this day or the next. I will pray long and hard for guidance."

"You must come with me to see Arlo, as soon as we have finished our morning prayers and broken our fast," the thane declared. "The Sandtun lies not far from our lands, and I am curious to know how badly the area suffered from this quake."

"Afterwards we must journey to the knoll from where we can see your land on Romney Marsh," Father Theodore suggested, as he led the way into his church.

It was a restless night for those returned from the Sandtun. Eadlyn stepped outside the next morning to find her sister by marriage was already preparing a pan of porridge for both families.

"You've put our clothes out to dry!" Eadlyn exclaimed. "I thank you."

"It is a small thing to do," Megan replied. "I know you'll be weary today." She adjusted her headscarf over thick red hair, which still glowed despite her forty years of age.

"When we are all together, we'll tell you what happened." Eadlyn placed a basket of wooden bowls on the ground near the fire. "Although it was all so quick, I don't know how we'll make sense of it."

Megan began to ladle the porridge. "Eadric told me that he and Clover weren't on the Sandtun when it happened. He feels the guilt for leaving his young brother."

"I know. They both do." Eadlyn put a handful of fresh blackberries on top of each portion. "But they could not have imagined what was to come."

In the summertime they shared an open fire, making cooking and eating a lively arrangement. Their two homes, and the shelter in which the metal was crafted, were set in a semi-circle. A third dwelling was part-built: its walls and rafters were in place, and a pit for the fire had been shaped in the centre of the floor. The roof would be thatched with reeds cut from the Romney Marsh within the next few weeks. By the time Eadric and Clover married, their new home would be complete.

Eadlyn's son, Cym, had not journeyed to the Sandtun that summer and was already at the cart with Arlo. Tall and bronzed from the sunshine, he was reaching for the intricate boxes, buckles and candle holders, wiping and placing them on a bench in front of the metalworking shelter. They worked alongside Penton and Eadric.

"Come and eat," Megan called. As she did so, Clover and Hilda appeared with buckets of water collected from the spring. The rest of the family members stopped their chores to gather for breakfast.

None of the story of the Sandtun and the night's suffering had been told before Thane Cenric approached, with Father Theodore at his side.

"News has reached our thane," Penton commented.

"I had a feeling he would be here soon." Arlo took a large spoonful of porridge.

"At least we will only have to tell the story once." Eadlyn's tone was positive, yet she resented the intrusion when they had rested for such little time that previous night. The damage and loss of belongings still needed assessing, so they were not planning on lingering over breakfast.

"Good morning, my friends." Thane Cenric raised his hand and beamed at them all.

The priest lowered his eyes, acknowledging the family members with a series of nods.

"Please join us." Arlo stood to greet them. He gestured to the benches, hastily vacated by Osric and Alfrid. "Will you excuse us if we eat while we talk? You will understand we are tired and have a day's work ahead of us."

"Eat, my good people." The thane seated himself and stretched his legs out before him. He was a man who always seemed satisfied with his life. "The first of my wishes has already been granted – I find you all in good health!"

"I thank you." The words were murmured by those who had travelled from the Sandtun.

Bit by bit the story unfolded with Arlo, who saw the tidal surge first, taking the lead. Then Eadric and Clover told of the collapse of the Roman fort on the hillside.

Finally, they described how they salvaged what they could, coaxed the horses to pull the carts free of the soft earth, and journeyed up the steep Shipway track. By the time the tale was told, the bowls of porridge had long been scraped clean.

"Penton, what relief you must feel to have your brother and sons restored to you." Thane Cenric was a man who took note of every family within his village. He understood how important it was that Penton's role in the family was not forgotten. Fifteen years ago, the metalworker had injured his leg; it had healed badly, making walking difficult and hindering his ability to provide for his family. Arlo, as younger brother, had stepped into the role as the one who laboured longest and travelled as necessary for the good of the family. Good-natured and strong, over time it was Arlo who commanded the respect of the local people. Little by little it was he whom people approached when they wanted an item of quality metalwork. By addressing Penton in this way, the thane acknowledged the worth of the man with his weak, twisted leg.

"I thank you, my lord. It was a surprise to have them return at night, and we thank God for keeping them safe."

"I will be offering my thanks to Him," Father Theodore spoke for the first time. "Join me in the church if you wish."

"I will," Penton replied. He had much to be grateful for, despite his injuries. To be blessed with a good wife and two strong sons, as well as a loving daughter, brought him contentment during the dark times when he struggled with the discomfort in his leg and, increasingly, his hip and back.

53

"Has much been lost? Your goods for sale? Clothing? Household items?" Thane Cenric now asked.

"The pieces for sale were secure in the cart, and much of it already sold," Arlo informed him. "Our tent is saved and all our bedding."

"Everything was bundled up in a hurry," Eadlyn said. "It was dark, and our concerns were for the horses and the people there. We certainly lost anything left by the fire, and items outside the tent. Megan has already laid our clothes out to dry." Eadlyn smiled at the woman who was like a sister to her.

"The people of Aldington will be good to you: a bag of wheat, a bale of cloth, wooden plates… You will not suffer for this," Thane Cenric assured them.

"We are blessed with our good neighbours." Eadlyn acknowledged the truth of his statement. She thought of her home village of Lyminge. It was a fine place with a stone church and minster on the hill. There was fresh water from the Nailbourne stream and shelter from the surrounding hills. However, once her husband had passed away, Eadlyn had struggled to live alongside his family who offered little support. As a grieving widow, she had been forced to labour in their tanning shed for no more than a bag of grain, a few vegetables or a lean chicken. Life in Aldington was indeed good for Eadlyn and the children from her first marriage to Todd Leatherman.

"Now I shall leave you people to your work." Thane Cenric rose, but his mind was still on the events of the previous night. "The good Father here has suggested that we stroll over to the knoll to survey the Romney Marsh." He gazed to the east, and continued, "We will leave when the sun has risen above the oak trees in the copse yonder. Come with us. Your account of last night's terrors will come to life when we have the marsh spread out below us. I can only hope and pray the sea has not claimed it all."

He has a way of making orders, without it seeming to be that way. "We said the same thing last night. I shall certainly come," Arlo answered.

The women and their daughters were the first to rise from the benches near the outside fire. Hilda, the youngest, went to collect eggs and milk the goats. Alfreda, the flame-haired daughter of Penton and Megan, collected the bowls, then wiped them clean. Clover collected the ingredients and bowls needed for breadmaking. Together she and Alfreda walked to the communal area where the women prepared the dough before sharing a space in the bread oven.

Eadlyn and Megan went to inspect the items brought in haste from the Sandtun. The clothes, blankets and sheets of material used for the tents, having been laid out to dry early that morning, were encrusted with saltwater and plant life clung to their fibres. "It will fall off the tent sheets in time," Megan observed. "But these blankets, and your clothes, will be all the better for washing in the soft water of the stream. If we all take them then the work will soon be done and, in this sunshine, they'll be dry by nightfall."

While Penton and his sons went to craft hinges for the carpenter and buckles for the leathermaker, Arlo set off to the knoll. He went with his son by marriage, Cym, and young Alfrid.

They didn't have to wait long for the other men, who joined them at the edge of the village. The five of them walked steadily up the gentle hillside towards a wooded area, with Thane Cenric still speaking of the flooding and seemingly unable to wait to see the view for himself but wanting to guess at what changes might be before him. Father Theodore said nothing, unless pressed to. Every so often he would murmur about great things to come from this shaking of the earth. "I felt it myself," he reminded them. "There was a message for me, and very soon it will become clear."

There came a brief respite from the sun when the group stepped amongst a band of coppiced trees. Arlo and Alfrid, weary from the previous night, were glad of the dappled light and found the woodland peaceful. Too soon, they reached the far side and were in the open again – this time facing the steep slope of a long barrow, under which the bones of Romans lay.

Here, Cym, who worked as hard as any man, but still remembered the fun to be had as a boy, looked at his brother in an unspoken challenge. Alfrid gave a broad smile and began to race up the mound, with Cym just a stride behind him. They slipped on flints, in rounded white and grey, reminding them of childish fun when they declared these were the bones of departed Romans coming to the surface. Sliding on the fine gravelly earth at the edge of burrows, the brothers recalled the times they longed to be a rabbit or a fox and explore the depths of the burial mound. Side by side, the summit was reached and, as young men, they were the first to survey Romney Marsh on this new day.

Chapter Six

Romney Marsh was spread out like a map below them. Long ago, when the Romans settled, the area had been more seawater than marshland. They brought their boats along the base of the hills to their fort, and most likely further still. The sea had retreated over the centuries and, sheltered by a shingle spit, the land began to dry. The view from the knoll was impressive, spanning the vast area of tidal creeks, whispering reeds, and small stretches of land, now dry enough to support cattle and sheep on their fertile soil. From this viewpoint, raised even higher than the natural ridge of the hill, narrow tracks could be seen leading from the base of the escarpment and across the low-lying marsh. Trees were sparse, and those braving the harsh environment were stunted by the strong winds.

There were men living humble lives in coastal communities. One which would, in the distant future, be named Demechurch, then Dymchurch, and come to be the centre of law and order on the marsh. Another was growing at a place where a long port had been created on the banks of the river Rother and already ships from distant lands were finding a safe haven. There were people living frugally on a diet of fish on an island they named Lydd, where the Romans had built a stone basilica. None of this could be seen and was only known about through reports from travellers. The wooden church at Longport, the fishing boats on the coast, the humble dwellings at Lydd or Middle Isle, the wooden cross crafted on a rise in the land by a travelling monk – they were too far away. Not one of them was large enough to be spotted by the most determined of onlookers.

"I imagined seeing the whole of it flooded," Thane Cenric exclaimed, after they had stood in silence for a moment, scanning the land. "I thought it would all be changed."

"It was just the one tidal wave," Arlo reminded him. "Although it came with a force never seen before, and its swell was greater than you could imagine."

"The ditches are bursting," Cym pointed out. "At least they are to the east."

"And the salt pans are full," Alfrid said. In the distance they could see the reflection of the blue sky and scattered clouds on the squares fashioned by men to hold saltwater.

"It is hard to know from this distance what damage the Sandtun has suffered," the thane conceded. "The lagoon is clear enough, but whether it reaches further than the usual limits… it is impossible to judge from here."

"I have a calling to see the tumbled fort," Father Theodore spoke for the first time. "It came to me when I was praying not long before we left to come here."

"A calling?" Thane Cenric repeated.

"Aye." The priest clasped his hands in front of him and gazed at his bare feet, as if reluctant to say more. "It came to me… a voice that said over and over that I must journey to the fort. There is something I must do

58

there. Perchance the fallen walls have unearthed something which the saints wish me to discover."

"What? What could it be?" Cenric quizzed. "Did you have a hint? A feeling?"

"It is not for me to question, but to discover the answer for myself," the priest replied.

"Then we must go there!" Already the thane was turning away from the view and preparing to find the easiest route down the steep mound. "This cannot be ignored. But, Arlo, my own interest will only be satisfied if your daughter and nephew were to travel with us. I should like to hear about the moment when the fort fell."

"I have no need for them. The calling did not mention these young people," the priest declared. "Mine is a spiritual quest, and I have no need for their storytelling."

"It will make little difference if we were to return for them now." Cenric was slipping on the loose soil of the barrow, so determined was he to fetch Eadric and Clover.

"My lord," Arlo interrupted, his voice clear and strong. "The sun is beating down upon us, and we are tired, having barely slept last night. Eadric is working alongside his father and is needed there. Clover is either in the weaving shed or helping her mother wash the saltwater from all the clothing and blankets we recovered last night. They will travel to the fort with you, but it will be tomorrow at first light before the heat of the day is too much and when they have rested overnight."

"Very well. I understand it is too much for them," Cenric conceded. "First light it will be." He turned to the priest. "You, Father, will you wait for us or must you go to the fort now?"

"I will wait," the priest responded. It was as if the fire had gone from him, as he considered his next move. "I will wait to seek further guidance from the Lord."

"We can trust that He will look kindly upon us all," Thane Cenric declared. "Without doubt we can already be grateful to see that the lands belonging to Aldington have been spared from the great flood I feared we would see below us. There will be salt to gather in our pans when the water dries, and our sheep still graze on the lush grass below us. We will return with this good news for our families. Meanwhile, Arlo will tell Eadric and Clover to be ready to leave at daybreak."

The following day, Clover and Eadric left their family homes, each carrying a small bag of provisions and a clay flask of weak ale. They reached out to one another, entwined their fingers, and kissed briefly before walking towards the village boundary. Still young, with a good night's sleep behind them, their strides were long, revealing an enthusiasm for the day ahead. Curiosity was roused: they were both eager to revisit the fort, to see if it was as changed as they believed it to be.

"Another fine day to cut the hay," Eadric commented. The sun had only just risen above the horizon and its light was mellow. But by the time they walked home, it would be beating down upon them.

"Aye, the boys will work hard today." Their younger brothers both laboured in the fields at harvest time. In return, they would each bring home a cartful of hay to store in the loft above where the goats were kept. Clover glanced back at the home they were building for themselves, and continued, "Soon the reeds will be cut, and our roof can be thatched!"

"I'll be thankful to see that done," Eadric replied. "Then we can be sure of it being ready."

"It will be ready." Clover was good-natured and resilient. In the evenings she was stitching the hems of blankets and embroidering the cuffs of the dress to be worn on their wedding day. Alongside her mother, she was filling a wooden crate with useful pots, bowls and plates to take to the home when it was finished. The women of the family would ensure the young people would be provided with the items needed for daily living, while the men concentrated on building the home.

"Good morning!" Thane Cenric was waiting for them. He was accompanied by his younger brother, a man of less than thirty years, who worked hard for the good of the village, and Father Theodore, who was never far from his side.

Greetings were exchanged as they followed the path leading towards the knoll and the edge of the hills, before turning to walk along the track to Lympne. They travelled mainly in silence, offering an occasional comment, and paying particular attention to the view of Romney Marsh when the trees cleared to reveal a vista stretching all the way to the Kingdom of Sussex.

"It doesn't look changed at all," Godwin exclaimed. "You said it wasn't, but I thought there would be some difference."

"I believe we will see a change, but not on our lands. It is the Sandtun and the area beneath Lympne which has suffered for this," Cenric reminded him.

Walking behind the brothers, Father Theodore raised his theories: "This has happened for a reason. I dreamt of it again last night and am certain the fort is calling me. It is for the good of our people."

Godwin dismissed this with a clear shrug, but the thane clung onto every word. "Tell us more, Father. What was the message?"

"If it were clear, a priest would have no need to pray and strive to do right," Father Theodore answered. "If there were no struggle, the reward would have little value. I must wait." He bowed his head a little, inviting no more talk of the matter.

Cenric walked faster, spurred on by the longing to see the fallen fort. His brother matched his step. They both wore good leather shoes. The priest wore no shoes. He was seemingly unaware of the stones and thorns underfoot. Eadric and Clover brought up the rear, listening to the conversation, but saying nothing more than a few words between themselves.

Open fields turned to woodland again, and soon they turned off the main thoroughfare to walk in single file, following a narrow path through the trees. On the edge of the escarpment, the woods ended, revealing the tumbled fort on the open hillside. With no horses or carts to consider, there was no need for them to descend the Shipway – a steep track which was always difficult underfoot due to loose stones and clay soil. Instead, a path led down the hillside from near the village of Lympne.

They stood in a line, trees behind them and the hill falling away at their feet. The walls of the fort were now slumped, no longer standing tall and proud, but leaning at odd angles. Stone blocks, toppled from their place, lay strewn on the ground, broken and helpless. Where the fort had stood weathering the storms for centuries, sturdier and more robust than any of its Saxon counterparts, it was now vulnerable. Defeated. The ground appeared to have sagged, no longer strong enough to hold the weight of the stone walls. Springs had broken out, where before there had been none.

"It really has fallen," Thane Cenric murmured. "You…" he turned to Eadric and Clover, "you were there when it happened."

"We were very lucky," Eadric replied. "Had we been in the fort we would have suffered injuries, or worse.

"I thank God we were above the walls." Clover felt her body chill despite the warmth of the day. She had an urge to step free of the shadows formed by the trees, and to allow the sun to drench her body with its heat. When the earth tremors came, she and Eadric had moved away from the walls, then along the hillside. The air had been filled with the thunderous rumble as the fort fell, but it had happened at nightfall, so they could only imagine the aftermath. Afterwards, they had been at the Sandtun, feeling the guilt for having left their families. Every second had been filled with thoughts of moving the horses and carts away from the flooded land, then up the Shipway. It wasn't until later, when they talked in private, they relived the moments on the hillside and shared gratitude that their lives had been spared.

Father Theodore, reflecting on Clover's words, appeared almost overwhelmed by the sight of the collapsed fort. "Indeed, we must thank God," he said. "I feel sure there is something here He wishes us to see."

"If there is, you, Father, will be the one to lead us to it," the thane declared.

"Of course," the priest agreed. "I saw this place in my dreams and now I must pray for further guidance." He took a few steps, then sank to his knees to pray.

They stood, watching for a moment before Thane Cenric turned his attention back to Eadric and Clover, wanting them to show him where they had been when the earth shook, and encouraging them to point out the path they had taken as they fled. When the priest stood, it was a sign that they could begin to descend the hillside to view the ruins at a closer range.

There were other people on the site of the fort. From a distance they looked like insects scrambling about on the uneven ground. "Now it has fallen, I expect the local men will want to make use of the stone," Clover suggested to Eadric as they picked their way down the path.

"I wouldn't want to be part of carting it back up the hill," he responded with a grin. "The people of Lympne have left the fort alone in the past, but they must have some use for the stone. It would be easier to take this than to quarry and cut new pieces."

"Perchance it is not just the men of Lympne who will want it." Clover inclined her head in the direction of their thane. Eadric gave a brief smile, showing his understanding.

They reached the outer walls of the fallen fort near a curved tower still miraculously intact, but leaning and almost on the point of collapse. "Look at the way the stones have been shaped to make this rounded room at the gateway." Clover had an urge to reach out to touch it. "Think of the time they spent creating a building of this size. The church at Lyminge, and the minster, are fine and solid, but this is so much bigger."

Thane Cenric had entered the area within the walls, stepping over worked stones and rubble. The others followed, keeping their distance from any area seeming likely to tumble, and moving into an open space. Here there had once been dormitories for the Romans to sleep, pens for animals, stores, and workshops – wooden-framed structures now long gone. Timber and reed thatch roofs had been easily removed by the locals once the fort was abandoned. The people of Lympne had made good use of these materials. There were also buildings for purposes unheard of by many Saxons: a hospital and bath houses.

Amongst these stones there were bursts of summer flowers: delicate red and white petals sprawling amongst the grass, bold spears of blue, and mop-heads of white vying with plumes of pink thistle heads. They offered an unexpected display of colour to appreciate before the practicalities of studying the building once more took the attention of the visitors.

Godwin knelt to examine clay pipework exposed by the movement of the ground. "Eadric, what do you suppose this was for?" He beckoned the young man.

Eadric frowned and turned to Clover. "Look at these." The three of them pushed back crumbling soil, ragged grass and rambling daisies.

"They were for warming the living areas," Godwin told them. "They heated water and it ran through a network of pipes, taking the chill from the floor. How would you like that in your new home?"

"I'm not at all sure," Clover countered. "How could they prevent the water from leaking? We already have a wooden floor in place and will fill the gap beneath it with straw after harvest time."

"Ah, you come from a family of skilled craftsmen and will warm your home in the Saxon way." Godwin smiled his approval.

They wandered freely within the boundaries of the fort, exclaiming upon how walls had pushed against one another, shifting from where they had been built six centuries earlier. Eadric and Clover recalled adventures shared as year after year they had explored the fort alongside their younger siblings. Later, they had returned there as lovers when the sun was setting, and their families sat around campfires on the Sandtun.

"I hate to think of us being under one of those walls when the earth shook," Clover said. Her voice was almost a whisper and she wrapped her arm around Eadric's waist.

"I know. To think of our families searching for us…" He placed a light kiss on her forehead. "But we shouldn't dwell on it. We chose to sit above the fort."

"It's all so different in the daylight," Clover reflected. "We didn't see anything of how it was ruined that night. I'm glad we came back."

"Aye, I was curious," Eadric agreed. "But now I'm ready to return to Aldington. As Godwin reminded us – there is a home to build!"

They had strayed to the bottom of the fort, to the place where no walls enclosed it. Instead, those long-gone Romans had relied on the sea as a natural defence. Through the line of trees, there were glimpses of the marshland – the shimmer of a tidal creek, the swaying of rushes in the breeze and the silvery flash of wading birds rising from the marsh to the sky.

"It looks the same as always." Clover frowned a little as she tried to gain a better view. The oak and beech trees were in full leaf, making it difficult to see through the ribbon of woodland between the hill and marsh. "I hope the traders will be back next year."

"I'm sure they will be."

They turned now, scanning the area for those they had journeyed with. Cenric and Godwin were standing in the centre of the fort, surveying the whole scene. "What's Father Theodore doing?" Clover wondered. "I have a feeling he is hiding something."

While they watched, the priest stood and made a show of looking at a fallen gateway, but all the time using his toes to push at the long grass and clusters of flowerheads. Then he glanced at the spot by his feet before strolling towards the thane, not once looking back. On meeting with the other men, he appeared to be animated, moving his hands as if to demonstrate the size or weight of something.

"It will remain a secret between the three of us." Father Theodore was saying as Clover and Eadric approached. He glanced towards the young people, narrowed his eyes a little and changed his mind: "It will remain a secret between all five of us. Eadric the metalworker is strong and will be one of the chosen few to help me in my quest. In my dream, I saw a man with fiery hair at my side and now it is clear that he is destined to be that person."

"He can be trusted without doubt," Thane Cenric spoke for Eadric's integrity. "We will make haste for Aldington and create our plans."

Chapter Seven

"We must be free of the trees," the priest insisted when questioned by Eadric. "We must be sure no one hears us," he reasoned. "Who knows where a hunter or woodcutter may be lurking, and we would be none the wiser."

They reached open land where to one side the hill was bare, with views across the marsh. To the other, the fields of pasture and crops sloped away to Aldington. Clover could see Eadric was losing patience with Father Theodore: his brow was furrowed and eyes dark. Concerned he may show disrespect to the priest, she slipped her hand in his, wanting to show her understanding, but Eadric shook it away, wiped his brow, and ran a hand through his red hair. Clover stepped back, hurt by his rejection of her.

"We are free of the trees now, Father. I would like to hear of your plans for me."

"Let us first pause to drink," the thane suggested. There was nothing more to do but wait while they quenched their thirst with cool ale from clay flasks.

He must be thirsty too, Clover thought, noting how Eadric refused to drink from his own bottle, as if showing there was no moment to waste. *I am curious too, but we will hear in good time.*

"I was looking amongst the fallen stones at a gateway, when something caught my eye," Father Theodore began. "I can only say it was God's will that I saw it amongst the hundreds, nay thousands, of stones. I was led to it by Him! This is how I know it is meant to be moved to my humble church."

"What was it?" Eadric asked, his disinterest apparent.

"An altar!" the priest announced. "And one very ancient for it was not in the place of worship as you would expect. It had come from another time, another fort mayhap, and was used in this one merely as a gate platform."

"A gate platform?" Eadric queried.

He listens without curiosity, Clover reflected. *To think of there being something more ancient than the fort, yet it means nothing to him.* Clover felt an urge to race back and see this altar for herself; there was so much to understand. *What is it about this stone that tells Father Theodore it once had such a sacred use? Is it the shape or its markings?*

"A stone on which the gateway was built," the priest confirmed. "Now I understand the full meaning of my dreams. I felt the tremor that night, you know, and it heralded something holy coming to us. We are to take this stone then install it as an altar in our own church!"

"And what do you want of me?" Eadric questioned.

"It will be cumbersome to pull up the hillside at night," the priest explained. "You will be one of two or three young men entrusted with assisting me." He began to walk, and the others followed. Now the countryside was open, there was no reason to be cautious of their talk as they made their way home.

69

"Father, we are indeed blessed with your foresight!" Thane Cenric exclaimed.

"Not mine," the priest replied. "I am merely the vessel for His good works."

Eadric said nothing more but strode out ahead of the others. At first Clover tried to keep pace, but when she stumbled he did not pause to check on her. She slowed and walked beside the other men.

"No doubt Eadric has work to do. Enough time has been wasted this morning," Godwin suggested.

"Aye, that will be it. He doesn't like to leave his faeder," Clover agreed, both appreciating the care shown by the thane's brother and embarrassed that Eadric's rare temper had been noted.

"I should be overseeing the harvesting of the wheat," he continued.

God did not favour Aldington when he chose Cenric as the older son, with Godwin as the younger. Clover considered the two brothers: both were good-natured and cared deeply about the welfare of the villagers. They treated the people well and showed respect for the most skilled, such as Penton and Arlo the metalworkers. However, Thane Cenric was devoted beyond all reason to the priest. Clover feared that he would follow the holy man without question, not thinking further than pleasing his every whim. *Is it wrong of me to think a person could be too faithful to a priest?* She was as loyal to God and the saints as anyone could be. *But I would not follow without question.*

"There will be items to replace after the flood," Godwin commented, pulling Clover back to the present.

"Aye," she agreed, thankful for his interest. "There was the pan holder, the frying pan and the few tools we had at the fireside. Eadric will be feeling that he should be helping the others, not taking time to go to the fort."

"They will understand he must do as his thane decrees," Godwin suggested.

"Aye, they will." Clover glanced at the man walking at her side. *If he had been the elder brother, we would all rest easy knowing Aldington was in good hands.* There were two males in the family and almost ten years between them. Where the thane was beginning to age, his brother was still as strong as a young man. There had been numerous sisters born, one still living in the village, others in settlements nearby and one buried in the plot of land not far from the church. *I fear for Aldington with Thane Cenric seeming to be making poor choices. If Godwin were to take charge all would be well, I am sure of it.* Clover took a deep breath then gazed across the fields. The sky was clear, and the harvest promised to be good. Soon the altar would be safe in their church and Eadric need have nothing more to do with it. They could finish their home while looking forward to their wedding. *I worry over things which need not concern me. All will be well.*

They parted at the village boundary. Clover walked past homes and animal pens to join her mother at the bread oven. Eadric had already returned to his father and uncle. He was fastening a leather apron around himself before beginning his day's work. The other men went to the thane's hall where they seated themselves on benches under the shade of the eaves.

"Brother, let us pause and think carefully," Godwin suggested. The women had just served them each a bowl of pork cooked with barley and root vegetables. It smelt good and was most welcome after the walk. "While an ancient slab may be valued by our priest, it belongs to the people of Lympne. If you wish to improve our church, why not bless it with a stone carved by our own masons?"

"Father Theodore was led to this altar," Thane Cenric protested. "Did you not hear of his dreams?"

"Aye, I heard them," Godwin replied. "At least I heard one thing after another which made no sense at all."

"It made no sense to *you*," the priest interjected. "You must understand it is for me to read the signs sent."

"I understand very well, but I have to question why something of such value would be used as nothing more than a doorstep." Godwin paused for a moment to consider how the priest could be swayed. "Think of how our own men would feel if a piece of good ragstone were brought here for them to carve. It would be you, Father, who would choose the design. In the centuries to come, the people of Aldington would still admire the altar stone commissioned by yourself."

"Nay, that would be prideful – to have people admiring my work." The priest gave a small smile and continued, "I am a humble soul, who looks only to listen to the word of my Lord and do as He wishes."

"We are blessed to have you," the thane responded.

"What about the people of Lympne?" Godwin persisted. "We have good relations with them. Our own sister lives a comfortable life there. Are you not going to ask their permission to remove the altar? I suspect not, if you plan to go there at nightfall then return by cover of darkness."

"They have had centuries to discover it for themselves, and there are plenty of building materials for both villages," the thane declared. "They have used the roof tiles and some of the worked stone, but I suspect now it has fallen they will think of making more use of it. They will not miss our piece."

"It is not *ours*," Godwin snapped. "It is not *ours* to take. What if they were to go to *our* pans and take the salt? Would they say it was not *ours* as it came in on the tide?"

"To take from our salt pans would be theft and they would suffer for it," Cenric raised his voice. "It is not the same at all. The people of Lympne did not make the fort. It merely lies on the land they now possess."

"Besides, we only follow God's wishes," the priest reminded them.

"I think my feelings are clear," Godwin stated as he stood up. "I thank you for the meal. I should be on the fields beside our men, not chasing after an altar. I bid you a good afternoon."

"I'm worried for Eadric," Arlo confided to Eadlyn as they lay in their curtained bed under the thatch roof. "I have not seen him like this before." His nephew had been sullen since his return from the fort, distancing himself from the family and spending less time with Clover.

Two days had passed since they first ventured to the ruins. Now Eadric was there again; this time he had left at dusk and travelled by night. He had journeyed with Cym and a local stonemason, as well as the thane and priest. All three young men were strong and chosen for being trustworthy. They carried a leather from a pigskin, with a tough rope threaded through holes cut in the thick hide. The plan was that the altar stone would lie on the leather then be pulled up the hillside. They were expected to return by dawn. Eadric had already claimed he would work through the next day without taking any sleep.

"He wants to be working on his home, so it is ready for when they marry," Eadlyn suggested. "Not labouring on the hillside for Father Theodore."

"Their home will be ready, and to please the thane is always beneficial." Arlo sat up, allowing the thin woollen blanket to fall away from his body. He swung his legs over the side of the bed, then leaned to kiss his wife briefly on the forehead.

"Aye, it is," she said. "He is a good leader."

"I'm going to wait for them to return," Arlo told her as he reached for his tunic and shoes, "and hope to see Eadric's ill humour has passed."

It was warm outside with a light breeze wafting over the village. The sky was a pale pink to the east. No other man, woman or child had stirred from their homes as yet. In the distance, Arlo saw the two watchmen riding their final lap before they retreated to their beds to attempt to sleep through the intense heat of the day. He strolled the other way, to the south, hoping to see the men approaching from the direction of Lympne, and was immediately rewarded. The priest had clearly been successful in his quest: the stonemason and Cym could be seen pulling a heavy load. Eadric trudged behind them; the slump of his shoulders made it obvious that, for him, there had been no pleasure in the night's adventure.

For Thane Cenric it was as if he had only just awoken from a night between his good linen sheets. He bounded forward like a man half his age to greet Arlo. "My friend, you have risen early to welcome us. We have worked like dogs all night, but our prize is great."

"I am pleased for you, my lord. May I come with you?"

"Of course!"

Arlo looked back at Eadric and received a nod of the head. His nephew didn't smile. He appeared exhausted, as did the other young men. But whereas they glowed from the physical exertion, Eadric's skin was pale and his eyes dull. Cym offered the rope to his cousin then stepped away from the heavy load.

"Can I take a turn?" Arlo asked.

"Nay, we are nearly done," Eadric replied. "I shall not wait to see this stone in the full daylight. There is work to be done with Faeder."

"Penton would prefer you to sleep, at least for a few hours," Arlo pointed out. "The day is still young."

Eadric merely shrugged in response. When they reached the church, the thane declared that the stone must remain outside for a time. It must be seen in its full glory, not in the shadows of the dimly-lit building. Father Theodore agreed and was soon indicating the exact spot where the altar could be displayed to the best advantage. The young men manoeuvred it into place and eased the pigskin from beneath it. With his work complete, Eadric dropped the rope and turned away, taking long strides back to the centre of the village. Arlo took a step, as if to follow, but faltered, knowing there would be no conversation between them. His concerns for his nephew had in no way been eased.

The thane and priest were poring over the altar, tracing the lines and curves of the markings with their fingers while wondering about its history. The stone was not long: the length of seven, perhaps eight, palms. Its width was about four palms. It was not quite flat, with a rise at one end; the other was broken off, making a rough triangular shape. On the surface there were letters – pointed and evenly spaced.

"What is this?" Thane Cenric asked, as he knelt on the grass, running his fingertips over rough growths on the stone. "It's not mortar. Look, that's a different colour and texture. This looks as if… but how can it be?"

"Barnacles!" exclaimed the priest. "Crustaceans! This altar has been, for a time, in seawater."

"How very odd," the thane remarked, echoing the thoughts of everyone crowded around the altar.

"If you could pass me your knife?" Father Theodore asked, his beady eye on the strong sharp blade hanging from Arlo's belt, "Then I could see how easily these barnacles will scrape off."

Arlo reached for the bone handle and passed the knife. They stood in silence as a few particles of shell were chipped away. A moment later, there was a change of heart from the priest: "Nay, it is not for me to remove the work of God's creatures," he proclaimed. "They are part of its story. I will only chip away at the mortar put here when it was reused in the gateway. Some of it has spilled into the carving and we must see these letters to their best."

There were six lines of markings. Soon each one was clear to see: plain in style with good straight lines and shapely curves. Although appreciating the orderly pattern, four of the men looking on could only wonder at their meaning. Not even Thane Cenric could decipher the words, but the priest recalled his learning.

He began to read and translate them, sometimes faltering: "*For Neptune*," he began. "*An altar. Lucius Aufidius Pantera, Prefect of the British Fleet.* This stone was dedicated to the Roman god of the sea. *Prefect* means commander. It was indeed an object of status. This dates it to the beginning of the first century."

"When the Romans were still worshipping their own gods and not our one Christian Lord," the thane pointed out.

"At a coastal fort it makes perfect sense to show their loyalty to Neptune," Father Theodore observed.

At this moment Godwin approached. He had not been a part of the pursuit to secure the altar overnight. "Good morning, friends. You have the stone," he stated. "Is it all you wished it to be?"

"Look at these letters," his brother pointed to the inscription. "They are as fine as the day they were carved – do you see? And the stone comes with a mystery for it is encrusted in barnacles!"

"Barnacles?" Godwin laughed. "How very strange, for I doubt the sea ever lapped so high against the hillside. Nay, it is almost impossible!"

"This was from its former life," Father Theodore pointed out.

"Before it was used in a gateway?" Godwin's words sounded innocent enough but told of his disdain for the plan to bring the stone to Aldington.

"A lack of respect." The priest bowed his head as he contemplated the actions of those Romans who built the fort on the hillside.

All day a steady trail of villagers went to gaze in awe at the irregular piece of limestone with the mysterious letters carved upon it. Some of them dared to trail their fingertips over the crustaceans, bemused at them being on an altar of such significance. In the late afternoon, the stone was shuffled onto the pigskin and pulled into the church. The priest closed the door, then spent some time in solitude, thanking God for the treasure while seeking His guidance as how best to present the altar.

That evening mead flowed freely amongst the noblemen in the village. Both skilled craftsmen and serfs supped strong ale – a rare change for the peasants whose palates were accustomed to the weaker form. A hog roasted over a huge fire in the centre of the village, and all were welcome to a portion of the tasty meat.

Stories were shared in the form of songs. They told of the almighty Neptune who ruled over the sea, according to those ancient Romans. This was at a time, they reminded themselves, before the Romans knew of the one true God.

Long after the sun set, the people of Aldington slumped in their beds. The night watchmen, their heads spinning with wine, their stomachs full of pork, bread and fruit pies, lolled at the boundary to the village. Eventually they slumped on the ground in a deep sleep.

An hour after midnight, the dry reed-thatch on the roof of the church began to smoulder. Within minutes the whole church was ablaze. By the time the watchmen were roused by the crackling of burning reeds and the creaking of dry timbers, it was too late to do anything but stand by and watch the house of God collapse upon the barnacled altar.

Chapter Eight

Two weeks passed before the remains of the wooden church were cleared from the site. "There are crops to be harvested," Godwin reminded his brother, the thane, repeatedly. "We can remove the charred timbers, but we must not work on this task day and night. Your men will not love you for it if food is not gathered from the fields, hay cut for our animals or straw collected in sheaves for the thatcher."

The villagers gave what time they had, each one doing a little to pull away the remains of the plank walls, then separate the char from the unburned sections. The Roman altar, removed from underneath layers of burned thatch, had been thoroughly scrubbed by Father Theodore and now rested in his humble dwelling.

The ground was swept clean, although no amount of care could restore the blackened earth. This would take several cycles of the moon. The ash had been removed by cart to be spread upon the fields. "Out of this sorry event, the church will enrich the land," Godwin said, trying to pacify Thane Cenric, as they watched a cart trundle off with a cloud of ash falling from the rear.

The salvaged wood, none of it any use for building, had been stacked in a neat pile. "We must offer this to the poorest of our villagers when the winter days are at their coldest," Godwin had suggested. "They will be thankful and know that God sees how hard they labour – that He wishes to offer them some comfort."

"The cross has been placed to the east of where the church was," Eadlyn told Arlo. She was stirring the pan of vegetables and barley which hung over the fire outside their home. "It's a good cross; I saw it when Clover and I went to fetch the water." Reaching for a bowl of fresh peas, she poured them into the thick stew.

"Aye, John Woodturner has been crafting it for days," Arlo replied. "He used his best piece of oak."

"Every time I look that way, I am surprised anew to see our church gone," Eadlyn said. She turned away from the fire and adjusted her headscarf, recalling the days when her hair fell loose down her back. *That was a lifetime away. Soon it will be Clover's turn to cover her hair after she marries Eadric.* The thought disturbed her. Not that her daughter would have to conceal her golden waves, but that the easy friendship and love shared by the young people for so long had suddenly and inexplicably turned sour. Eadlyn glanced towards the metalworking shelter. "How has he been today?" she asked.

Arlo, knowing who his wife referred to, shook his head slightly. "Eadric labours hard, but there is still an anger when he works the metal. Penton is reluctant to give him any delicate tasks."

"If anything were to become spoiled it would only add to his frustration." Eadlyn understood the processes involved in producing quality workmanship.

"Is he being any gentler towards Clover?" Arlo asked.

"Nay. She told me she had suggested that they walk to the knoll this evening, thinking they could talk, but he

80

said that there were plans to work on thatching their home." In fine weather, the knoll was a romantic place for young lovers to walk, giving them some distance from the elders.

"We agreed to start on the thatch," Arlo responded. "But I'd gladly let him go if I could see him walking with Clover's hand in his and looking at her with warmth in his eyes."

"They're coming to eat now." Eadlyn looked towards the centre of the village to see the women of the family approaching. Megan, her flame-coloured hair streaked with grey, was carrying two loaves of dark rye bread, while the younger generation were leaving the weaving shed together. They made an attractive group – Megan's daughter, her red curls caught back at the nape of her neck and tumbling down her back, alongside Eadlyn's daughters, their waves the colour of ripe wheat. They wore just their loose dresses with a belt at the waist and their skin glowed from the months of sunshine. Clover was carrying a bundle of woollen cloth in a pretty shade of moss green.

"I've been given this, Modor." Clover lifted a piece of the material to show its weave and thickness. "The women heard how our shawls were ruined on the Sandtun. We can cut and stitch it so there is a shawl for each of us: you, me and Hilda."

"How kind of them," Eadlyn replied, "and what a beautiful colour. If you put it in the trunk, we can work on it in the evenings."

Clover turned away, entering their home through an open doorway and disappearing into the dark interior. Eadlyn turned back to the pan of pottage then called, "Hilda, can you pass the bowls around, please?" She began to fill wooden dishes with nutritious beans and vegetables while the members from both families gathered at the long table not far from the fire.

The talk over the meal was about the newly constructed wooden cross. They then pondered on the future of the altar, wondering what plans the priest would have now there was no church for it to stand in. "It was a foolish idea to bring it here," Eadric said, the irritation in his voice clear. "Is it right to have an altar dedicated to a Roman god? Is it right to have moved it when perhaps they placed it there for good reason?"

"It leaves a sour taste in my mouth," Penton agreed with his son. "But it appears Thane Cenric will do all he can to satisfy the whims of our priest."

Eadric stood, pushing his bowl aside. "I thank you for the meal, Eadlyn. I'll take a walk across the fields rather than hear any more of this altar and whatever the priest may think of next." He stepped away from the table, slipped through the gap between their homes and was gone.

Eadlyn gazed at her eldest child. Clover was picking at the dirt under her fingernails. *My daughter is to marry her best friend in less than two cycles of the moon, yet for the first time I worry for her future.* She glanced towards Penton and Megan who were both looking in the direction their son had gone. *Will they speak with him? Although I fear it will make no difference. This anger is something Eadric will have to resolve for himself.*

Walking with no purpose, other than to take himself away from the prying eyes of his family, Eadric found himself on the village boundary. He flopped down on an

82

area of pastureland where the grass was parched from the sun and worn thin by sheep. It was bound to rain soon, and the earth needed moisture, but he hated the thought of the interior of his home becoming spoiled. *It will soon dry*. Eadric heard Clover's voice and it irritated him. Then he felt frustrated for his disloyal feelings about the good-natured woman he was fortunate to be marrying. It was like this all the time at the moment: one thought was followed by another, each one conflicting with the last.

"Life is good. What's wrong with me?" the young man spoke aloud. These words had been uttered so many times over the last two weeks, yet the answer became no clearer. Eadric pictured the altar with the letters cut into it. He had gone back to see it on the day of its arrival in the village. Curiosity had got the better of him, so they had walked to the church together, he and Clover. Even on that day, there had been a tension between them and Eadric knew it to be his fault. He recalled being terse for no reason other than his own bad mood. "It is as if taking a part in bringing it here has cursed my life," he muttered. "Ridiculous thoughts. What can a stone have to do with my low spirits?"

There was a stream not far away. It meandered through a copse of ash trees, then forged a path through the soil. There were a couple of people sitting on the banks near the trees, their feet dangling in the water, but if he were to walk a little further downstream Eadric could find the solitude he craved. Picking his way past hillocks and sheep droppings, he climbed over a fence then strolled down the hill to the water's edge. Here, the grass on either side was lush and there were patches of well-trodden earth where the women of the village gathered water and washed their clothes. Glancing towards the copse, Eadric noted that the people he spotted earlier were now within the shadows of the trees. He wouldn't have known they were there had they not been seen earlier. *What brings them here? If they were from our village they would not have retreated into the trees.* He splashed the cool water over his face, cupped his hands and drank deeply. For the first time since learning of the Roman altar, Eadric felt at ease. He took his shoes off and sat on the bank with his feet resting on a flat stone, allowing the water to flow around his ankles.

The young woman approached silently, and he became aware of no longer being alone. Looking up, as he lifted his feet from the stream and scrambled to his feet, Eadric felt confused by her presence. She wasn't tall, at least not as tall as Clover, and her skin was the colour of a fawn. Her eyes looking into his own were deep brown pools, full of mystery. There was no headscarf covering her straight, dark hair, indicating she was unmarried. The stranger was gesturing to her clothes and Eadric realised she was attempting to apologise for them being no better than rags. He hadn't noticed before that her dress was both tatty and dirty, and she wore no shoes. Her eyes, full lips and button nose were so seductive that the rest went unnoticed until she drew his attention to them.

"Good afternoon." The words were somehow squeezed out, but immediately Eadric felt foolish. A blush began to rise in his neck. She had been speaking while showing her spoiled clothes and the words were like none he knew – this person came from foreign lands and the thought of it filled him with wonder.

"Felice," she replied to his awkward greeting.

"Felice?" he repeated. Then he understood. "Felice!" Eadric placed his hand on his chest. "Eadric."

"Eadric!" she echoed.

The dark-eyed woman held one hand over her flat stomach, and raised the other to her mouth, as if eating. Imploring Eadric to bring some food, her voice reminded him of honey: her tone was so sweet, yet a little husky. He wanted to hear more, although the gentle sounds meant nothing to him. The urge to care for her was strong, and already he knew that she had a hold over him. "You need food? I'll get you some," Eadric said, knowing she would understand the words came with kindness. He pointed to the sun and moved his hand until it paused before reaching the hilltop. "When the sun is here, I will be back."

Reaching forward, she touched his hands and he allowed her to take them in her own small brown ones. Words flowed and her smile was radiant, showing rows of white teeth. The woman's understanding and gratitude were clear. She pointed to the trees, reminding Eadric of the other figure he had spotted. *They must be hiding out there for some reason.* He was curious to discover why, but there was metalwork to be completed, so he simply nodded and stepped away.

Eadric's thoughts were on the strangers in the copse while he worked the bronze that afternoon. His father and uncle left him alone, assuming the young man was dwelling on the altar and its coming to Aldington. As soon as he was able, Eadric set the intricate buckles and his tools aside, then left. *It may be days since they last ate and they are expecting me to help them.* He slipped into the home and grabbed at a

85

selection of food, placing it in a small bag before darting off to the copse.

Felice was waiting. Her smile was wide but coupled with a desperate look in her eyes. The greeting they exchanged was brief – all her attention was focused on the meagre collection of berries, nuts and cheese he had brought. She almost snatched at the food, then darted off with half the offerings. *Why does the other person not come forward? What does he or she have to hide?* Felice returned to devour her share, seemingly taking no notice of what she was eating in her desperation to stave hunger pangs. When the nuts and berries had gone, she thanked him in a stream of unknown words and her sweet smile.

"I'll bring some more tomorrow," Eadric told her, pointing to the east to indicate the new dawn. She nodded her agreement, also pointing to the sky.

The following morning, Eadric left at sunrise for the copse. He had the last of yesterday's bread in the folds of his tunic, while a small bag of plums with some cheese were stowed in a jug, later to be used for water. Hurrying along, he passed by the village homes and only paused on reaching the remains of the wooden church. Here, he glanced back to see the neat line of thatch secured on the roof of his new home. Already it had caught the morning sun, shining bright amongst the tops of neighbouring dwellings where the reed-thatch had aged. Then he darted down the slope of the field towards the stream and cluster of trees.

The interior of the copse was a smoky dark, but Eadric sensed the young woman was watching his

86

approach. "Felice," he whispered the name, liking the way it flowed over his tongue, eager to see her again.

As Eadric neared the trees, there was a crack of a twig and the young woman stepped forward. She stood against the curving trunk of a tall ash, watching him approach. He quickened his step and slipped into the copse, standing close to her. "Eadric!" she exclaimed. The 'ee' of his name was accentuated, making it sound unusual. It delighted him!

"Felice," he replied, wanting to say more in her own tongue but unable to. He held out the food, then took his knife from the belt at his waist. There was a fallen branch on the ground, and he cut a piece of bark. Its bowl-like curves were perfect for the cheese and plums. The bread she took in her hand.

At that moment, the man emerged from the darkness of the centre of the copse, raising his hand in both greeting and thanks. This was the first time he had shown himself. Eadric frowned, knowing him, but for a moment not being able to place this person from foreign lands. Then another scene flashed before him. He was standing on the beach at the Sandtun with the other traders and their carts. Boats from Francia were pulled up on the shore while those who had sailed on them were gathered on the sands. They fawned over the metalwork, leather goods and items crafted from wood, wanting to secure the best pieces to take back to their homes across the sea. This man had come from the Sandtun. It made no sense at all.

The stranger began to babble, and a grin spread across his face. Reaching out, he clutched at Eadric's hand, recognising the young man. Then he began to explain, in words which meant nothing to the young

Saxon but, coupled with gestures, the scene began to fall into place. His arms portrayed a great wave and the man moved, showing himself rocking and tumbling. He indicated being washed up on the beach and looking for something, perhaps his boat. It appeared that everything was lost for this man – his open arms were combined with a look of dismay. Then they were walking, both hungry and searching for shelter.

"Thomasse," the man tapped himself on his chest.

"Thomasse," Eadric repeated. He pointed to the sun before sweeping his arm through the sky, indicating the passing of time. Then he tapped his stomach to show he understood their hunger. "I'll bring more food later."

With her lips slightly parted and the bread still in her hands, Felice stood watching the exchange between the men. As Eadric turned away, she spoke, no doubt indicating her gratitude and he raised his hand in response. Stepping into the light and away from the copse, all his thoughts were on the woman. Felice had been at the Sandtun, yet he would have known if he had seen her; she must have been hiding away on the boat. Who was she? What was the relationship between herself and the man? Was he her father, brother, or husband? A dart of envy shot though Eadric's chest forcing him to put his hand to his heart. *Not her husband – he is too old, and she wears no head covering. Most likely this man is her father.* The dark-eyed stranger filled his thoughts, easing the bad temper he had suffered since his return to see the Sandtun after the earth tremor.

The fire was already burning when Eadric pulled on his apron in preparation for a day's work. A selection of buckles were to be fashioned for the leathermaker's new belts. It was a job he had started the day before and held no challenge but would be enjoyable.

"Good morning." Arlo looked up from the dish he was shaping at the workbench; the tin was draped over a wooden mould and a small hammer rested against it.

"It's a fine day," Eadric replied. "We should make good progress with the thatch this evening."

"Aye, we will." Arlo frowned slightly. He lifted the hammer and continued to tap away whilst Eadric selected the lengths of material needed for his task.

Throughout the morning, all was peaceful in the metalworking area. Eadric toiled alongside his family members, but now with care, whereas recently mistakes had been made through being heavy-handed. The anger of the past two weeks had dissipated. He noted his father and uncle glancing at him every now so often, perhaps unsure of his mood and curious as to the apparent change.

The day was warm, and they frequently stepped away from the fire or benches to reach for a clay flask of weak ale. Before their midday meal, they walked to the stream to slosh cool water over their faces and arms. Eadric glanced towards the copse, his heart pounding with anticipation, but Felice and Thomasse were secreted in its depths.

The midday meal with the mothers, Eadlyn and Megan, presiding over the food, was a merry affair. Even when the talk returned to the stricken church and the Roman altar, Eadric remained unperturbed. His mind was full of plans to gather food for the man and woman who sheltered in the trees.

89

It wasn't until late evening Eadric was able to remove himself from the family group. He walked quickly, with a small bag of bread and cheese held against him. On entering the copse, for a moment it seemed as if he were too late and that the strangers had gone. Then Felice stepped forward into a pool of dappled light; there was no sign of the man.

"I've brought some food." Eadric offered the bag, and she opened it to look inside. "It's not much." He wanted to give her more: some pork carved from the thane's hog, sweet honey dripping from a comb or summer fruits cooked with apples. All he could do was shrug an apology.

Despite the meagre offering, Felice smiled, and her words appeared to be full of gratitude. She placed the bag so it hung on a broken branch, then stepped forward taking his hands and placing her full lips on his own. All sense was driven from Eadric's mind. He thought only of that moment and the sensuous young woman whose tongue now flicked into his mouth. His hands circled her slim waist. The moment lasted seconds before a bird rose squawking from the tree canopy and Felice extracted herself from the embrace. Stepping back, she reached for the food, murmured some words of thanks and retreated into the shadows.

Chapter Nine

"If the church had been made of stone, it would not have burned," Cenric stated, as he drank wine with his brother and their families outside the thane's hall. His tone was mild as if it were merely a fleeting thought.

Godwin knew better. His body ached from working alongside the men on the fields, but his mind was still alert to his brother's whims. He said nothing.

"We cannot continue to worship at the wooden cross," Cenric continued. "Aldington is a prosperous settlement, on the Roman road from Lympne to Pevensey. Think of how often we have travellers staying in the barn, and the news they tell of other places. With all this new land on Romney Marsh, we can afford to be thinking of a stone church. One that would be easily spotted from a distance, and then people will say: 'Ah, there is Aldington! We can be assured of a welcome and shelter for the night.'"

"They can still be assured of those things, and God will look down on us just as kindly," Godwin suggested.

"No!" Cenric spoke with passion. "God *does* look favourably on Aldington but think how pleased He would be if we were to have a stone church. We must not be slack in these matters."

"Where would the stone come from?" Godwin asked, knowing full well. "The task of quarrying it and the expense is mighty compared to constructing a fine wooden building."

"From the fort of course!" Cenric exclaimed. "I cannot think why you had not thought of it yourself."

"I am busy harvesting," Godwin responded. "We will thank God with a fine festival as the summer ends."

"There is to be a wedding at the same time," the thane said. "We must bestow Eadric Smith and Clover with a suitable gift."

"Aye." Godwin thought of the young couple and frowned. "Eadric's spirits are low. I wonder why?" He sipped at his wine from a pewter goblet. "He has a fair bride, known to be gentle and hardworking, as well as a home beside that of his parents. What reason could there be for his ill temper?"

"No doubt he has needs to be satisfied but has not taken a village wench," Cenric suggested. "You speak of his fair bride, and Clover is all that any man could wish for: she is sweet of both face and nature. How old are you, brother? Twenty-seven years?"

Godwin nodded. "Aye."

"We must find you a bride, for I fear your voice softens when you speak of Clover. If you wish for golden hair with a slender figure, a woman will be found for you."

"It is time,' Godwin conceded. "After the harvest." His brother was right; there was no need to delay the quest for a wife and, after the crops had been gathered, the matter would have his full attention. He had his health, a decent home, and now there was an urge to father children with a good woman.

"Before then, I will journey to Lympne and take Edina. She is pretty enough, and the thane there has a son of about twelve years old. Perchance it will be a match which interests him, and an agreement can be made, God willing." Cenric referred to his eldest daughter, a docile child of ten years. "Her mother will be gratified that she will not be far away once married, and our sister, Edina's aunt, will be pleased to keep a watchful eye over her when they are of an age to marry."

"It would be another union between our villages," Godwin agreed. "As for myself, until now I have been happy enough in my work, and the company of the widow woman from Mersham."

"She has taught you well, no doubt, but in a wife you will need someone younger," the thane suggested. "Mayhap you will be wanting to marry before our stone church is built. I won't make you wait for that."

"What does Father Theodore think of your plans for a new church?" Godwin returned to the previous subject.

"Father Theodore is a man of few needs," Cenric declared. "He demands nothing and is overwhelmed by the thought of being able to serve God from a building of status. It would be a fitting home for our altar slab and all he asks for are some candle holders crafted by Penton or Arlo."

"That would be a fine commission for them," Godwin approved.

"And I thought a cross…" Cenric continued. "I shall speak to them in the morning."

The weather had been fair for weeks and the following day was no different, although the wise ones who knew the signs were foretelling rain by the Sunday. The land needed it, and thankfully the grain would be harvested by that time. The thane, with his usual exuberance, set out to visit the metalworking shelter as soon as he had broken his fast. Father Theodore scurried at his heels, clouds of dusty earth brushing between his bare toes.

"Good morning!" Thane Cenric's voice was loud and clear. "I come with good tidings for you both." Had Godwin accompanied his brother, the younger man would have noticed the look of concern – or was it fear? – flash across Eadric's face before he turned his back and retreated to the woodstore under the eaves. But the thane was so filled with the joy of this moment, he did not realise that everyone else might not share his pleasure.

Penton and Arlo repeated the greeting: "Good morning, Thane, and to you, Father." Work had not yet started in earnest. There was the slumbering fire to bring to life, then the day's duties to be discussed.

"I have exciting news!" Cenric began. "We have been speaking of building a stone church – a place to be admired by all who pass through Aldington. Somewhere to honour God, Jesus and the saints. We have our altar, and I want you to craft a pair of fine candle holders, and a cross… a cross to hang on the wall." He closed his eyes for a moment while raising his face, as if seeing the cross high up on the stonework. Then, struck with a new idea, Cenric continued: "And another… another less decorative one to fix on the ridge of the building, so there is no mistaking its purpose!"

"A stone church!" Penton said. "That will be a worthy project for our masons. Will it be ragstone or flint?"

"It will be ragstone from the Roman fort!" the thane replied. "I plan to journey to Lympne tomorrow to discuss the matter with our neighbours there. When the harvest is complete, there will be work for every strong man and boy. The stone will be brought here over the wintertime."

Despite his back being turned, Eadric could not help but hear of this plan. The good thane's voice boomed as he expressed his enthusiasm. Eadric's rage, which had calmed over the last few days, now came to the surface. Before he showed disrespect to the thane and his revered priest, he stepped out of the confines of the metalworking shelter then stalked off, past the village boundaries and into the countryside.

With no plan in mind, Eadric walked away from the village. He would have liked to kneel at a stream, splash water over his face and refresh himself. However, the women were at the water, filling jugs and washing clothes. To hear them fuss over his presence would only bring further irritation. Just thinking of them telling his mother and Clover led to further tension. His steps took him to the other side of the copse where Felice and Thomasse spent their days. As he neared the trees, determined to walk by and not be drawn into seeking out the newcomers, there was movement from within.

Perhaps it was an animal sheltering in the copse, birds flying within the canopy, or even the movement of leaves in the light breeze. Eadric turned his face towards the open fields and lengthened his stride. *I cannot continue to feed them. It is not my place to care for these people. If they were to approach our kind-hearted thane, he would provide food, shelter and work.*

Eadric had tried to explain this the best he could with gestures – pointing to the village, offering to take them, indicating a roof and sustenance. Yet they had been adamant in their wish to remain in the copse. *It is too small. Too near the village if they wish to hide away. It is a foolish choice.* Even to himself, Eadric did not admit why he wanted them gone now.

For five days he had provided food both morning and evening. Each time Thomasse kept his distance, while Felice thanked their protector by pressing her lips on Eadric's. Every kiss lasted a little longer and, as they parted, she murmured sweet words unknown to him. Wanting it to stop, yet returning for more, caused him to wake at night thinking of the dark-eyed woman, and wondering if he would return the next day to find her gone. It was becoming harder to pull away from her.

Unable to resist, Eadric glanced towards the trees. Felice was there in full view. *I cannot stride on now, as if I have not seen her,* he reasoned. *It would be rude.* She waved, beckoning him. The decision was made – the young man turned abruptly, heading for the copse.

This time there was no food to be given and no gratitude to be offered. As he approached the shady area of oak and ash, Felice stood back. They met within the shadows of the outer trees and stood, inches from each other. No words passed. Not even a smile. The air between them felt as thick as honey; it was as if they were the only two people on earth. Reaching for his hand, she drew Eadric closer and they kissed with an urgency he had never known before. Her hands roamed his body, finding a way under his tunic. His cupped her small breasts and then her buttocks. Stumbling, unable to pull apart from one another, the lovers slipped further into the copse, where the moss was dry and grass thin. He wondered where her father was, but the thought was fleeting as Felice consumed all his senses, and his mind was filled with nothing but her. The natural bed on the floor of the copse appeared to be ready-made for them. While the fire in the metalworkers' shelter burned, and the lengths of iron waited to be crafted, Eadric fulfilled his desires for the young woman from Francia.

"Arlo told me that Eadric was disturbed by talk of the stone church today," Eadlyn said, as mother and daughter stitched the hems of new shawls. "It seems that he can tolerate no word of the altar, although his part in bringing it here is over."

"He has been happier in the last few days," Clover replied. Her needle paused as she gazed towards the roof of her new home. Eadric and Cym were astride the roof beams, securing the bundles of tied reeds. They called to the men on the ground and banter passed between them. It appeared all was well. "Happier, but not as he was. It seems as if his mind is elsewhere."

"I thought the same," Eadlyn agreed. "It appeared the worst of his temper had passed, but today the thane and priest came to speak about metalwork to adorn the new church. Eadric could not bear to hear about the altar and left. Arlo said it was some time before he returned."

"Afterwards, was he better? Did he speak of it?"

"They continued to work and there was no mention of the altar."

"I don't understand." Clover pressed the needle through the wool, then pulled it, her stitches small and even. "For one night, Eadric worked for the thane, yet the resentment still brews. I've never known his mind to be disturbed like this."

"Is he gentle with you?" her mother asked.

"It is not one way nor the other. It is as if he is the woodworker, the mason or the thatcher – friendly and polite, but not my Eadric whom I am to marry." Clover frowned before considering her next words carefully. "Modor, do you think he no longer wishes to marry me?"

Eadlyn did not want to rush her answer. It would be wrong to disregard her daughter's concerns, yet there seemed to be no good reason for the young people to have become distant. She believed that once they were married and moved into their home, any rift would be healed. "There must be more to Eadric's ill humour than the altar slab and his distaste for it," she began. "But I can see no excuse for it, and I am sure he'd not change his mind about the marriage. Look at the pride he is taking in the home."

They watched the two generations of men working together. Then Clover turned her attention to her sewing, and they sat in a companionable silence for several minutes, the needles moving smoothly through. The moon had almost completed one cycle since their return from the Sandtun, and the young woman contemplated the change in her closeness with Eadric. She recalled the time she had reached to take his hand, but he had stalked off. Then her suggestion that they walk to the knoll, but he claimed to be too busy. Eadric was pleasant enough most of the time, yet there was a lack of the affection which used to come so readily. "Modor," Clover began "I am nervous about the marriage. Nervous that it will be no better."

"Perchance you are both anxious?" Eadlyn suggested. "Eadric is a good man. I'm sure he will settle once you are married." To cancel the wedding now would cause untold difficulties. The two young people already lived as cousins, and their home was almost finished, making a third within the tight cluster of homes, animal pens and metalworking shelter.

"Aye, the home will soon be finished, and all will be well."

Nearby, Eadric jumped from the low roof to the ground. He was followed by Cym, and the two young men stepped back to survey their work. Turning, they grinned and slapped each other on the back. They had done a fine job: the bundles of reed were now pegged down securely to form three tight rows of thatch on each side. Arlo was trimming the bottom edge with a sharp knife, while Penton tied more bundles.

"We'll have the ridge completed tomorrow, or the day after." Eadric walked towards Clover then sat on the bench beside her. "I was worried that we wouldn't have it ready in time, but the weather is kind." He gave a broad smile and ran a hand though his red hair.

"It will be one of the best homes in the village!" Clover responded. She reached out and placed a hand on his thigh. He didn't flinch. These moments of closeness were rare, and tears began to form. Blinking them away, she continued, "You can be proud of all your hard work."

"I can!" Eadric placed a kiss on her forehead before jumping up. The loose reed needed tidying away before the work would be complete for the day.

Two days later, the thatch was finished, and the floor swept clean. Eadric was in good spirits. *By the time I marry, Felice and her father will be gone,* he reasoned while walking to the stream to wash the sticky sweat from his lean body. *There is nothing here for them, so they will travel on to another village, begging for food or scavenging in the fields and hedgerows. Tomorrow, or the next day, I will bring less food so they see I cannot be relied upon. The day after, I will bring less again. But before they leave, no harm will be done for my enjoying her company a few more times. It is Clover whom I love, and when we marry, I will be the good husband she deserves. Felice may lure me to her, but it is Clover who has shared my life since we were children. She will be the modor to my sons and daughters.*

Eadric had already enjoyed the pleasures to be found in the shady copse earlier that day, but once refreshed with the cool water, his path took him to the trees once more. Usually there was a sensation that Felice was watching and, as his eyes adjusted to the shadowed area, he would spot her waiting. This time, there was no sign of the young woman. Eadric frowned. *Of course, she would not be expecting me, but it seems as if she always knows when I am nearby.* He stepped into the copse, paused on the edge, then listened. There was near silence: the slightest rustle of the leaves above, the creak of one branch rubbing on another.

Moving further into the copse, Eadric scanned the area as his eyes adjusted to the darkness. There was no sign of Felice or Thomasse, and soon he found himself blinking as the trees thinned on the far side. Turning back, he searched the area thoroughly. It was as if they had never been there. Hurt by them leaving without saying goodbye, and stunned to think of the sudden absence, Eadric stumbled out of the trees. Unable to think of going home, he headed to the knoll to be alone and reflect on the times spent with Felice.

Not too far away, in another village, someone was thinking about the family in Aldington. A plan was forming and when it came to fruition two others would journey under the guise of doing good deeds, but intent on causing disruption.

Chapter Ten

Bertana of Lyminge knelt at the edge of the Nailbourne stream, with her back to the stone church built on a prominence overlooking the village. The air was warm on her skin, and the water icy as it trickled past her hands. Small flying insects hovered. One settled on her legs; she batted it away. Water flowing through the rags in her hands was turning brown, causing a dark cloud to weigh heavy on her shoulders. Two days ago, her monthly bleed had come.

It was the fault of the earth tremor, she silently raged. *If I had not had to labour so hard to save our leatherwork, his seed would have settled, and my son would be growing.* Bertana pummelled the rags on the bed of the stream, then flung them into a small bucket. She rose, stretching her long sturdy legs, and walked to the heart of the village where her loaf of bread was cooling near the communal oven.

If only she were blessed with sons, life in Lyminge would suit Bertana very well. She glanced beyond the church, seeing some movement – a pair of nuns drifting along clasping baskets of herbs, or pots of honey. Bertana gave a small snort of distaste. Countless times she had gone to them, securing potions for herself and Alwin, but with no success. Her womb remained empty.

Taking the loaf from the cooling racks by the oven, Bertana tucked it under her arm and retraced her steps, crossing the Nailbourne then striding up the slope to her home on the edge of the village. Her husband and his older brother were leatherworkers and the nature of their craft meant that the workshop was located on the outskirts of Lyminge. The tanning of leather was a filthy business, with the stench unbearable during the hot summer months. However, the goods they produced were of high quality, affording the family a great deal of respect in the community.

Although set apart from the workshops, the smell of animal skins and the tanning process still penetrated the row of three timber and thatch dwellings. Bertana reached her home, then turned to look back. Taking a deep breath, she considered the advantage of living here – the view of the homes and animal pens clustered about the stream. From the elevated position, she could watch the inhabitants go about their daily lives in the shallow bowl-like dip in the hills where the village nestled. Every day was different and to look on from a distance was fascinating. Lyminge captured her imagination: there were always stories to be told of the first Christian king who built a royal palace here, and his daughter who founded the minster on the opposite hill.

Bertana glanced at the stone church again, admiring the shape of its curved end wall and picturing the altar: almost smelling the scent of the candles and the glow of the red sanctuary lamp. She recalled her wedding day and the sword presented to Alwin, so in turn he could pass his sword to their first son.

Movement from within the leathermaking shelter brought the woman from her reflective mood and back to the present. Fourteen years had passed since her marriage; she was no longer a girl but had matured to over thirty years of age. *Still young enough to bear a child,* Bertana reflected. *A son.* There were plenty of girls in the family: Alwin's brother, Cedric, had fathered five of them. Most were married now, and it was not the place for a woman to be curing the leather or shaping it into belts, shoes or bags. She sniggered, her upper lip curling a little. There was a time when Eadlyn had done the very worst of the tasks, those usually given to the boys from poor families in the village. Bertana had enjoyed seeing her sister by marriage pressing chicken droppings into the animal skin or using a sharp flint to remove the hair and fat.

It had been thirteen years since Eadlyn had married again, leaving Lyminge for Aldington, but every year she unwittingly taunted Bertana with her two fine sons and handsome husband. An image of Cym flashed into his aunt's mind. He was blond, like his mother, not dark like his father and uncles. The boy was tall too, and good-natured. If she were to have a son, Bertana imagined he would be like her nephew in both appearance and personality. Only three nights beforehand, there had been much talk of Cym at the fireside; now Cedric and Alwin approached, the same topic again on their lips.

"We must fetch the boy," Cedric declared.

"It's clear he should be here with the men of his family," Alwin agreed. "It is time for him to learn from those who share his blood." He was thinking of the recent news that Cym was working alongside a leathermaker in Aldington.

"No doubt he'll be pleased to hear of our offer." Cedric nodded, his satisfaction clear to see. "But first we must eat, then plan for him coming." They were now passing the home of Bertana and Alwin.

"My belly is grumbling for food," Alwin declared, slapping his wife on her full backside. "Bring the bread, as Ora is sure to have the bowls ready to fill." He referred to Cedric's wife who had prepared the midday meal for both families.

The brothers walked by and Bertana scowled at their backs. She stepped into her home, took a slab of wood and a knife from a basket, and followed the men.

After they had satisfied their hunger, the conversation returned to their nephew. "I should never have allowed him to go to Aldington," Cedric declared, and not for the first time. "I thought we would have more sons born to our family – that his going would cause no harm." His wife lowered her eyelashes and began to gather the bowls.

Bertana's eyes flashed in fury, but when she spoke, her voice was calm. "If Cym returns to Lyminge, I would welcome him into our home. He cannot live with you and your daughters; it would not be right. The boy will be comfortable with us, but I wonder if you were rash in settling your daughter up here in a leathermaker's dwelling?"

The third home in the line of dwellings had once belonged to Todd and been the childhood home of Clover and Cym. Now Cedric's eldest daughter lived there with her family of daughters. Her husband was a thatcher, which proved useful, but traditionally it was the domain of the leatherworkers.

"How old is he?" Cedric asked. "Fourteen?"

"Sixteen," Bertana informed him. "Old enough to cast his eye about and look for a wife soon. Cym will not stay with us for many years but will be made comfortable while he does." She pictured another home being built, a wedding in a few years and new hope for healthy sons being born into the family. "I was sorry not to see him at the Sandtun this year, but he was growing into a fine young man last time we met. There will be no shortage of local women for him to choose from."

"Sixteen!" Alwin repeated in wonder. "There is plenty of time to construct a home for him when he chooses to marry."

"He might look no further than one of my daughters," Cedric suggested.

Cedric's daughters! Bertana may have mentioned the women in Lyminge, but her heart was set on her brother's daughter. *If Cym marries Annis of Ottinge, she will come to live nearby, and I will have the family I wanted. Their children will carry my blood. He will not be lured by Cedric's girls; they seem a little sickly and it is always a wonder when they live through the winter.* "There is no need to talk of his marriage yet," Bertana snapped. "First he must be brought to Lyminge. Alwin and I will travel to Aldington to speak with the family."

Her husband smiled his approval, although his heart was pained. Only three days ago, Bertana had been forceful in her belief that she was finally carrying a child, declaring there was no need for another male to be brought into the Lyminge family. Alwin knew the monthly bleed had arrived so, yet again, her hopes had been dashed. For a few days he had almost believed it himself though, and imagined his son running about the place. His thoughts flitted to Eadlyn. He had been

106

foolish there – pushing his desires on her, then not allowing her enough time to consider marriage. His wife was a fine woman, strong and healthy, but Eadlyn had already proven she could provide a son.

"Very well," Cedric agreed. "There is nothing to stop you leaving within the week."

"There is nothing to stop us leaving tomorrow," Bertana retorted. "In the meantime, I must prepare." She left the men, taking the bread knife and wooden board. "I thank you, Ora," she called to Cedric's wife.

Following the tracks beaten into the ground over the years, and skirting the molehills with long strides, Bertana once again headed towards the village centre. In her basket she had a pair of leather shoes. *A generous gift. It is time I made my peace with our neighbours in the minster.* The tension was in her own heart, and it had led to her donations being less than charitable over each year that she had not been blessed with a son. *The nuns did their best to help,* she conceded. *Each potion, each bag of herbs, was given with love. It must be that my husband's seeds were so weakly there could be no hope of success. My own health and vigour are without question. If it were not for the earth tremor, I am certain we would have no need to fetch the boy from Aldington. This must be God's path for me: I will nurture a young man, rather than a child. He will still need feeding, caring for, and will be seeking guidance as he becomes used to his uncles and their ways. Cedric will have his own plans.* Images of the sickly daughters flashed into her mind and Bertana scowled. *I will be the trusted one to guide my new son.*

107

Once amongst the homes, animal pens and workplaces in the centre of Lyminge, Bertana's path twisted and turned as she negotiated children labouring with carts, animals being herded and villagers about their labours. The Saxons had no plan to their settlements, no orderly lines of plank and thatch constructions; they had discarded the Romans' influence and Lyminge was typical of a place this size. However, there were some buildings giving a clue to an illustrious past: the remains of a royal palace, now reconfigured to suit the needs of the current thane; the stone church; the minster founded by a widowed queen.

Offering a swift greeting or a brisk wave, Bertana forged onwards, showing no frustration at the obstacles in her path. Respected by the villagers, she had no close female friends, nor any enemies. After crossing the stream by one of many plank bridges, she glanced to the church and was soon marching up the steep slope towards it.

The church was tall and narrow with a roof of wooden shingles. There was something calming about its solid presence and Bertana was drawn to it. On a Sunday when the priest said Mass the villagers remained outside. There was barely enough room for the thane and his extended family. At that moment, she felt a rare urge to enter the building: to breathe in the rich dampness of stone walls and the smoky scent of the candles. With a light press of her hand on the narrow door, it swung open, allowing Bertana to step into the holy place. It was largely unadorned – a cross on the wall above the altar, some tapestries of the saints and, of course, the altar itself the focal point, set in the curve of the eastern end. A couple of benches for the elderly or infirm ran along the walls; the rest of the congregation stood, as did those who gathered outside. One carved chair was placed in a shadowed corner, perhaps for the priest – although no one had ever seen him use it. Through small windows, high in the walls, shafts of golden summer light beamed. In the lofty roof space, and in the corners where the stone walls met, it was permanently dusk in the church.

The altar was the priest's domain, and even Bertana would not think to encroach. Instead, her eyes fell upon a cushion, heavily embellished with a needlework cover. This small comfort had been gifted to the priest by the thane's wife and daughters to ease any discomfort to his knees. *If I am to pray well in this church I must kneel, and the dirt will never wash away from my dress. This cushion will soften the floor, making my prayers all the stronger.* She picked it up from where it rested on a bench and placed it on the stone slabs.

"Mary, mother of Jesus, look kindly upon my desire to bring Cym back to the loving fold of his family. I pray that you understand the need for him to learn his faeder's trade in the village of his birth. I ask you to look upon us with mercy and enable his smooth return to us here in Lyminge." Bertana didn't believe in embellishing a prayer or giving undue flattery to the saints. Her desire to have the boy return was in no way unjust, and so to dash out a prayer was merely a way of ensuring all avenues were open. With that in mind, she rose from kneeling, replaced the cushion and left. Once more Bertana was bathed in the warmth of the sun.

From the churchyard, a path led to the minster buildings. It trailed through a gap between the abbess's chamber and the guest lodgings, then the extent of the property was before her. To Bertana's right she saw the chapter house, with the monks' dormitory above, the church and a small oratory, both built of stone. To her left there were the rooms where the business of running the minster was planned, and above them the nuns' sleeping quarters, then the refectory and kitchens. Bertana appreciated the clear sense of structure in the minster, otherwise lacking in the rest of the village. With the buildings set in lines, there was an elegance to be found in their tall walls of strong oak plank or stone. Only at the far end, the storerooms and workshops appeared to be built here and there in a less orderly fashion. The sounds of the minster were muted, so when there came the clatter of a pan in the kitchen or the scuffle of birds on the roof, they jarred on the sense of tranquillity.

As Bertana paused for a moment, the door to the refectory opened. Monks and nuns filed out, their heads slightly bowed. They moved in silence, their habits rustling slightly, simple shoes brushing on the dry earth and withered grass. Again, it was a contrast to life in the village where nothing was done without exchanging the news of the day, ensuring noise and bustle filled the air. In the minster, these godly people were like rows of worker ants, each knowing exactly what they were doing and where they needed to go. The line split: the monks to the fields, the brewhouse, the woodworking area, and the nuns to the stillroom, the beehives and weaving shed. Bertana watched them go before continuing on her way.

As she passed the church and oratory, the stillroom beckoned with its curtained door open. Standing on the threshold, Bertana paused to appreciate the aroma. Freshly gathered lavender filled the air, its scent powerful as it mingled with rosemary. There was something different – fresh and uplifting – mint! One of the nuns was tying dried lavender heads, then hanging bunches from the ceiling. The other was pounding a herb or flower head in a clay dish. They wore veils so their features were hidden, but a blue vein across a hand, thin white skin, the wisp of a stray strand of hair and the tone of their words gave clues as to the age and appearance of these women. A whisper of welcome, no more than the soft sound of reeds swaying or a woollen sleeve brushing against a skirt, came from their lips.

"Good afternoon," Bertana said, keeping her voice low. "I would like some cream for soothing the skin and a bag of sweet scents for the home." She moved her basket in a subtle movement to show the leather shoes. The nuns would know the trade was to be a generous one. "It is for my sister who now lives in Aldington; I wish her to be reminded of our modor through marriage."

To use the word 'sister' was something which jarred. True, they had been related through marrying brothers, but Eadlyn had long been the wife of Arlo and there was no friendship between the two women. Yet at this moment, Bertana knew the nuns would look kindly on the display of affection and she knew the gift of cream would bring memories of love and friendship between Eadlyn and the old woman she had called Elder-Modor. There was a nod of understanding while the nun tying lavender placed it on the long wooden table, then turned to the shelves behind her and, having selected a small clay jar, filled it with a thick creamy lotion from a larger pot. The top was sealed with a cloth previously soaked in wax. Then she gathered an assortment of dried flowers and placed them in a hessian bag, pulling the cord tight.

"God bless your sister, Eadlyn, and her family," the nun murmured, each word so softly spoken, they were barely discernible.

"I thank you," Bertana replied, before turning and walking back into the sunlight. "She will be grateful for your blessing."

Glancing across the fields where the monks toiled to gather the bean harvest, Bertana strode past chicken coops and tool stores before she reached the brewhouse and, beside it, a smaller shelter where the mead was brewed then stored. The smell on entering was both sweet and potent. One monk was at work there, his hood falling down his back, showing his face and neck to be sticky with perspiration. A slim clay bottle was soon filled with the golden liquid.

"Peace be with you," the monk said, as the mead was placed on a small table.

"I thank you." Bertana bowed her head a little, then turned to stride back towards the minster kitchen. Here, in a small, sheltered area, she placed the leather shoes crafted by her husband. Gifts to the monks and nuns were given with thanks, but never directly to them. In return, they asked for nothing, accepting that some of the villagers had nothing to offer. As she slipped past the abbess's room and walked through the churchyard, Bertana glanced at the goods in her basket. "These will bring pleasure to our family in Aldington," she murmured.

Chapter Eleven

The next morning Bertana pulled back the curtain covering the opening to their home and gazed up at the sky. She was satisfied to see some cloud to the west. "It will make our journey easier if the sun is shaded a little," she said to Alwin, "and I wouldn't mind a little rain."

"Aye, better than having the sun beating upon us," he replied, while rolling up a blanket and using a strong leather cord to secure it. They hoped to be offered a bed for the night, but it was always wise to travel with some items to make their stay more comfortable.

They had already poured ale into clay flasks, then placed bread, cheese and fruit in a bag with the gifts for the family. Now Bertana returned to their home to stir the porridge. She reached for the wooden bowls to fill. "Do you think Cym will return with us? He will come at some point soon, of course; the boy is Lyminge born and should be here alongside his family. But will he come immediately?" She glanced towards the second bed in the room. The previous evening, they had stuffed the mattress with fresh hay and swept the area clean.

"Nay. He will think of his modor and give them time to become used to him leaving," Alwin suggested. "There will be preparations to make."

"It is no distance at all," she scoffed. "There is nothing to prepare for. A tall young man can walk from Lyminge to Aldington long before the sun has reached its highest point. We shall prove that today, and we are neither young nor tall." She glanced at her husband, "At least *you* are not tall."

He ignored her jibe as he placed the rolled blanket beside another on the bench outside their home. Then, having taken his bowl of porridge and tossed some nuts on the top, Alwin seated himself so he could look across the village while eating.

Bertana left her porridge inside and appeared instead with her arms full of a sheet of thin, brown woollen cloth. "This must be given to Ora," she said. "It can be washed today and no doubt her daughters will help as they have set their minds on Cym being a husband for one of them." She looked towards the nearby home where Cedric and Ora lived with their unmarried daughters, and confided: "I think he can do better for himself; those girls are neither attractive nor robust."

Before Alwin could answer, Bertana was marching towards the next dwelling. He watched as she called for Ora, handed over the material and barked some instructions. She opened her arms showing the extent of the material, clearly expressing how the cloth would hang as a curtain, offering privacy for the young man who was to be staying in their home.

Not long after, their hunger satisfied and the fire left to burn out, Alwin and Bertana checked their shoes were well-fastened, then each slung a leather bag over a shoulder. The time had come to set off to Aldington and claim the son they had not been blessed with.

114

They walked from their home on the gentle hillside, through the shallow dip in the land where the Nailbourne flowed and villagers were beginning their day. Skirting the church and minster, they noted a line of monks and nuns walking in pairs. Even from a distance, a sense of peace radiated from the holy buildings with their orderly grounds. But the scene was nothing new to the leatherworker and his wife; they felt no curiosity about the lives of those living there. All thoughts rested on the journey ahead and the talks which would take place that day.

Soon the lane taking them away from Lyminge became narrow with high banks and trees. Sunlight pierced the covering of leaves above them, emphasising a gnarled root here, a tangle of blackberries there, showing the grass to be a youthful green, whereas in the open fields it was tired and ragged. The air was cool in the sunken lane and this was appreciated as soon the path they trod would be open to the sun.

They had been walking steadily upwards, and when the trees thinned Alwin and Bertana now approached the Roman road from Lympne to Canterbury. At the junction, they paused to take mouthfuls of ale while appreciating the view. This scene never failed to cause Bertana to gasp with pleasure at the beauty of the Kingdom of Kent. The fields and woodland rolled on and, although unseen, she knew there to be small villages with clusters of homes not unlike their own. Signs of the summer harvest were everywhere. Not too far away men with horses and wagons gathered beans or peas. A cart trundled by on the road, holding the pickings of a fruit harvest. The old man who led the

115

horse gave a nod of acknowledgment. They returned it, gathered their bags from the ground, then turned to the south-west, soon turning off the main thoroughfare and back into a narrow lane, this time leading downhill.

Time passed. The clouds, which had promised to shade the sun, moved slowly from the west and eventually offered some respite from the heat. There was no rain, but the cooler air was welcomed. They walked for a while with little sign of human life: a horse and cart on a distant field; the crack and a shout as a tree was felled; the girl who seemed to appear from nowhere, scurrying along with a small basket of eggs. The lane meandered past woodland and pasture; sometimes a stream followed it for a short distance before turning in another direction.

When the next settlement came, it almost caught them unawares as it was shielded by trees, affording only a little view of it from the track. "What is this place called?" Alwin asked his wife.

She frowned, considering his query. "Sellin… Sellindge… I believe."

No more had passed between them before they were approached by a couple of men, swords hanging from baldrics. Clearly wanting no trouble, one of them spoke: "Good morning, friends. What brings you to Sellindge?"

"I am Alvin of Lyminge. We are travelling to see our family in Aldington."

"We wish you well," the other said. "It is a fair day for walking. What is your trade?"

"We are from a family of leatherworkers," Alwin informed them.

"You are well-skilled then," the first remarked. "May God keep you safe as you journey onwards."

"I thank you," Alwin and Bertana responded.

Continuing along the track, they came across a scattered settlement watered by three streams. There was a wooden church to their right. "We turn again before the church," Bertana reminded Alwin. "Then we will pause to enjoy some bread and cheese. Aldington will soon be in sight, but we cannot be sure of our sister welcoming us to her table."

"I believed you were sure of it," Alwin remarked, a slight smirk on his lips.

"I am sure of them wanting the best for Cym once the matter has been discussed," Bertana snapped. "But to have us come and catch them unawares, it will cause confusion and disruption to their day."

"We should have sent a boy to herald our arrival," Alwin suggested.

"I am merely the wife of a leathermaker, and daughter of a farmer," Bertana reminded him, her voice stern. "Our arrival will be enough."

Stopping only long enough to eat, the travellers walked the narrow track which would lead to Aldington. The ground was dusty underfoot, at first still downhill, then rising a little until there were once again magnificent views over pasture, woodland and fields. Here, the most direct route was no more than a path, and they turned onto it, finally able to look across to the settlement they were bound for. Bertana increased her speed, taking longer strides until she paused, turning to her husband, and expressing her confusion: "How

117

many times have we been here? Two or three? I was certain there was a church, over there. A tall building?"

"Aye – a fine structure built in oak, with a neat row of windows under the eaves," Alwin confirmed. He scanned the area, taking in dwellings, animal pens and communal areas such as the weaving shed and bakehouse. Set apart from the area where the humble folk lived and worked, there was the thane's hall, and other homes belonging to his family. It was much the same as any settlement of a fair size in an area of good land, and had definitely been blessed with a church, where smaller villages often had just a cross. "There is a story to be told here," Alwin declared. He walked on, quickening his step with anticipation.

The path across pasture became steep, leading down to bridge a stream, then rising again. On nearing the village boundary, they noted three men with a heavy horse and wagon approaching. One separated himself from the others, walking towards the newcomers. "Good morning. What business do you have in Aldington on this fair day?"

Alwin bristled slightly, noting this man's height and broad shoulders. He appeared to be nothing more than a worker on the land, with no need to question the arrivals.

"We have come from Lyminge to see our sister, Eadlyn of Lyminge," he informed.

"I trust all is well in Lyminge?" the man asked.

"Aye, life is good for us."

"If anyone else asks about your presence here, tell them you have spoken with Godwin of Aldington," the man told them, before adding, "brother of Thane Cenric."

118

"I will," Alwin replied. When they had put a little distance between themselves and Godwin, he remarked, "Brother of the thane! I thought him no more than a field worker."

"He has the stature of someone who works on the land." Bertana watched the other man go, appreciating his height and figure.

"I wonder where we'll find Eadlyn?" Alwin changed the subject.

Now slowing, they strolled past the site of the church, noting the burned ground, and the lonely wooden cross where the people worshipped. The village homes were now before them, and soon they wound their way past buildings and animal pens towards the group of homes where the metalworkers lived, while scanning the area for a familiar face. A flash of red hair under a headscarf and another with her fiery waves loose, led Bertana to exclaim, "Look! Megan, wife of Arlo's brother. Over there with her daughter."

"Should we wait until the family stop for their midday meal?" Alwin queried.

"Nay, word of our arrival will soon spread, and they will be eager to know of what brings us here."

"Perchance they will not be so pleased to see us when they know of our reasons." No longer in his home village, and with strangers all around him, Alwin suddenly wondered about how warm their welcome would be.

"They will be pleased – I am certain of it!" Bertana declared.

As she said the words, her distinctive stature was noted by the woman she called her sister with an affection previously unheard. Eadlyn, stunned by the arrivals from Lyminge, knew they meant no good for her and slipped out of sight, moving between the buildings until she reached her husband who was hammering a sheet of tin on his workbench.

The air was still in the metalworkers' sheltered area. The fire burned white hot. Its heat radiated towards the benches, stores of metal, and items both part-made and complete. The roof trapped the warmth, so it hung, wrapping around the men who laboured with a sheen of sweat across their bodies. Eadlyn stood on the perimeter and paused, knowing Arlo would soon look up and see her.

"Hello," he grinned. "Are you in need of a buckle or a bowl, or does something need repairing?"

"I'm wanting to know what Bertana and Alwin are doing here in Aldington," Eadlyn answered, her expression serious. "Can you come with me, as I don't want to find out on my own?"

"Have you spoken to them?"

"Nay, I saw them and came straight here to you. I can't imagine what they could want, but they must be here to see us."

"Janna? Cedric?" Arlo suggested, referring to Eadlyn's sister from Lyminge and the older brother of her late husband.

She considered this, but soon dismissed the idea: "They would not care enough to give news of Janna, and Cedric... if there were news of him, a messenger would be enough. Nay, if they are here it is for their own purposes, and I fear they mean no good to us."

Arlo placed his hand on Eadlyn's shoulder. "We'll go together and face whatever brings them here."

120

Eadlyn smiled her appreciation. They walked past the backs of the family homes, then turned towards the shared area with an outside fire, benches and a long table. Bertana and Alwin were approaching Megan but, on seeing their prey, they turned with wide smiles on their faces.

"Sister!" Bertana stepped forward, holding out her hands to take Eadlyn's in hers. "How well you look. How we worried to think of you after the earth tremors and we could only pray you had returned home safely."

"All is well, as you can see," Eadlyn responded, pulling herself from the other woman's clutches and stepping back.

"I thank God for that," Alwin declared, raising his eyes to heaven. "Which reminds me – I see only a wooden cross where once there was a church."

"Our sister need not bother herself with telling the story of the church," Bertana butted in. "Clearly there has been a fire. The ground is burned. There were no injuries, or worse, I hope."

"No one was harmed," Arlo replied. "Our good thane has plans to rebuild in stone."

The travellers from Lyminge nodded their understanding and appreciation.

"You have not come to talk of our church, nor to reassure yourselves of our wellbeing," Eadlyn commented. She would not please them by using the familiar terms of brother or sister; they had never spoken to her with those terms of affection before now and their use of those words disturbed her.

"What brings you to Aldington?" Arlo added. "I will fetch cool ale to quench your thirst while you tell us."

The four were soon seated on benches outside. Nearby, Megan was preparing vegetables to add to meat and grain stewing in the pan. She and Eadlyn shared an uneasy look, then a few whispered words: "Stay close by; I know they mean trouble."

"We missed seeing Cym at the Sandtun this year." Alwin cut straight to the point. "He grows to look more like my brother as every year passes."

"He does, despite the fact that Todd was dark and Cym fair," Eadlyn agreed. "We planned to travel to Lyminge after the harvest as usual. You would have seen him then." *It is the same every year; there is no need for a visit to Aldington.* The unsaid words screamed through her mind. *Why are you speaking of my son and his resemblance to his faeder?*

"We were eager to see you before." Alwin smiled, but his dark eyes narrowed. Age had hollowed his cheeks and his face appeared thinner than ever. "He follows in his faeder's path and is learning to craft leather, I hear. How proud Todd would have been."

"Aye, and proud of Clover too," Arlo pointed out. "She is a lovely young woman."

Bertana sat beside her husband, her back straight. She allowed her husband to speak but now the words burst from her: "Will Cym return here for his midday meal? We are eager to hear how he is enjoying learning the skills of his forefathers."

"Although he learns them at the hands of others," Alwin added.

It is Cym they want. Eadlyn felt her body stiffen and she answered, the words abrupt, "He'll be here to eat with his family."

122

"The leatherworker Cym works beside is well-respected," Arlo told them.

"He may well be, but would you want your son or nephew to learn with one who is not their blood?" Bertana asked.

"If Cym's faeder were here my son would be taught at his side," Eadlyn reminded her. "But that was not to be." She placed her hand on Arlo's thigh – a gesture to remind him of how thankful she was for the love he offered both her and the children of her first marriage.

"But Cym can learn with his family," Bertana stated. A flash of jealousy pierced her. She swept it aside, not wanting the display of closeness to distract her from the purpose of this visit. "He is the only son to be born from Cedric, Todd or Alwin, so now he must return to us. His uncles want to teach him as their father taught them."

"It is how it would have been if Todd were alive," Alwin continued.

"I know," Eadlyn admitted. At that moment it seemed as if it were the true path for her son. Standing abruptly, she took a few steps away from them and said, "I'll tell Megan you'll be eating with us today."

"Cym is a man, so will make his own choice," Arlo said. "He will be here us when the sun reaches its highest point. Until then, I must return to my work and no doubt Eadlyn has her duties." He walked over to his wife and placed a hand in the small of her back. "Go, my love. Collect the water, or the bread. Take yourself away from these people for a moment."

"We brought gifts," Bertana called. "From the minster." Her words were ignored.

Chapter Twelve

The pull of Lyminge was strong for the young man who had left as a child of only three years. He recalled the excitement felt when standing by the stone church and saw the village afresh each year. Despite tales of hardship forced upon his mother by his uncles after she was widowed, Cym had found his uncles to be amicable towards him. The girl cousins, Cedric's daughters, had made good playmates on the visits when he was younger, and there was a secret admiration for the strong-willed Bertana.

"I am content here in Aldington, but it would be an honour to learn leather-making in the place where my faeder crafted," he said, having been faced with the unexpected offer on his return for the midday meal. "I don't remember my faeder," Cym continued. "But I do know my modor was blessed when she met Arlo, who has given us a fine life here."

Eadlyn, her meal of beans, barley and summer vegetables lying heavy in her stomach, said, "You already follow in Todd's path, but if you were to choose to learn beside his family, we would understand."

"But I hope you choose to be here," Clover cried out. "Don't make it too easy, Modor. He can learn to craft leather here *and* be with his family."

"I can," Cym agreed. "I won't decide in a hurry. It is a choice I had never thought of."

"Let us meet again this evening," Arlo suggested, "and say nothing more of it. Cym has enough on his mind. I will take our visitors to Thane Cenric and ask for shelter in his barn overnight. If Cym has decided by tomorrow, they will know. If he wants longer then it is no trouble to travel to Lyminge with a message."

That night Bertana and Alwin retired to an area reserved for travellers; they laid their blankets on hay-filled mattresses set on wooden pallets. Bertana was quietly triumphant. Conversation at the fireside that evening had been agreeable, and she saw Eadlyn would not try to force her son to remain in Aldington. *I have been cruel in my feelings towards her*, Bertana admitted to herself. *She is a good mother to give her son the freedom he must have.* With these warm thoughts in her mind, she wrapped her arm around Alwin's waist and kissed him soundly before falling asleep.

In their home, Eadlyn was subdued. *I should be thankful they waited until he was fully grown.* She tried to find comfort in the many years shared with her son. *They could have fought for Cym when he was a boy of ten or perhaps twelve. Old enough to begin scraping the fat and hair from the skins and sweeping the floors. I should be thankful that it is no distance to Lyminge, and my son will be well-cared for. But today and through the days that follow, I cannot be kind in my thoughts towards these people who have intruded on our lives.* She reached and grasped Arlo's hand. He gave hers a squeeze, then kissed her gently on the forehead.

The following morning, Cym rose before dawn. His mother heard him swing his legs out of bed, dress, and leave the home. She allowed him to go without question, resisting the temptation to follow. Walking around the village boundary, Cym gave a wave to the night watchmen finishing their work and saw his neighbours emerge from their homes as the sun broke free from the horizon. He completed his route, then seated himself on a log outside the barn where his visiting relations had spent the night. Now a decision had been made a sensation of calmness settled on the young man and he was content to wait.

When Bertana stepped out, it was as if she knew – a broad smile spread across her face and she called to her husband: "Make haste. Cym has come to see us." As soon as Alwin appeared, Bertana asked her nephew, "Do you have news for us?"

"Aye." He gave a small smile. "I would like to come to Lyminge, but there are matters to settle here first. For a start, our good thane is asking for all young men to help move cut stone to the site of the new church. I would like to be a part of that. Then I will see my sister marry and after that I'll travel to Lyminge. This will be in two cycles of the moon."

Bertana looked at Alwin. He stepped forward, clasping his brother's son on the shoulder. "That is wonderful news! You will be most welcome in Lyminge. We will say farewell to your family here, then return with the good news."

"I am sure your modor will be visiting as soon as you are settled," Bertana reminded Cym. "She makes her annual visit after the harvest." The goodwill towards Eadlyn was now boundless and her sister by marriage continued, "Mayhap one visit will not be enough, and she will journey to Lyminge twice a year."

"I can travel to Aldington; it is no distance." Cym glanced towards the site of the church. "I will be keen to watch the stone walls rise, as well as see my family."

Alwin and Bertana left the village when the sun had risen clear of the woodland to the east. She was overflowing with a sense of well-being, her mind full of how she would nurture the young man who was to be living with them. Imagining herself in the weaving shed creating the blankets for his bed, or in the home adding honey and nuts to his porridge, Bertana smiled to herself. The walk to Lyminge was an uphill trudge, but this was nothing to the woman who was quietly victorious and reached for her husband's hand as a gesture of them being truly united.

"I should not want a woman like that for a wife," Godwin remarked to his brother. "She is more man than her husband could ever be."

"What woman?" the thane asked.

"The wife of the leathermaker. Do you see them, walking across the fields? I hope they did not come to cause trouble, but I have a feeling it was so."

"That woman!" a grin spread over Cenric's face. "I should take her as a lover, but not a wife! You see her as a man? Nay, she is a strong woman though."

"I would not take her as a lover!" Godwin exclaimed.

"Of course. You have romance on your mind and seek a loving wife. I have not forgotten. Let us see if Lympne has a good woman available."

A plan was in place to visit the thane in the nearby village. The day before, a messenger had been sent and, as they breakfasted, horses were being prepared. Cenric's wife and their daughter Edina would accompany them, as well as Father Theodore who now approached, his hand clutching at the cross resting on his chest.

"I have prayed long for guidance," he declared.

"Then you must be in need of sustenance," Cenric replied.

"My needs are few," the priest reminded his benefactor. "Some porridge would be welcome, but I have no want for it to be sweetened with fruit or honey."

"What guidance do you seek?" Godwin asked.

"I wish to be sure that our Lord knows the stone church and its adornments are there only to serve Him, and that for myself I would pray in a hut if the message sent to the heavens was as strong." The priest spoke with passion. "I need to be sure that a stone church is His wish."

"Very wise," Godwin responded. He reached for a couple of plums and bit into the golden flesh.

"You are too good!" The thane was quick to offer his opinion. "It is in the hands of our friends in Lympne, for I am certain the Lord knows how true to Him you are."

By mid-morning, the thane's family and his priest were riding along the road towards Lympne. They had passed the open land offering views across Romney Marsh, and now entered a wooded area. Godwin, with the two stocky men who escorted them, each kept one hand on the hilt of a sword, while their eyes scanned the shadowed areas under the trees. They passed through with no incident, the only sign of life being that of wild boar and birds, then entered a clearing where the settlement was scattered not far from the edge of the escarpment.

Villagers turned from their daily business to watch the arrivals, at first with suspicion in their eyes. The newcomers were soon recognised as being from nearby Aldington, and a few nodded a welcome. The thane's hall was set apart from the other dwellings, near the church. A fire burned in a pit outside the hall, and over the flames a hog was roasting.

"A fine welcome," Thane Cenric said to his wife and brother. "I pray our good relations with Lympne are long-standing."

"I suggest you are modest with your request for their stone," Godwin murmured.

Cenric ignored this, turning to his daughter. "Edina, this is a splendid place, don't you think? You would only need to step through those trees and the whole of Romney Marsh would be in front of you. Think of that: you can see land belonging to Aldington from the thane's hall here in Lympne! I believe he has a son who may like to meet you."

"You know very well he has a son!" Godwin countered, amusement in his voice. "But look, Cenric, here is our sister, Cate…"

At that moment Thane Selwyn of Lympne strolled towards them, accompanied by two women. One rushed forward, as best she could: the curves of her stomach showed her to be heavy with child. "How wonderful to see you!" Cate clasped her brothers to her, one after the other, before taking the arm of Cenric's wife and holding out her hand for Edina.

The second woman, wife of the thane, expressed her pleasure in having visitors, then busied herself producing cups of wine. Children gathered and, by the time they were seated, Brice, brother of Thane Selwyn and husband to Cate, had arrived. Greetings were renewed as they congratulated him on the forthcoming birth of his first child and wished their sister well. Amidst the sharing of news, flying from one to another, Father Theodore slipped away to the solitude of the church.

Before the hog was served, the men took a stroll around the village boundaries. Standing by the church, the view of the Sandtun and Romney Marsh was breathtaking. "Has the Sandtun returned to how it was?" Thane Cenric asked.

"Aye. A fresh layer of sand and shells lies upon it," Thane Selwyn answered. "There were a couple of men from Francia who patched up their boats with help from our men, then returned to their country. Sadly, another man was lost and there has been no sign of a body. His shattered boat washed up on the beach and no doubt we will do something with it. His was the only loss of life we know of."

Cenric moved a little, placing himself on the edge of the escarpment, and looked down on the slumped fort. There were a couple of men moving amongst the fallen stones. The colours of the blocks and mortar remained fresh where the walls had come apart; it was too early for them to weather or for the tenacious roots of tiny creeping plants to settle within the cracks and pores.

"No doubt you will be using some of the stone," Thane Cenric probed. "What plans do you have?"

"We are thinking of a stone church," Thane Selwyn informed him. "The stone here is already cut and it has lain unused for too long."

"Have you heard…" Cenric spoke with an innocence which led his brother to raise his eyes to the heavens, "… heard that our church has suffered from fire? It is entirely ruined."

"Reports of this came to us," the other thane responded. "We were saddened to hear of it. Do you know the cause? Could any of it be saved?"

"It was ruined!" Thane Cenric replied, more than a hint of drama in his voice. "What a thing to happen! It brings me to think that our own holy place would be better if built in stone."

"A worthy ambition," Thane Selwyn agreed.

"Brother, do you have any plans about where to quarry?" Godwin asked, a glint in his eyes.

"It seems as if there is no need to quarry when our good friend here has enough for us all," Cenric suggested. The men still stood on the edge of the hillside, gazing down at the fort and, beyond it, Romney Marsh. "What do you say, Selwyn? We are as good as family, in fact I have more to say about that when we are with our good wives again. I daresay you would not miss some of the stone cut by those long-gone Romans?"

Thane Selwyn turned his back to the fort and scanned his settlement. His eyes rested on a beautiful grey mare with dappled flanks and neck. "I say, Cenric of Aldington, you have a fine mare there."

Godwin could not hold back a snort of laughter. His brother had certainly met his match!

131

The men now caught sight of Father Theodore and Cenric was keen to have the priest at his side. "There he is – my worthy priest. Do you know he sleeps in a shelter no better than I give my pigs? He asks for nothing and it would give me such pleasure to reward his good works with a new church. How we mourn the wooden structure. You may recall its height and the fine workmanship in some of the wood carvings?"

"I do," Thane Selwyn answered. "But even in a stone church you will need wooden beams and a door, so your carpenters will be well employed."

"If there is stone to be brought from here, all our men will be a part of it," Thane Cenric enthused. "All who are strong enough will be hauling the blocks back to Aldington, while others can still be involved. I would like to pray in your church for their strength and for God to look kindly on all who labour in order that we can praise Him in a building worthy of His holiness." He raised his voice and called to the priest, "Father Theodore, let us pray together. Side by side."

"In the meantime, Godwin can accompany me, and I will make myself known to this fine beast which you have so kindly offered as a small token of appreciation," Selwyn replied. "Come, Godwin, let us look at the mare. Then we shall eat."

The talk at the meal table was of family matters before, to Thane Cenric's pleasure, it turned to the practicalities of hauling the stone up the escarpment to the summit and transporting it to Aldington. They spoke of the oxen to be used and whether there was enough strong rope.

"Will the men of Aldington be eager to labour in such a way?" Thane Selwyn asked. "Even with the oxen, they will need all their strength to manoeuvre the stone."

"The men of Aldington are fit from working on the land and if their bodies tire, their hearts will be filled with zeal, giving them strength to continue," Cenric informed him. "My men are honoured to be a part of this project. When they see the stone church rising beside the ashes of the other, they will feel proud to have been a part of it."

"I am glad of it," Selwyn responded.

"The men have indeed worked long hours, and the harvest has been good," Godwin added. "No stone will be moved until all our crops have been gathered and stored. Only then will there be the men free to transport the stone."

"Alongside those who work on the land, we have others who are strong enough," Cenric enthused. "Thatchers, leatherworkers, woodworkers – all the crafts you can think of. They will all be a part of it."

Father Theodore, sitting slightly apart from the others, listened intently and sipped at his noggin of good wine. The women spoke quietly amongst themselves, while the children were watchful, waiting for the time they could slip away. Hovering nearby, the servants offered more meat, then fruit, and finally honey cake. Both wine and conversation flowed easily.

"How pleasant it is to be with our neighbours and family," Thane Selwyn remarked.

"We should talk of our families uniting further." Cenric glanced towards his young daughter sitting beside Selwyn's son. "I would be pleased to think of Edina being under the care of her aunt when she

133

reaches an age to leave us. To have her settled at Lympne would mean my daughter remains close by and strengthens the bond already forged when our dear sister married your brother."

The manor of Aldington was large, with land not only on the hills surrounding the village but spreading in vast tracts across Romney Marsh. This fertile land brought great wealth. Thane Selwyn of Lympne was aware of the benefits of being on close terms with his neighbours. The girl, Edina, was quiet with a healthy glow to her skin, shining eyes and glossy hair. Her aunt was proving to be fertile and Edina came from a family where the children were born strong. Selwyn of Lympne glanced at his wife, who had clearly heard the suggestion. She gave a small smile, and he returned it with a broader one.

"I suggest we speak more of this in private," Selwyn replied. "It is a union which can only be favourable to us both."

When the family from Aldington, and their priest, left Lympne, Thane Cenric was satisfied by the outcome of the visit. The only regret being that he was astride his dappled mare for the last time. She would be returning to Lympne on the following day and soon be snatching at the fresh grass in the field on the edge of the escarpment.

Chapter Thirteen

"Look, Modor, Hilda's stitches are so neat now." Clover beckoned Eadlyn, who was gazing towards the charred ground where the church had been.

"Thane Cenric appears to be marking out where he plans to have the new church built," Eadlyn observed, as she turned to her daughters who were sewing in the evening sunlight. "He has Godwin there, stonemasons and the priest, of course."

"He will be keen to start work," Clover commented. "Our good thane is passionate about the new church and if it were not for his brother's influence, I am sure the men would already be moving the stone."

"Aye, Godwin was adamant the food must be harvested first," Eadlyn agreed. "I thank God for the younger brother and his steady ways. But never mind about that – there are hems to be sewn."

Hilda tucked the needle into her beige linen, then held it up for her mother to see. All the girls and women in the family were having new dresses. There was a fold on the hem of the skirt, and she was completing the second row of small, even stitches. "Is it straight enough?" she asked.

"You have done well." Eadlyn smiled at her younger daughter. "The task is dull, but you will be glad of this on your sister's wedding day. And you have the brooch your faeder made last week; it will look fine against this cloth."

The summer evenings gave the family an opportunity to relax in the golden warmth of the sun. On a nearby bench, Arlo and Penton were sipping wine, while Megan and her daughters sat on a rug, threading small clay beads onto leather cords. The third family home was now complete and Eadric was already living there, ready to be joined by his new wife within another cycle of the moon. Clover glanced towards the man she would soon marry and smiled. His bad mood had passed. All was well again.

In the village, the pace slowed as the sun began to drop behind the trees to the west. The people gathered their animals for the night or strolled to the stream to fill jugs. As they sewed, Eadlyn and her daughters looked up occasionally to watch their neighbours go about their tasks. A young woman meandered through the settlement, looking this way and that. Her hair was dark, and her figure slight.

"I didn't know we had a visitor to Aldington," Eadlyn commented. "Do you recognise her, Clover?"

Clover watched the woman's progress for a moment. "Nay. I've not seen her before."

"We'll hear soon enough." Eadlyn turned back to the line of stitches on a sleeve.

A moment later and Clover glanced up to see the young woman walking directly towards them. As she neared, it became clear her clothes were ragged and feet bare. Brown eyes roamed over the women sewing, then to the men with their wine. At that moment Eadric stepped out of his new home, holding his hand to shield his eyes from the sunlight. The stranger paused, then took a few more paces. Penton called to his son, who laughed and was about to respond when the smile fell from his face. Clover saw him shrink back a little; her skin began to prickle and her mouth dried.

"Eadric?" The young woman said. Her husky voice made his name sound different.

He flashed a look at Clover, and faced the newcomer, but said nothing in reply. The woman took another step towards him. Clover noticed her legs were dusty; she must have been walking all day.

"Eadric," she repeated, now standing at the edge of their family group. Everyone had turned towards her. No one stood or offered a welcome. They merely waited. The sun gave the scene a richness of colour lacking when it was at its full height. The fire smouldered. Beetles scurried across dry soil and ragged grass. In the distance, a flock of starlings rose from the trees.

"Felice." Eadric's voice was low, while it seemed as if his skin had paled.

The young woman, whose name was now known to them all, took another step forward. Where her eyes had appeared fearful, and expression serious, she now smiled. "Eadric," she repeated, moving forward once more, then placing her hand on her flat stomach in a protective gesture.

Already sensing danger, the mothers, Eadlyn and Megan, stood. They glanced at one another and Eadlyn placed her hand on Clover's shoulder. The young man was still unaware of the scene about to play out before them all, but the women knew and were helpless to protect their grown children. Megan walked to stand by her son's side, then asked, "Who is she?"

137

"I found her hiding in the trees with her father," Eadric said. "They were there for several days and I took them food. Then they were gone." His voice was low, so the others nearby could only guess at the words exchanged between mother and son. "Now Felice has returned for some reason. Perchance she is hungry? We must feed her."

"Aye, she is hungry," Megan agreed, "but that is not why this woman seeks you out. She is carrying your child."

"Nay!" The horror on his face was unmistakable. "How could that be?"

There was no need for Megan to respond; they both knew how a child was conceived. Yet how the dark-eyed Felice had lured Eadric was, as yet, a mystery. Seeing his distress, the stranger moved forward, needing to claim her possession of this man and comfort him. She placed her hand on his arm, speaking softly with words which meant nothing to Megan, further mystifying her as to where the woman came from.

Once so alluring, the husky softness of her voice and the pressure of her hand now filled Eadric with fear. He saw nothing to tempt him in her brown eyes, while the dark hair was dull with grease. There was a stale whiff about her, where before there had only been sweetness. The touch of her hand on his arm was intolerable. Eadric swung away from her. As he did so, the vomit rose in his throat, causing him to expel the contents of his stomach by the doorway of his new home. Without pausing to glance at the family, and unable to face the hurt in Clover's eyes, he ran, slipping between the homes and past his workplace.

138

The earth was hard; Eadric felt every stone and ridge under the leather sole of his shoes. His mouth was sour, his ears pounded and thoughts formed no reasonable pattern in his mind. Having raced some distance beyond the village boundary, he now slowed to a walk, then found himself by a narrow stream. The water was sluggish, but he cupped his hands and sloshed a little over his face before rinsing his mouth. Now, on the far side of the copse where Felice had first been spotted, Eadric glanced, out of habit, towards the trees. With the evening setting in, they were dark and foreboding. The young man stood, turned, and began his steady trudge up the sloping fields to the knoll.

With Eadric gone from the family group, a stunned silence hung over those who remained. Rather than fleeing from the scene, Felice sat on the ground, tears rolling slowly down her cheeks. Megan, left standing near the newcomer, leaned down to give an awkward pat on her shoulder, before walking towards Clover and Eadlyn. She knelt, placing a hand on each of their knees.

"Who is she?" Clover whispered. "What does she want from Eadric?"

"My sweeting, I think she wants him for herself," Megan replied. There was no hiding the truth of it. "This stranger speaks with a foreign tongue. Who she is will no doubt be revealed in time."

"But she is nothing to him. He was sick to see her."

"No woman repulses a man to such an extent that he vomits, unless there is good reason to fear her," Eadlyn suggested.

"She would be beautiful if it were not for her ragged appearance," Clover observed, her voice leaden. "I wonder if she were once beautiful to him. Look at her eyes." The other women turned and looked at the dark pools, brimming with tears, begging them for help.

"I should send her away," Megan suggested, "but it would make no difference. Perchance she would hide out nearby in wait for him."

"Does he want her?" Clover asked, half to herself.

"Nay!" the mothers protested.

"I hear you, but there will be no way of knowing until I have spoken to Eadric." Clover stood, shaking off the comfort of their hands. "Even if he does not speak, I will know when I see him."

They watched her leave, somehow finding the strength to walk past Felice. The stranger dropped her gaze to the ground.

"How did this happen?" Eadlyn whispered.

Megan repeated Eadric's words about how he had come to know Felice. "And when I said she was carrying his child, the sickness rose," she continued. "I fear he knows it could be true. I am so ashamed that my son has brought this woman to our family and worry there is nowhere else for her to go."

Felice remained sitting on the ground, her knees drawn up to her body and hands clutching at her calves. Her hair hung in lank tails across her shoulders and down her back, while her eyes roamed from one person to another. She had watched Clover leave, admired her long golden hair and the healthy colour of her skin. Sometimes she glanced towards the men, but mostly it was the women who were observed. Felice knew it was

Eadric's mother with the red hair who would most likely decide her fate.

"What shall we do with her?" Eadlyn asked, wanting to march Felice to the village boundary, but knowing it was too late to undo the harm caused. "Whatever she has done – they have done – she is hungry and no doubt exhausted."

"My heart aches for Clover," Megan began, "but this girl – she is hardly a woman – is starving and has used all her strength to come here to face us. I will feed her, then offer a bed." She glanced towards the third dwelling. "I cannot allow her in the home which is to be Clover's. Penton and Osric can put up the tent. It will be better than she has been used to these past weeks. Will you speak with them, and I'll go to her?"

"I will," Eadlyn rose from the bench. She turned to place her hand on her younger daughter's shoulder. "Hilda, my dearling, please fetch the blankets we brought back from the Sandtun; they are ragged but clean enough. She will need something to sleep on."

Megan walked towards Felice, wondering how to communicate. Putting a hand on the young woman's arm, she prompted her to stand. The stranger gave a slight smile, but Megan gave none in return; she would care for her but could not extend a welcome. Felice allowed herself to be seated on an empty bench, her eyes following the progress of Eadric's mother as she walked into the home, returning with a plate of cheese, bread and plums. The food was accepted with a smile and words expressing thanks. While Felice devoured it, Megan placed a pan of water over the fire to warm.

"Alfreda, we cannot leave this young woman in rags. I would give her one of my dresses, but I am tall, and it would only drag on the ground." Megan approached a trunk in their home. "Can she wear one of yours until her own is washed and repaired?"

"I am to give my dress to a woman who has come here to snatch my brother from my dear friend and cousin?" Had it not been dark within the home, her mother would have seen the fury flash in Alfreda's eyes.

"Aye. That is what I ask of you," Megan admitted. "But also, to offer clothing to a stranger who is desperate and starving. Look how thin she is."

"Take it." Alfreda opened the trunk, pulling out a dress of thin woollen thread, then an apron of a rougher material.

Megan took one of her own linen shifts to be worn underneath. "I will bring her in here to wash," she told her daughter.

"I will go and sit with Hilda." Alfreda stalked out, tossing her head, causing her long fiery hair to ripple down her back.

When Megan returned to the fire, the water was hot. She poured it in a bucket and beckoned Felice to follow her into the home. Leaving the young woman in her shift, so as to give some privacy, Megan took a bar of scented lye soap and a clean rag, then began to wash first her face and neck, before starting on her upper body. While doing so, she tried to shut out the fear of harm coming to the family, thinking only of cleaning the dirt from Felice's young skin.

Clover caught up with Eadric as he approached the knoll. No words were exchanged. They walked on without looking at each other, but she sensed he did not mind her being there and that was enough for the moment. They crossed a track which followed the line of the hills, offering glimpses of the marshy lowlands. Then began the ascent of the knoll. At the peak, Eadric slumped on the dry grass, facing to the south.

The colours of Romney Marsh were rich in the evening light: strands of golden-topped reeds marking the trailing waterways; the dark green of lush growth in rich boggy soil; mysterious pools of blackening water, seeming still from a distance yet rich with tiny insects. A formation of geese flew high above the flat land.

When the reds and oranges in the sky had deepened further, Clover spoke, "The Sandtun is back to as it was before the flood. From here it's as if it never happened."

"But it did happen," Eadric said, his voice expressionless.

"Aye, and now we are changed." He said nothing in response, so after a moment Clover asked, "Have you chosen to be with her, Eadric? Who is she?"

"I would never choose her over you," he replied with force. "At least not if I were in my right mind."

"Or if she were carrying your child?"

"How can they know, my mother and yours?" He turned to look at Clover, and she saw the dread in his eyes.

"They are used to reading the signs," Clover suggested. "There must be a chance, or you wouldn't be here now. You would have faced it if there were no reason for it to be true."

"I know."

"Who is she?" Clover asked again.

"I found her hiding out in the copse with a man. Her father, I presume. They wanted food."

"Where has she come from? She does not speak our tongue."

"Francia. Their boat was broken up in the tidal wave." He gazed into the distance, as if picturing the scene.

"I have never seen a woman at the Sandtun," Clover remarked.

"Nor me," Eadric agreed. "She must have remained on the boat, or perchance they had just arrived. I don't know."

There were sheep grazing on the land from which the knoll rose. Clover watched them snatching at the grass and began to put together the pieces of the story, coming to understand how Felice had entered Eadric's life.

"You've betrayed me," Clover said at last. "Should I be glad that she came before we married? Before it was too late for you to take her as your wife instead?"

"Take her as my wife?" he repeated.

"Look at her, poor and ragged. Would you have your child born to a life of hunger and fear, when you could care for it?"

"But I am to marry you. Our home is ready."

"Nay, Eadric. It cannot be. We both know that." Clover stood and began her descent of the knoll. "Your home is ready for a wife. Not the wife you first chose, but another."

"I'm sorry," he called out.

Clover heard the fear in his voice. Their future had been planned for as long as both of them remembered. Drawn to each other as children, they had met at the Sandtun every summer to explore the nearby beach and marshland, with younger siblings trailing behind.

144

Later, they became cousins through marriage, living side-by-side and sharing family life. The two young people became best friends then, later, lovers. Now, for the first time, they looked to the days and weeks ahead and saw themselves on separate paths.

Chapter Fourteen

"Perhaps there is no child," Penton suggested. "How are we to be certain?"

"She has been sick for the last three mornings," Megan pointed out.

"I'd be sick if I came to snare a husband and found him about to marry a woman as lovely as Clover." Penton shifted a little to ease the discomfort in his withered leg.

There had been four days of Felice drifting about on the edge of the family group. She ate with them and spent her days walking on one of the many tracks leading from the village into the surrounding fields or woodland, then resting under the cover of the tent's cloth walls. The newcomer offered to help the women with their chores as best she could, but they declined her attempts to follow them into the weaving shed, to knead the bread alongside them, or prepare the meals. It was too soon to accept her impending place amongst them.

On the first morning, Megan had taken Felice to the stream and washed her long dark hair. Then the young woman had seated herself on the bench near the fire and combed it through. Now it hung in a sheet of glossy brown. The women noted that she took care to comb it daily. Her skin had been cleaned, and the ragged clothes taken to be washed and repaired. The stale odour was replaced with a sweetness, aided by a small bag of lavender hanging from a belt.

"Today I must find her some shoes," Megan said to her husband. It was the fifth morning since Felice had come into their lives.

"Today we must decide what is to happen with her," Penton replied, his voice firm. He turned to Eadric who was sitting near his parents. "She can't remain here like this, living amongst us but not part of the family."

In the past four days, Eadric, sullen and silent, had worked long hours at the metalwork, then retreating to his new home before sunset. Unable to bring himself to communicate with Felice in any way, he barely glanced in her direction. The attraction, once so strong, was nothing to him now.

"Son, will you speak with her?" Megan asked.

"She does not speak our tongue," he countered.

"Take her for a walk, to the knoll… or through the fields, and ask yourself if you can send her away, knowing both she and your child will suffer," Megan suggested.

"Clover suffers," Eadric pointed out.

"Aye, she does," Megan agreed. "No one wants Clover to be hurt, but she has the love of her family and Felice has no one. You cannot ignore this anymore."

"Your modor is right," Penton said. "For the sake of everyone, a decision must be made. There is no choice between them as Clover will not marry you now. You have to decide if you can treat Felice with kindness and care for her as your wife."

"How can I do that?" Eadric questioned, his voice tinged with anguish.

147

"You found it no hardship to leave her carrying a child, and now you must ask her to be your wife," Penton insisted. "I hear your modor speaking of you choosing either to keep her with us or sending her away, but we cannot have her cast out of this village. Take her somewhere away from prying eyes and ask her to be your wife. Say you will care for her. She is pretty enough, as you well know, and seems docile too. This stranger is not the wife I would want for you, but after the wedding I am sure she will prove willing enough to please you."

"I cannot bear to look at her," Eadric murmured. He had never known his father to be so unyielding.

"Are you denying that you have left her with your child?" Penton asked.

Eadric did not answer. They all knew there had been a time when Felice had tempted him. Now he had to find the strength to approach her and begin to plan their future. It was still early in the day, and no one else in their family group had emerged from their homes. The young man stood and walked the few paces to the tented shelter where Felice slept. He flopped onto the ground beside the entrance, waiting for her to emerge, resigning himself to communicating as best they could.

The woman who had crossed the sea from Francia was already awake. Eadric could hear her shuffling about. He wondered, for the first time, how it felt to be alone in a new country with no home or family to give comfort. The man who appeared to be her father had gone. Eadric considered if he had abandoned Felice on learning about the child, or if, between them, they had decided she would fare better in securing a husband without the older man at her side. Thinking back to

148

those intimate moments at the copse, he wondered if they were planned in the hope of planting his seed in her and making a home here in Aldington. *I did not object at the time. Not once did I try to stop, even though the loveliest woman was waiting to be my wife. And when she left, I returned to the copse day after day, hoping for her return, reliving the memories of the times we shared. I told myself I was glad she had gone, that I could not continue the burden of feeding her, but my thoughts were still with the temptations of her body. Would it be so difficult to marry Felice and take her to the home I created with Clover?* He glanced towards the newly thatched roof and the pale oak plank walls. *Would it be that bad to take Felice to my bed every night?* There was a stirring in his treacherous loins while Eadric considered that it would not be at all unpleasant to take the dark-eyed young woman as his wife.

At that moment, there was movement at the doorway of the home of his uncle, Arlo. Clover stepped out, her long golden hair swinging in ripples across her shoulders and down her back. She carried a jug in one hand and paused to lean down to fasten one of her shoes. Still crouching, she glanced up and saw Eadric sitting on the ground outside Felice's tent. For a moment, their eyes met.

I cannot do as my parents wish, the thought screamed in Eadric's head. He bounded past the benches and the fire in its pit, then stood in front of Clover. "Please come and speak with me. Now. Speak with me away from the family."

She shrugged her shoulders, looking at him with no emotion in her eyes, and placed the jug on the ground.

They walked a short distance from their homes before Clover asked. "What do you want from me?"

"I want to marry you as we planned or sooner," Eadric replied.

"We cannot marry." Clover set a brisk pace along a track to the south. She did not slow down or turn to look at Eadric as they spoke. "I will not marry a man who is so easily swayed by another woman."

"Nay, Clover. It will never happen again. I have done wrong and beg you to forgive me."

"Why were you waiting outside her tent?" she asked.

"To tell her to leave us alone," Eadric lied, raising his voice to express the passion he felt. "To tell her she means nothing to me."

"Your child grows within her," Clover stated. "What plans do you have for it?"

Eadric stepped off the path, no more than a track worn smooth by use, and onto the grass. He flopped on the ground and gestured for Clover to sit beside him. "How can we talk at such a speed?"

"If I do not rush about and keep busy, I will see her face watching me, and if I allow myself time to think, then I fear that I will never stop the tears from flowing." Clover sat on the ground beside Eadric, drew her knees up to her chest and wrapped her arms around her legs as if to shield herself from harm.

"I'm sorry," Eadric said.

"I believe you and pray that one day I will be able to forgive."

"My parents feel a duty to care for Felice and the child," Eadric told her.

"Your parents are good people."

"The child will not suffer, nor its modor." Eadric began to clutch at a plan barely formed in his mind, having only just considered it when he sat down by Felice's tent waiting for her. "If we were to leave, we could make a home elsewhere. Perchance your family in Lyminge would welcome us? Or somewhere new? Anywhere. I will take my tools and soon prove my skills. It will not be easy to leave our families and the home we made, but we shall be together."

Clover turned to look at Eadric. Her gaze ran over his red hair and blue eyes, the callouses and burns on his hands from the hours spent working metal, his long, freckled limbs. She twisted a little, preparing to stand and walk away. "I'm sorry you are suffering, but there is nothing I can do to ease this. Leave if you want to, but I will have no part of it.

As she stood, Clover felt a movement under her dress and the gold pendant slipped out from its secret spot. She placed her fingers on it, feeling the dome of the ruby and the splayed ends of the cross. Wearing it around her neck brought a comfort. Clover had taken the pendant out of its small box on the day Felice arrived, then worn it day and night, falling asleep with her fingers tracing the golden swirls and smooth red stone.

No more words were exchanged. Eadric, still sprawled on the grass, allowed her to walk away from him on the path to the village. On the same route, the thane and his brother approached.

How unusual to see Thane Cenric at this early hour, Clover observed as the men neared. *I would expect him to be with the priest or eating alongside his family. His days follow the same pattern, as far as I can tell. His*

151

brother is different and can often be seen working in the fields from dawn. They seemed to be deep in conversation and Clover expected no more than a brief greeting on passing them. However, the thane, his beady eyes alighting on the pendant cross, could not allow the young woman to pass.

"Good morning. Another fine one!" Cenric boomed. "The good Lord seeks to bless us with a fine day."

"Aye, he does," Clover murmured. The unexpected suggestion from Eadric had left her agitated. She thought ahead to pummelling clothes at the stream or kneading dough, and, stepping off the path, intended to move past the men.

"What a decorative pendant you wear," the thane remarked. "Was it crafted by Arlo Smith?" The words were said with assumed innocence, for Thane Cenric knew full well that the striking cross had not been worked in Aldington.

"Nay, it was a gift from my faeder, Todd of Lyminge." Clover reddened a little, longing to ease the cross into its hiding place under the material of her dress.

"Where would your faeder have been honoured with such an exceptional piece of jewellery?" Thane Cenric probed. "He must have been in great favour with the Thane of Lyminge?"

"Come Cenric, leave her alone." Godwin saw Clover's discomfort and his tone was sharp. "I have no time to stand here bothering Clover."

The young woman flashed a look of gratitude towards Godwin, but his brother took no heed.

"May I take a closer look?" Cenric asked. "Was it a gift to your faeder?"

152

"I... don't know," Clover replied, tugging at the leather lace which was caught up with her hair at the nape of her neck. "It was found with him when he died." She handed it to the thane.

"A mystery!" He held it to the light, while they all gazed at the pinkish-red of the smooth ruby, the splayed cross and ornate scrolls on its surface. "This gold has some weight to it. Do you wear it every day?"

"I rarely wear it. But sometimes I want to think of my faeder, although I barely remember him." Clover reached to take the cross from the thane and folded her fingers around it, feeling it secure against her palm.

"You are privileged to have it," Thane Cenric said. "I would suppose it has religious significance and once belonged to a very holy man. Our own priest, with his humble aspirations, would never presume to wear an item such as this."

"His own cross is fine enough," Godwin was swift to point out. "You are right, Father Theodore would want nothing so elaborate." He noted the look of fear on the young woman's face, and the knuckles on her hand whiten. "Keep it very safe, Clover. I will say nothing of the precious gift from your good faeder and wish you well. We must make haste, brother."

Clover took her chance to move away from the men. She quickened her pace, eager to return to the village and secrete the pendant cross in the area of hollowed ground under the bed she shared with Hilda.

On nearing the home, Clover saw the family had risen for the day. Not far away, Felice squatted on the ground outside her tent, her dark eyes following those who went about their morning tasks. Darting into the home, Clover found herself to be alone and swiftly pulled back the hay mattress, slipped her hand between wooden bed slats and retrieved a box of silver with brass inlay – a gift from her faeder to Eadlyn. She placed the golden cross inside and returned it to the hiding place. Outside, the jug remained on the ground, reminding her of the first task of the day before Eadric had asked if they could talk.

"Let us go to the copse where we first met." Eadric raised his arms to indicate trees above them and gestured for Felice to follow. This was the first time he had spoken to her since she returned to Aldington. On seeing the surprise and gratitude in her expression, he felt ashamed. True, she had lured him to her, without shame, but he was not blameless.

They walked side by side, exchanging no more words. *How can I take a woman as my wife when the sounds flowing from our tongues mean nothing to each other?* Eadric reflected on the times they had been together. *We had no need for words then. It was enough to kiss and explore each other's bodies.* He glanced at his companion, noting the hair hanging down her back was now glossy. *My good modor has washed Felice's hair. I have allowed her to care for this stranger and not even given thanks. What has happened to me? I grew from child to man with the love and care of my parents, yet now I cannot see all they are doing for me. I have brought shame on my family.*

Reaching towards the dark locks, Eadric brushed his fingers over them. "Your hair is beautiful," he told Felice. "Beautiful."

Smiling, she pointed towards the stream, then held an imaginary jug above her head and made a show of lathering her hair with soap. Eadric nodded his understanding and led her to the far side of the copse where they could enter without the eyes of the villagers upon them.

It was cool under the trees and Felice wrapped her shawl tight around her. There was uncertainty in her eyes when she lifted her head a little, offering her lips to his. Her body was all she had to give him and Eadric felt fresh shame that the young woman believed he had brought her here for no other purpose than to satisfy his lust. The kiss he gave was light, with none of the passion previously known, enough to tell her that there was another reason for them walking to the privacy of the trees.

Placing the palm of his hand on her flat stomach, Eadric smiled his understanding that a child grew there. He took her hand in his and traced the shape of a ring on her finger. "I think we should marry," he said, then indicated a roof over their heads.

The smile on Felice's face lit up her eyes. She nodded her acceptance, babbling away in the husky voice he had once found so seductive. Leaning forward, she kissed him again, this time allowing her hands to roam over his body. Eadric gave himself up to the pleasure for a moment, but soon backed away. "No, that is for when we are married," he said, repeating the action of a ring on her finger and the shelter of a home.

Taking his hand, Felice led them to the edge of the trees. She pointed to the sky indicating the movement of the sun again and again.

"Ah... when will we marry? How much time?" Eadric considered this. The home was ready, but for him and Clover. The wedding date was set, but for him and

155

Clover. He would have to speak to his father, then decide how best to marry Felice with the minimum of attention on themselves. Eadric copied Felice's action of the sun moving through the sky, but only a few times. "Soon," he said.

"Soon," she repeated.

Chapter Fifteen

The huge doors were pulled open at both the front and back of the metal-working shed, but not a whisper of a refreshing breeze passed through the building. While lifting a rod of red-hot iron from the fire, Arlo glanced to the west. Storm clouds were gathering in a mass of dark purple and grey. Soon the much-needed respite from the heat would come. He moved with the iron, already turning back to grey at the edges, then placed it on the thick oak workbench. Its surface showed the scars of a decade of metalworking.

As he prepared to beat the rod into shape, Arlo's gaze rested on Eadric for a moment. The young man seemed calm today. *There is no knowing how his temper will be from one day to the next. I suspect I would be no different if I had been so foolish as to lose the love of Eadlyn and were fearful of my future with another woman.* The previous day, Megan and Penton had spoken to him, Eadlyn and Clover. Their expressions were serious as they told them that the decision had been made: Eadric was to marry Felice. *I wonder if he will treat his new wife well? We never had a moment of concern about him, but I have seen how Eadric avoids this stranger who has come into our lives. It is clear that he feels nothing for her.*

But Arlo understood the longings of a young man. *She would not be carrying his child if there was no desire for her, and she seems placid enough. I wonder what thoughts are in that head of hers? She studies us with her dark eyes, but how does Felice feel, knowing the faeder of her child was about to marry another woman? Should we be glad they were not already married?*

At least for today he seems to be at peace, and we must be grateful. Perchance Eadric will be happier now the choice has been made. Arlo picked up a hammer, then turned his attention back to the metal, eyeing the places it was cooling. Lifting the tool, he made the first strike.

The sky darkened over time and, on moving to the open doorway, Arlo could now feel the air had cooled despite the sun being almost at the midway point of its journey that day. Before turning back to his work, he spotted the thane approaching. *He will be wanting to see how the candle holders are progressing,* Arlo thought, glancing towards his brother who was bending delicate strands of copper into place. Penton had started on the work, knowing it would not be needed for months but also aware their thane was eager to see the finished objects. *It will do no harm for us to have a visitor today. In fact, we will welcome him taking our thoughts away from the wedding and the hurt caused to both our families.*

Thane Cenric was soon upon them, standing at the doorway while exclaiming over the storm clouds steadily approaching. Penton held up the first of two candle holders; the straight sides and scrolled top were beautifully crafted but the thane was unusually

158

dismissive: "Fine workmanship, Penton, but you must excuse me, I am here to speak with your brother."

Arlo placed his tools on the bench, then retraced his steps to the doorway. "What can I do for you, sir?"

"I saw your daughter, Clover, wearing a golden cross," Thane Cenric began. "Something so beautifully crafted that any king or archbishop would have a pride in it. I was honoured to hold it, if only for a moment."

"It is very precious to the family," Arlo informed him. "The pendant was found with her father, Todd of Lyminge, when he was murdered." He knew the moment the precious cross was mentioned that the thane coveted it for himself. His body chilled. "Nothing could be more precious to my wife and the children of her first marriage," he added in desperation.

"I can see that, so I know they will be gladdened to hear what I have to say." Cenric beamed, raising his eyes to heaven. "The cross must be gifted to our own Father Theodore. His needs are few and he would never desire such an object for himself. Yet when it graces his neck, our good Lord in heaven will look kindly on our priest and those who thought to bestow the cross on him."

"I am sorry," Arlo ventured to reply. "The pendant belongs to my wife and her children. It is not for me to offer it to our good priest. We have no idea where it came from, but it gives a great comfort to them."

The thane opened the pouch hanging from his belt and pulled out a small leather purse. He handed it to Arlo. "Payment for the cross. Your wife or Clover can bring it to me later. They will gain pleasure from knowing that when our stone church is built, our priest will be suitably adorned."

"I want nothing for it," Arlo stated. "It is not mine to give."

Thane Cenric placed the purse on the workbench. As far as he was concerned, the pendant cross was his. Turning to Penton he said, "Now let me see this candle holder. How good it will look placed upon the ancient altar."

Arlo said nothing else but noted the horror on the faces of his brother and nephew, before turning his back on his work to leave the metalworking shed. In the distance, the clouds were pierced by forked lightning, followed by the rumble of thunder. He moved through the gap between the family homes and was relieved to find Eadlyn and Clover alone at their chores. Looking up from the vegetables on chopping boards, their smiles soon faded on seeing his troubled expression.

"Are you wearing your faeder's cross?" Arlo asked Clover, his tone uncharacteristically sharp.

"Nay, but I have worn it," Clover admitted. "I hoped it would bring me comfort. It's hidden away now."

"Thane Cenric has seen it."

"Aye." Clover gazed at him straight in the eye. There was fear in hers.

"He wants it for his priest." Arlo paused, allowing the significance of this to sink in.

"Nay!" Eadlyn gasped. "He can't… What does a humble priest want with something as fine as our cross?"

"It has nothing to do with Father Theodore's needs," Arlo surmised. "Our thane is determined to bestow great things on him. In two days' time they begin the task of hauling the stone back here. He is to build a magnificent church for his priest and wishes to adorn him with a cross worthy of an abbot."

"He can't have it!" the words burst from Eadlyn. "It is not his to give."

"Cenric is our thane. We live on his land," Arlo replied, his voice glum. "I told him how important it was to you, but he was so keen to gift it to Father Theodore, it was all that filled his mind. I was given a purse of sceattas, with the order that he expects the pendant today."

"It's all my fault." Clover turned to walk into the home as the first raindrops fell.

Eadlyn pushed the chopped vegetables into a bowl and followed Clover. "You wore it to comfort you," she said. "What is the point of us having your faeder's cross if we cannot gain strength from it at difficult times?"

"But now it's gone."

Eadlyn considered this and, as she did so, the tension drained from her body. She felt confident in her reply to her daughter: "The thane will take our cross, but in time it will return to us if its purpose is to be with our family."

Clover, knowing the story of the cross, drew comfort from her mother's words. "I thank you, Modor. I will let it go, knowing it will return."

The rain hammered down on Aldington while the women lit fires in their homes, then placed pots of vegetables and beans to hang on their stands. Clover, who dashed to the bakehouse to retrieve their bread, saw Felice looking doleful from the doorway of her tent. Both young women turned away, not ready to exchange a passing greeting. The family ate in near silence, all

161

brooding on the thane's visit. Dark skies, combined with a chill in the air, reminded them of the winter which would soon be upon them, and the struggles they would face over the upcoming months when the days would shorten, and long hours would be spent huddled under blankets in smoke-filled homes.

By mid-afternoon, the sun was shining again, although the thunder still rumbled on sporadically. The women were able to venture from their homes. Eadlyn picked her way past pools of water gathered on the hard ground and walked to the thane's hall with the pendant cross held in her clenched fist.

The wife of Thane Cenric was outside their home. She was a mild-mannered woman of about thirty-five years and Eadlyn had no argument with her. "Good afternoon," she said, holding out her hand to show the cross nestled in her palm. "The thane has asked that I bring this to him."

A frown flitted across the fair face of the other woman. "It is beautiful," she responded. "I heard him talk of it." She paused recalling the discomfort felt when told that the pendant cross was to be taken from a good woman in their village and gifted to Father Theodore. "I will call for Cenric."

Eadlyn watched as the thane's wife retreated into her home, returning a moment later in the wake of her beaming husband.

"You have brought the cross!" Thane Cenric's words were full of jubilation.

Eadlyn handed it to him and attempted a pleasant response. "Aye. I hope your priest knows he will be honoured to wear it."

"My priest is a humble man," the thane reminded her, "but it is our Lord in heaven who will see your gesture and look kindly on your family."

Eadlyn gave a brief nod to show her understanding, then turned away. Passing the younger brother, Godwin, she offered a flicker of a smile and, wrapping her shawl tight around her shoulders, walked back to her home.

"Is all not well with the family of Arlo Smith?" Godwin asked his brother. It was rare to see Eadlyn in low spirits.

"Life is very good for them," Cenric beamed. "Their path to heaven will be greatly eased by their gift to Father Theodore." He displayed the pendant cross in his open palm, moving it slightly so the sunlight lit up the ruby.

"This is the cross we saw Clover wearing!" Godwin exclaimed.

"Too good to be hidden away," Cenric stated.

Godwin recalled their meeting Clover not far from the village boundary, just the day before. She had looked distressed. At the time, the urge to ask if she was well had been strong, but he had known better than to pry. This was just as his brother had noticed the cross hanging amongst the folds of her dress. Something told Godwin that there was a reason why Clover wore her faeder's cross and most likely it was to bring comfort. Now Eadlyn and her children would suffer the loss of an item precious to them, as well as seeing it adorn the neck of their priest.

The exasperation, so often endured when witnessing the ideas and schemes hatched by his brother, bubbled up inside Godwin. No longer able to

163

hold back his disgust, he snapped, "Cenric, you have taken it too far. First a Roman altar brought here by night, then plans to build a new church and now… and now you take a precious gift from a dead man to his family. You take it to give to that priest of yours."

"Eadlyn is pleased to have a purse of sceattas," Cenric boomed, seeing only goodwill and happiness.

"She doesn't need sceattas. Eadlyn has a good husband and a decent home." Godwin stood before his brother knowing he was helpless to change his mind. "Eadlyn and her children want the solace of holding the golden cross which was found with Todd of Lyminge after he died."

"They kept it hidden. Otherwise, we would have seen it," Cenric argued. "Now they will have the pleasure of seeing it worn by our priest. When they pass to a better life, their gift to our priest will smooth their journey."

"The people of Aldington are interested in whether they have enough logs for the winter, enough grain for their bread and in keeping the damp from their homes and clothes," Godwin roared. It was not often he lost his temper with his older brother, but Cenric's foolish ways were becoming dangerous. "If it were not for me working alongside our men, giving them faith in our leadership, this village, and all that our forebears worked towards, would be a shambles. You would have them bringing stone from the fort while the crops rotted in the fields."

"It would all be done." Thane Cenric dismissed these words. "It has been done. The crops are stored away and tomorrow we start bringing the stone back."

"It is done because I stopped you from taking the men from the fields when you first came up with this ludicrous plan."

"And now the ground will be treacherous underfoot," Cenric stated. "The men and oxen will slip on the hills. Everything will take twice as long."

"But the men will be thankful to have food in their bellies and be glad to know the crops are safe."

They were standing in the open doorway of the thane's hall. The sky was cloudy, but the rain had passed. Water dripped from the thatch roof and the fire in the pit outside smouldered.

"You need a wife," Cenric declared, and not for the first time in the past few months. "The widow woman in Mersham does not keep you satisfied. Choose someone young with sparkling eyes and fine breasts, then you will spend less time thinking you should be thane and more indulging in your own pleasures."

"There is nothing more I can say to you." Godwin turned and strode towards his home. He snatched at his cloak hanging from a peg, took an apple from a dish, and chose the track to the north-west which would take him through the village and on to Mersham. The walk to the smaller settlement would ease his temper and the company there was sure to distract his thoughts.

Godwin, who usually had a smile and a word for everyone, kept his eyes firmly on the ground when walking by the village homes and workplaces. It was only on passing the boundary that he slowed a little and looked up to take in his surroundings. The landscape undulated gently: a patchwork of pasture, harvested fields and woodland. Hedgerows were rich with rosehips and clusters of rounded berries. Nuts already

165

fell from the trees, and fruits, such as apples and plums, ripened with a soft blush to their skin. Apples were gathered, then stored in trays on the rafters to last over winter, while berries would be dried. This was the time of year when the women and children foraged for the autumn treats to be eaten over the cold months. These foods would keep their skin from greying and their eyes from becoming dull.

After a while, Godwin passed an area of woodland and saw a figure crouching in the shady area at the edge of the trees. She had a basket and was gathering mushrooms. On hearing his footsteps, she turned, her long golden hair rippling.

"I hadn't expected…" The words came before Godwin had a chance to consider what to say, if anything. Clover turned and stood. Her expression was serious, and he saw there were unshed tears in her eyes. Godwin's heart swelled with warmth for the young woman. He sensed her family were troubled and was momentarily overwhelmed with a desire to hold Clover in his arms – to bury his face in her hair. Instead, he stepped back, saying, "I am sorry. Sorry about my brother and his obsession with the priest. There is nothing I could do to stop him." It appeared as if Clover were about to respond, but Godwin, overwrought and needing to distance himself from his brother, turned and gave his parting words: "I must go, but please know I am not a part of this."

The widow woman of Mersham was of good birth and understood the need for the thane of the village to be steady. She knew the man who now lay beside her would have made a fine lord and was much admired.

166

However, he was the second-born son and likely to remain at his brother's side, rather than be the excellent leader he would make if it were not for the order of birth. She had frequently listened to Godwin's frustrations and found it no hardship – he was a handsome man and good company. Now she had something to say to him, echoing Cenric's words: "You must find yourself a wife, Godwin. What are you – twenty-seven, twenty-eight years of age?"

"Twenty-seven," he replied, placing a kiss on her neck.

"It is a good age, and I cannot see you anymore."

"Cannot see me?" There was indignation in his voice and Godwin sat up, the linen sheet falling away to reveal a chest with a light covering of curling brown hair.

"I am getting married again."

"Ah." He frowned, not expecting this outcome. It always seemed likely that it would be he who married. "I wish you well. Your husband will be a lucky man."

Godwin returned to Aldington before dark. The news of the marriage neither pleased nor distressed him. He shrugged it off. They were right, his brother and the widow woman – it was time to find his own wife. But he would have to remain in Aldington. The fortunes of the settlement relied on his steady nature.

Chapter Sixteen

The following morning, the men who were young enough and strong enough to help with the movement of stone gathered on the track leading towards Lympne. Those who worked on the land or crafted leather, wood and stone, came to be a part of this momentous occasion. Looking on, Arlo wondered if it was loyalty to their thane or the hope of an easy path to heaven, which spurred them to toil up the steep hillside with blocks of ragstone once worked by those long-ago Romans. There was a set of oxen, and six strong horses with wagons and ropes. A donkey and small cart carried barrels of ale, bread, cheese and fruit for the workers. There was an air of celebration and no wonder – life for the villagers was much the same day after day. To be involved in creating a stone church was something to be proud of. For generations to come, the story of this building would be shared in the form of songs at the fireside.

Cym was there, standing beside Arlo, who had been a father-figure to him. He was to help the thane and men of Aldington for ten days. Then he would be ready to move to the home of his family in Lyminge. For Eadlyn, left at home, the movement of the stone marked time passing until her son departed. As the piles of ragstone blocks were hauled up the hillside and along the tracks, each day the thane would glory in the rising stack while Cym would feel that his duty to the village was nearing completion.

"Good men of Aldington," Thane Cenric bellowed. He stood on a slight rise in the land, with his brother beside him. "Let us make haste to the Roman fort and begin the task of bringing the stone back here. May the Lord look down on us and appreciate our endeavours to make a worthy church in which to worship him."

There was a great cheer; the men needed no more encouragement. Arlo and Cym grinned at each other, feeling a wave of enthusiasm run through their bodies as they headed away from the village. If Eadric's absence had been noted, no one spoke of it. "I am working on the cross to be placed on top of the roof," he had reminded his uncle. "My faeder and I are needed here. How would he feel if we were all to be working with the thane, yet his injuries have forced him to remain in the village?"

"I wonder if Penton and Eadric will finish the cross today?" Cym said to Arlo, as they strode along.

"How strange, I was thinking just the same thing," Arlo remarked. "I'm glad Eadric chose to stay with his faeder."

They walked on, long strides taking them up the slight incline towards the road to Lympne, and each of them preoccupied with his own thoughts.

By noon, two dozen blocks of ragstone had been hauled by the oxen up the hillside. Thane Cenric's prediction that the ground would be slippery underfoot was correct – the men were constantly changing their path rather than treading the same perilous route. As

169

the stocky beasts took the weight, men were endlessly checking that the ropes were in place and the knots strong. They manoeuvred the stone, guiding it around the lumpiest of hillocks, and encouraged the oxen to lumber onwards. But before any of that could be done, each cut stone had been eased from its place amongst the ruin and rolled or lifted into the cradle to await its journey up the hill.

While most of the labourers took a break, sitting with a beaker of ale and their food, others made the return journey to Aldington with the horses and carts. These men carried crusts of bread and slices of cheese in their hands. "You will always remember that you were the first to deliver the stone for our church," Thane Cenric encouraged them.

Back in the village, the foundations had been excavated beside the site of the wooden church. When the first stones arrived, those suitable for the footings were selected. By nightfall, the first stone had been set in place and blessed by Father Theodore. The building of Aldington's place of worship had begun.

"This church will stand strong for centuries," the thane announced, "and I shall be remembered as the one who thought to create it here!"

Despite their aching legs and calloused hands, the men who had toiled long hours, cheered and clapped their approval. This was the first day and every man who could spare the time laboured for the thane. In the coming weeks, most would return to their daily work and help when they could. But the men who slaved for the thane, usually on the land, were to spend most of that autumn and winter moving the stone.

"There will be no marriage between Eadric Smith and Clover," Father Theodore stated, sprinkling nuts across his porridge. "Instead, he is to marry a stranger to us all."

"Eadric is to marry someone else?" Godwin repeated. The words struck a blow as if it were news of his own family. "How can that have happened?"

"In haste," the priest added.

"In haste?" the words catapulted from Godwin's mouth. "How can that be?"

"Surely you have some understanding of these matters?" Cenric replied, a hint of a smile on his face. "You do not travel to Mersham to sup wine with the widow woman."

Godwin ignored his brother's snipe and asked the priest: "When will the wedding take place?"

"Today!" Father Theodore responded.

"I have word that there is a pair of strong oxen for sale in Ashford." Thane Cenric remarked, seeming to have no interest in the forthcoming marriage and the unrest it would cause amongst the good people of Aldington. "I suggest we travel there together, Godwin, and see for ourselves which women of good birth are seeking a husband. I hear your preference for golden hair, but we must also take care to ensure your bride has an upright figure and clear skin. She must be built for breeding."

Godwin shrugged. "Aye, I'll come to Ashford with you. I will look for a sweet smile and pleasant nature alongside the golden hair. Brother, you do right to buy a couple more oxen as hauling the stone will be laborious."

171

Clover had not wanted to know when the wedding ceremony would be. She could not bear to be counting the moments until Eadric and Felice exchanged vows, and the dark-eyed newcomer took her place as Eadric's wife in his bed. It would be soon though and she accepted it. The families ate separately now, although their food was still ladled from the shared pot hanging above the fire pit. *It will be easier when the leaves fall from the trees and the days become cooler. We will be forced to hide away in our home, so I will not have to see her as much.* But even as those thoughts wrapped a blanket of comfort around her, Clover knew Felice could not be avoided. *She will be there in the weaving shed, at the bread oven or by the stream. By the time the branches are like skeletons, and the days are darker, I will see the swell of his child growing within her belly.*

'How will I bear it?" Clover whispered to Alfreda, the young woman who would have been her sister through marriage, and now had to accept the difficulties of welcoming another woman as her brother's wife.

"I wish I could find the words to comfort you," Alfreda replied. "As time passes, we will all become used to Felice in our lives. Eadric has been a good brother, but I am saddened to see the hurt caused by him. He will regret it."

"I believe he already does," Clover said, revealing nothing of Eadric begging her to leave the village with him. The young women were washing clothes at the stream and now stood to wring water from the sodden cloth. In the distance, Father Theodore walked from the thane's hall to the ground prepared for the new church. Clover watched his progress, wondering if he wore her father's cross under his tunic of rough wool. "Everything is going wrong," she blurted out. The silver sceattas, stored where the pendant had been, were no replacement for the treasured golden cross.

When damp clothes had been folded and placed in baskets, Clover glanced towards the wooden cross where the villagers worshipped. Her chest tightened on seeing the priest had been joined by Penton and Megan, with Eadric and Felice. For a moment, she was unable to return to her task.

"Osric and I refused to go," Alfreda said. "They understood. At least Eadric does, I don't know what Felice thinks."

Clover placed her hand on Alfreda's forearm in a silent show of gratitude, then turned back to the basket of washing. She picked it up and they walked together back to the family homes. Having busied themselves with spreading clothes on the ground to dry, Clover eventually broke the silence: "In time we will learn to live together."

"I wish Faeder would ask them to leave," Alfreda blurted out. "I wish *I* could leave."

"Cousin, our hurt *will* pass," Clover insisted. "Now I am going to gather wild berries. When they return, I'll not be here to see them."

I wish I could leave. Alfreda's words rattled about in Clover's mind as the milk flowed from the goat's teats in a thin stream. Eadric's sister had shown a steady support since the arrival of Felice, and now four days had passed since Eadric's wedding. His wife remained subdued but there was an aura of quiet victory about her. Gradually she was integrating herself into family

173

life. Clover found herself spending more time on her own, although content in the company of her mother or Alfreda. In the mornings she tended the goats, squatting on a stool in their pen and soothed by the repetitive action of milking them.

I wish I could leave. There is no need for Alfreda to go, but if I were to make my home away from Aldington, mayhap I could find peace. Modor has shown me how a brave woman can find ways to manage. There is no need for Arlo to find another man for me to marry. I have the sceattas and my family in Lyminge. There is no need for me to feel alone in this kingdom when I can seek comfort elsewhere.

Memories of other times and places flitted through her mind. Clover frowned, recalling a childhood walk with Eadlyn. She remembered running alongside a stream and there being a steep hillside nearby. Hunched men pushing small handcarts gathered flint on the hills, and there was a humble settlement towards which she and her mother were heading. The walk home had been tiring, as they now journeyed with three goats. The beasts were too strong for a child of only seven years but, like Eadlyn, Clover showed determination to lead them back to Lyminge.

"Do you remember the goats we had when it was just you and I with Modor?" Clover asked Cym, as he leaned against the wooden division between the pen and the living area in the home.

"Aye. You learned to milk them," he replied. "I was too young."

"You were only three." Clover's fingers continued to tug at the teats. The flow of milk into the bucket was mesmerising and, as it eased, she removed the bucket, then gave the goat a scratch between its horns. Turning to Cym, Clover shared the thoughts which had been lingering in her mind over the past few days. "It has been twenty days since Felice came here and fourteen since she married Eadric. They live in the home which we built for my wedding."

"I know." Cym waited.

"Soon we will see the signs that a child grows within her," Clover continued. "Before long they will be celebrating the birth and she will truly belong to our family."

"You will marry a better man," Cym suggested. He saw his sister's hurt but did not know the words to comfort her. Thankful that his work took him away from the family who spent their day in the metalworking shelter, he too felt Eadric's betrayal. From a young age, Cym had looked up to the older boy, who grew up to become a man to be admired. Now that respect was lost, to be replaced with confusion. He started to turn away, pausing as Clover spoke again.

"You were planning to go to Lyminge after my wedding. Can we go sooner? The family there will be pleased to see you, and I shall go to our modor's sister."

"We?" Cym repeated. "When…?"

"I am free to do as I wish." Clover picked up the bucket, then moved towards the partition between the animal pen and home. "I can take a silver sceat or two from those given to us by the thane. There is no need for me to arrive in Lyminge and beg for a place to sleep or food to eat. Janna would welcome me if I had nothing, but with money I can begin to take care of myself."

"Clover, you *will* become used to Eadric and the choice he has made."

"I pray that I will, but there is no need for me to wait for a man to offer a home and an escape from having to live beside Eadric and Felice." As she voiced her thoughts, Clover felt the strength returning to her young body and the clouds that lay thick upon her began to lift. "I am leaving with you, Cym. We will go to Lyminge together whether it is on the day you decided or earlier."

"We will leave before," Cym replied. "But not too soon. You must speak to Modor, who will suffer for the both of us leaving."

Later that morning, Eadlyn and Clover worked water into barley flour, then added the froth from fermenting ale. They were baking for the two families – *three now that Eadric lives in his home with his wife,* Clover realised. The mixture, at first too dry and then too sticky, became more pliable as they each kneaded dough on wooden boards near the communal ovens. Women and girls of the village worked alongside, while others were occupied in the weaving shed, washing clothes at the stream or perhaps foraging for berries and nuts.

Having marked the top of their loaves with their unique pattern, mother and daughter left the dough to rise, then each picked up a bucket with a jug stored inside it. They walked from the centre of the village, past their home and towards the thane's hall near the site of the new church. Pausing for a moment, they gazed at the progress made in just six days. Already, the foundations of irregular stone blocks were supporting a layer of smooth-facing ragstone. At the eastern end, where the Roman altar would stand, the wall was rising to a greater height and, as they watched, another piece was eased into place. An inner layer was also taking shape, for there was to be no stinting in the quality and strength of this church. In the distance the sound of an axe could be heard as the straightest, most noble of Thane Cenric's oak trees were being felled for roof beams.

A moment passed. They walked on, following the course of the stream until they reached an area with shallow pools of clear water. Now at a distance from the other women of the village, Clover broached the subject on her mind. "Modor, soon Cym will leave for Lyminge."

"Aye, he will," Eadlyn responded. "And you will go with him."

"I… I hadn't said."

"But how could you not think of it? Your brother is leaving, and you must long to be away from Eadric with the reminders of how he hurt you."

"I have thought of it," Clover admitted, "and I want to go to Janna."

"She will welcome you," Eadlyn told her. "My sister has a kind heart."

Clover scooped water from the stream and poured it into her bucket, then reached to pick out a leaf. "Mayhap I'll learn to accept Eadric's choice and be able to return, but until that time may I go to Lyminge with one of our thane's coins? I remember how wise you were, using Faeder's sceatta to care for us all. When I go to Janna, there must be a way to make my home in Lyminge without her support."

Eadlyn stood and lifted the bucket so it was supported by both arms. "Aye, you and Cym will both have a sceat. I want him to be free of Alwin and Bertana

177

if he wishes. He must be able to build a small home of his own."

That day Arlo was once again working for the thane, leading the heavy horses from the top of the escarpment to the site of the growing church. On his return to Eadlyn that evening, she said to him: "I was right. Clover is to go to Lyminge." He wrapped his arms around her shoulder and nestled his face in her hair, understanding her hurt but also Clover's need to leave.

Chapter Seventeen

The day Clover and Cym left Aldington, the skies were overcast. Clouds hung low, while the lightest of misty rains settled on their cloaks. The leaves on the trees, so glorious with shades of brown and gold when lit by the sun, were dulled and drooping. The weather suited the sombre moods amongst those who gathered at the edge of the village.

After hugging all the family there was only Eadric left, standing behind the others. Clover's eyes met with his then she stepped towards him, feeling an affection thought to be lost to her. "You will always be my much-loved cousin," she said. Before he could respond, Clover turned away, unwilling to prolong the moment. Cym stood by, his expression serious and fingers resting on the handle of a small barrow. No longer able to speak, her throat tight and eyes brimming with tears, Clover glanced at her brother, adjusted the bag slung over her shoulder and took the first step away from the life they had known for the past thirteen years.

They picked their way down the slope and crossed the stream before following a narrow track leading steadily upwards. It was only when they reached the top of the hill that they paused and allowed themselves to look back at the settlement. The small gathering of family members was dispersing. "Life will continue

179

without us," Clover reflected. As if to support her words there came the call from a man and the cracking, ripping sound of a tree being felled. "When we next stand here, we will be looking down on the new church."

"Aye. We will." Cym's reply was brief. He had no need to express his thoughts, but it was unlikely that they would venture to Aldington until after the winter snows had cleared, and there had been a period of dry weather allowing for the roads to dry out.

They continued, following another track which eventually led them to the small settlement named Sellindge. They passed through without taking a break. The journey to the village of their birth was far more uphill than down and, by mid-morning, it seemed as if the whole Kingdom of Kent was spread out before them. Here they followed the tradition of many years, pausing to gaze across the landscape of pasture, harvested fields and woodland. They pointed out the now indistinct Sellindge, then looked for clues to show them where Aldington was. The river and Ashford, spreading either side of its banks, was too far away, but they knew it to be there.

"I didn't expect to see the sea today," Cym remarked. The *Oceanus Britannicus* was no more than a grey smudge, while low-lying Romney Marsh merged as murky green into a smoke-grey sky.

"I'm glad we did," Clover replied. "I wonder if I can go to the Sandtun next year? You will. You'll go with Alwin."

"I hope so."

They shared food carried in a cloth bag and drank weak ale from clay flasks, turned their backs to the view and took the lane to Lyminge. The barrow trundled onwards, pushed by Cym. It contained the tools collected during the years he had crafted leather, as well as clothing and blankets. Small gifts for the family were tucked amongst the material. Whereas Cym was expected, albeit not for another week, Clover's arrival would be surprising, although not unwelcome.

The approach to Lyminge took them through the land owned by the minster: small fields with well-ordered areas for different crops, as well as pens for goats and poultry. Then the minster itself dominated the scene, rising high on the hillside, with its stone church, and tall wooden buildings. Here the monks and nuns worked, slept and ate, following the routines set by their abbess. As they took in the scene, the pair returning to their birthplace watched the habited figures trailing from the fields and outbuildings towards the church.

"It must be their hour to pray," Cym observed.

"Aye. How peaceful to watch them go about their duties without noise or fuss. It feels good to be home."

They passed the perimeter of the minster and approached the church, standing on a promontory in the land. From here they looked down on Lyminge, with the thane's hall and Nailbourne stream being the central points around which village life revolved. An agreement to visit their father's grave was unspoken, and they walked across the grass to where Todd Leatherman had been buried for the past fourteen years. With heads bowed they stood for a moment, both reflecting on sparse memories while wondering how the patterns of their lives would have varied if he had lived.

"Now we must go to Janna," Cym said.

"Aye." Clover responded. For the first time the enormity of her being here sank in and tiny doubts

181

began to gnaw at her. Cym was expected, but she was to go to her aunt and ask to stay with no word from a messenger or a hint of what was to come. She hitched up the bag hanging over one shoulder and followed her brother down the winding path until they reached the head of the Nailbourne stream. Once more following the family tradition, they both knelt to drink fresh water from cupped hands.

Now in the heart of the village, they were, of course, recognised and greeted familiar faces as they scanned the area for Janna. They found her at home, slicing bread to go with the pottage.

"Janna!" Cym called.

She turned, her initial smile turning to a frown. "You're not meant to be here yet, Cym, and Clover... is everything well? Your modor?"

"All is well, Janna," Clover was quick to reassure. "Modor, Arlo... Alfrid and Hilda." She stepped towards her aunt, who looked so much like Eadlyn, but with nut-brown hair, rather than fair. Clover could say no more and, as Janna's arms wrapped around her, she began to cry as she hadn't in all the weeks since learning of Eadric's betrayal.

Bertana had prepared the home for Cym's arrival not long after their return to Lyminge. Every day she plumped the mattress filled with sweet hay, lest it should lose some of its softness before he slept on it. She had hemmed linen bedsheets and repaired soft beige-coloured woollen blankets. These had been washed at the Nailbourne, then rinsed in sweet marjoram and rosemary water. A cloth had been hung to make a curtain, offering the young man privacy in his

182

new home. There was a sturdy chest and iron pegs for his clothes.

"I will kill a chicken myself on the day he arrives," Bertana had said to Alwin. "Cym will be left in no doubt of how welcome he is in our home."

"Then we will see how skilled he is," Alwin had replied. "What is it, two or three years working under those who are not his blood? Who knows what bad habits have been learned?"

"Nothing that cannot be changed under the watchful eye of yourself and Cedric," Bertana had soothed.

Now, as she placed the bread on the table outside their home, Bertana wondered if the weather would remain mild for much longer. She wanted Cym to see Lyminge at its best before winter settled in. Glancing across the shallow valley to the village and over to the church, she appreciated the position of her home in its setting a little apart from the main cluster of the settlement. One of her pleasures was the view, enabling her to watch the people going about their daily business.

Something, or someone, caught her attention. A young man was walking away from the stream and cluster of houses towards the eastern slope where the leather-makers lived and worked. He pushed a small barrow, pausing at times to adjust its position on the narrow path. *What brings him here? Why does he bother himself with taking the barrow up this hillside?* Watching the young man's progress, a thought came into her mind, and she studied the figure more closely. A sense of jubilation soared through her: *It is him! How can it be?* With no consideration of the meal in the pot that might need stirring, or the flies that would settle on

183

the fresh bread, Bertana was following the rough track down the slope while waving her greeting.

"Welcome! What brings you here early?" she called. "Let me help you with your barrow." She walked beside it, ready to put out a steadying hand if needed.

"I thank you. It was easier when I had Clover to help."

"Clover? Here with you?" Bertana could not keep the joy from her voice. She thought nothing of the possible events that could have led to Cym arriving early.

"There will be no wedding," Cym told her. Then showing an astuteness beyond his years, he continued, "But please say nothing to Clover about this. She's come to stay with Janna."

"Will she travel home before winter?" Bertana asked. A mild curiosity had been spiked, but the girls of the family held little interest, not now Todd's son was with them.

"Nay, she will stay."

By the time they had pushed the cart into the home, and Cym had thanked Bertana for the care she had taken in preparing his bed, Alwin was home. The men discussed the journey, agreeing it was a long slog uphill, before settling down to eat the midday meal.

"I was going to kill a chicken!" Bertana recalled, as she dipped her bread into a broth of beans and root vegetables. "I'll do it tomorrow!"

At dawn, when Janna lay awake with Egfrid snoring beside her, she recalled Mildrithe, the wise woman from the woods. She often thought of that good woman who had brought her the comfort of her only son, Leof.

184

Fearful of never keeping a child in her womb, Janna had visited the woman who lived in a shack amongst the trees and wildlife. Over the years, thirteen now since Leof had come into this world, she had returned to Mildrithe, taking small gifts to show her appreciation.

In that time before the day began, Janna pondered on Clover's heartache, certain that if she were to go to the wise woman, something could be done to alleviate the sorrow. The last time Janna had seen Clover, she was happy and healthy with clear skin and bright eyes. On her arrival at Lyminge, the young woman looked to have lost weight, while the delicate skin under her eyes appeared grey. It had been disturbing to see her like this, although to be in her childhood home would hopefully bring some peace.

That morning, three days after Clover and Cym's arrival, Janna left her niece with tasks to keep her occupied and walked away from Lyminge. She took the ancient track where the trees grew high on either side then, when they cleared, turned towards the village of Postling. She met no one, which suited her well; her thoughts were company enough. It was a pleasant walk, and in the distance she saw men working on the land: a lone man tending sheep, some with handcarts collecting flint from the hillside, and others preparing the soil for next year's crops.

Before reaching Postling, nestling within a fold in the hills, Janna took a track across pastureland towards a small wood. She stepped beneath the trees, her shoes on the soft bed of fallen leaves. There were some local women who were fearful of Mildrithe and only ventured to see her out of desperation, but Janna knew her as a gentle soul who meant nothing but good to

185

those who sought her help. The air was cool and damp, rich with the scents of fungi and rotting leaves. There was a whiff of woodsmoke, indicating human habitation, but the only sounds of life were the birds high in the branches, along with that of Janna's shoes pressing on twigs and brushing aside fronds of bracken.

Mildrithe knew Janna was approaching. Most likely she sensed it long before footsteps could be heard in the woodland. "I thought you would come," she said, taking the pot of honey and the small sack of grain with a nod of thanks.

"I never forget the comfort you have given me," Janna replied. "My son is thirteen years old now. Strong and healthy."

"You will never need to seek my help for him," Mildrithe told her. "Your sister, is she well? Many years have passed since we met."

"Aye, she is well enough." Janna shrugged a little. "There has been some upset in the family, but it will settle."

"It will. You can be sure of it." Mildrithe glanced over the cobnuts she was sorting, and picked one up, eyeing it for signs of boring insects or rot. Casting it aside, her attention returned to Janna. "I have nettle tea in the pot, will you take a cup with me?"

"I thank you." Janna knew this invitation came from the many years of building up the trust of this woman who chose to live a lonely life. Not many who entered the wooded area were invited to stay. She watched as Mildrithe shuffled about, ducking into her low home and returning with two clay cups.

Once seated on a roughly-hewn bench, Mildrithe continued: "Your sister has been parted from the golden

186

cross, and there is a dark-eyed young woman who came to cause harm within the family. I see her carrying a child, but whose child?"

Janna said nothing. She took a sip of the tea, finding it soothed her.

"This child is a mystery to me. The answer will come, but not yet. There will be a sign and I will understand. But your sister, and her daughter named after the flowers in the pasture… they will have the cross restored to them. I see the cross worn around the neck of the young woman. It is hers and no longer needs to be hidden. There are good things coming to her. The lethargy you see will soon lift. In the meantime, she suffers, so I will give you a bag of dried flowers to make as a tea. But it is you welcoming her into your home which is giving more comfort than I can offer. Bring her to me, my friend. I would like to meet this woman whose spirit is strong and pure."

Her heart filled with gratitude and all Janna could do was give her thanks. She could not repeat these prophecies to Clover but had no doubt of them coming true. They spoke of other things – the change of season, life in Lyminge, the story of the stone church being created in Aldington. Then Janna rose to leave, promising to return within days, and bringing Clover with her.

On his fourth day in Lyminge, Cym worked on leather straps for one of the thane's carts. Already he was beginning to feel at home at the workbench provided for him by his uncles. "This is where Todd worked," Cedric had told him and, reaching out to touch it, Cym had felt honoured to be there.

187

Putting the straps on the bench, then placing his tools in an orderly line, Cym turned to the door and stepped outside. He took the chance to gaze across the village and appreciate the view to be enjoyed from the hillside where his uncles lived and worked. Usually, the midday meal was taken at the home of Bertana and Alwin, with his aunt fussing to ensure he was well fed. This time he had been invited to eat with Cedric's family.

Three of Cym's girl cousins were older than him, and two younger. They all appeared much the same in his eyes, but with varying heights and signs of maturity. As he approached alongside Cedric, the girls watched his progress, before returning to their various tasks without any word of greeting. *If these were the daughters of Bertana, they would not be so meek!* Cym reflected. *They would be jostling and chattering away.* He grinned, accepting his admiration for the overbearing woman.

During the meal, the talk centred around life in Aldington and the differences in the two settlements. The two unmarried daughters spoke little, unless prompted by their mother. For Cym this was strange. *At home the girls, Hilda and Alfreda, make themselves heard and speak freely. Perhaps it will change as they become used to me. I hope so or I will miss the company.* The homes were strung in a row and he glanced to the next one – the place he had lived as a child. Another of the five daughters lived there with her husband and children. *More girls!* Cym grinned and dunked his bread in the tasty broth.

From nearby, Bertana looked on. "I hope Ora isn't trying to press one of her sickly daughters on him," she

188

said to Alwin. "It surprises me every time one of them finds a husband."

"Cym is too young," Alwin mumbled, while spooning peas into his mouth.

"Too young to marry," Bertana agreed. "Not too young for an arrangement to be made. I'd not stop him finding pleasure in women before he settles."

"Let him make his own choices."

"I am sure he will choose his own wife," Bertana replied, an unusually mild tone to her words. "Did I say that my brother and his daughter are to visit in two days? I look forward to seeing Annis again; she is growing into a fine young woman."

Chapter Eighteen

By the time the leaves had fallen from the trees, the walls of the church came up to the shoulders of the men who worked on it. A narrow, round-topped doorway had been formed and the floor laid with wide oak planks. Then the rains came. Day after day water poured down the grey stone walls. It seeped into the cracks, washing away fresh mortar. The men replaced it and strengthened the space with chips of stone. There was a fear that the walls were not strong enough to face the onslaught, and that if the mortar were to be lost, the whole building would collapse.

"The foundations and lower walls are strong," Thane Cenric insisted. "It is only those constructed in the last week which need watching."

"You should have stopped work when advised to," his brother said. They were walking towards woodland where workers were shaping shingles for the church roof from sycamore. "There are other tasks the men can continue with."

"You, Godwin, are not the thane." Cenric increased his pace, the soles of his shoes slapping down harder on the wet earth. His legs became mud splattered and he slid a little, almost toppling to the ground.

"I am not the thane," Godwin agreed, "Nonetheless, I have instructed our cousins to ensure the men prepare your land for crops. For a week you have insisted they battle on with the removal of stone. One of the horses is lame, the oxen cannot keep their footing on the escarpment, and John Thatcher had a nasty fall. I pray that the injury to his shoulder is not permanent. Your wife is to visit the family today with a basket of food."

"Aye, she told me." Cenric was forced to slow. Having slipped, he now suffered the humiliation of his brother's quick reactions being the only thing stopping him from ending up on the ground. "But Otha must take care: my son will be coming into this world shortly."

"Otha is in fine shape. Your son or daughter will not object to a gentle stroll around the village," Godwin remarked. "It will do no harm until he or she joins the family, and the whole of Aldington will share your joy when the child arrives." Thane Cenric was known for his generosity in the form of a hog-roast to celebrate the birth of his children.

Having arrived at the woodland, Godwin was pleased to note that the men worked under a makeshift shelter of twigs, saplings and fern, giving them additional respite from the rain alongside the bare branches of the trees. There were many months of work ahead of them and the more comfortable they were in their efforts, the more shingles they would produce.

"Ah, look at this!" Cenric said, when they spotted the shingles stacked in neat piles. "My good men, I thank you. These will look fine on the roof."

They stopped for a moment to examine samples of the wooden tiles, and to exchange a few words with the woodworkers, before returning to the village.

"These men can work safely in their shelter," Cenric concluded. "I can only hope that the building of the church walls can continue soon." After four days of rain, it had been decided that it was unwise to continue but instead to ensure the area was safe.

"You were wise to stop," Godwin observed, as they trudged back towards the village. "Mistakes happen if men work in difficult conditions."

Soon they were approaching the church. Although only two men were on site, all the signs were there that work could proceed as soon as weather conditions allowed. There was a stack of worked ragstone, cut into neat blocks by those Romans who had taken care to create a substantial fort, and a separate pile of stone of lesser quality. Platforms of upright wood and planks, lashed together with rope, had been constructed to raise the men as the stone was placed on the ever-growing walls. Cenric cast his eyes over the scene and was not satisfied.

"How long will this stone last us?" he asked, before continuing, "A day? Two at the most. As soon as the rains stop, we must choose another path to lead the oxen up the hillside. We must keep working them and continue to build the church." He walked over to a small pile of flat red bricks. "These will be used in layers of three at the base of the windows."

Godwin and Cenric both looked up to where the windows would begin to take shape. They would be high up, just below the eaves: a row of three on each side, narrow with rounded tops.

"They will look fine," Godwin remarked. "Will there be one above the altar?"

"Aye." Cenric saw it all. "Above the sacred Roman stone."

192

It rained for a whole cycle of the moon. In that time the thane's rejoicing in the safe birth of his child – a daughter – was celebrated with a basket of food for each family. However, his spirits were diminished by the lack of progress in the building of the church. All stonework had ceased, and the only comfort was the growing stack of sycamore shingles for the roof.

Godwin was frustrated by the slow progress in preparing the fields for next year's crops. "If it were not for using the men to move the stone, the ground would have been ready long before these rains came," he muttered to himself. Working long hours, he no longer enjoyed the respite of his visits to the widow-woman of Mersham. By the time the rain ceased, the work on the land was complete, but the men were despondent.

In the homes, fires smoked from the burning of damp wood. Sodden clothes hung about steaming and moisture lingered in the material, causing the air to become stale. Even the best of roofs began to leak, and bedding joined the clothes needing to be dried. If the mattresses were spoiled, those who slept on them faced many months of rotting hay beneath them if they could not afford to replace it. Thatchers worked long hours, and men scavenged for dry wood, while women sought to feed the families and dry their clothes.

"Never has Aldington suffered so badly," the thane said to his wife as she nursed the baby. "The people are feeling low. They move about all hunched up as the rain presses down upon them. I can hardly believe they will know how to stand straight when the sun shines upon them again."

"This time will pass," she reassured him.

193

The families of Penton and Arlo Smith fared better than others. The men worked beneath a sturdy shelter, with the heat of the fire wrapping itself around them. Their younger sons, Alfrid and Osric, were sent to bring wood for the fire but had the luxury of that same fire being fierce enough to dry their capes and mud-splattered trousers. They began to learn the skills of their ancestors: the shaping of metal and the beating of patterns.

With her thickening waist, Felice began to integrate into family life, joining Eadric's mother and sister as they went about their daily tasks. She learned the words for common items then began to string them together. The women of Aldington watched her but were unable to satisfy their curiosity. That Felice carried Eadric's child before the wedding, they had no doubt. However, they were yet to learn where she had come from, or how a good man had been lured to stray from the woman he had intended to marry. There was no chance of encouraging the newcomer to tell them. She did not know enough words, so they merely nodded and smiled. Amongst themselves, the women agreed that Felice had done well to marry Eadric Smith and sometimes she looked a little sad, but more often appeared quite pleased with herself. Her new family learned no more about her life, other than she had been at the Sandtun when the earth had quivered, and a great wave had thrown her from the boat.

Now the rain had come, and night fell early, Eadric began to spend more time with Felice. *She is still a stranger to me,* he reflected, *yet Clover, who I know so well, is gone. How am I to spend my evenings alongside Felice, now the days are short and I am forced to remain in the home*? He cast aside the woollen thread and needle used to repair his trousers. "The light is not good enough," he muttered, pointing to the lone candle.

In her usual calm manner, Felice picked up the discarded items then put them on the table. She pointed to herself and the trousers, before saying: "I sew."

Eadric stood and gave her a light kiss on the top of her head to show his thanks. "What happened to the man, your faeder?" he tried to ask, indicating with his hands the presence of another man.

Felice shook her head and used a word recently learned, "Nay."

"You know about my life," he said, knowing there was frustration in his tone. "I know nothing of yours." She shrugged. The words were just sounds. So, Eadric picked up the bucket from the corner and relieved himself in it. He placed his cloak on a hook and his tunic on the top of a wooden trunk, then reached for his nightshift. *If only I could spend the evening with my family, but to leave Felice on her own would be cruel.* He reflected for a moment on her needs. "You must miss being able to talk to other women." She gazed at him and gave a slight smile.

From the bed, Eadric watched her check on the fire and prepare for bed. She slipped in beside him and lay on her back, then pulled his hand to the swell of her stomach. The baby pressed outwards. After a moment he moved his hand upwards to her rounded breasts and lifted himself a little, so their lips met. They communicated in ways other than speech on the mattress that had been filled with sweet hay by Clover and Hilda.

The tracks leading from the village and those winding between the homes, animal pens and places of work were difficult underfoot. The men cleared slippery leaves, but thick mud was perilous for the elderly and weak. The streams, where the women filled buckets, burst their banks, leaving swathes of boggy land to be negotiated so as to reach the clean fast-flowing water. When the rain finally abated, the weather remained mild, but the hardships arising from twenty-eight days of rain continued to make life difficult for the villagers.

"It will be easier to move the stone when the ground becomes firmer," Godwin told Cenric as they drank cups of warm wine by the fire in the thane's hall.

"Then we will have snow!" the thane declared. "We cannot expect the horses and oxen to work in those conditions."

"Or the men," Godwin pointed out. "But you are wrong – there will be a time of frost with dry weather before the snow comes. The days will be short but there will be no work to be done on the fields. Our men can move a lot of stone in that time. Wait a couple more weeks, brother, and work will start again."

With the baby sleeping in a sling against her breasts, Otha poured more wine for the men, then some for herself. "That will make our daughter strong," Cenric approved.

"There is a fever in the village. Have you heard?" Otha said as she seated herself. "One of the women collapsed in the weaving shed. They say her skin was grey, and dress soaked in a sour sweat. She is one of four women who have taken ill while others are complaining of their foreheads aching."

"This weather has been no good for anyone," Cenric replied. "We must remember them in our prayers and hope she recovers."

"Which women are these?" Godwin asked. "Are they from the same family? Is there anything we can do to help?"

"They are from several families who live close together in the north of the village," Otha told them. "Their husbands work on the land, or the new church, and the families have been suffering for the lack of work."

"We gave food when our child was born," Cenric observed.

"Aye. They would have been grateful, but perhaps they need more. I will visit tomorrow and see what can be done."

"Not with a baby," Godwin interjected. "She is only ten days old. I will speak to our cousins, and between us we can arrange help for the families."

"I thank you." Otha adjusted the sleeping child in the sling. "I cannot leave our people to suffer."

Two days later, talk of the fever was rife in the village. "Mary and Eda have died," Eadlyn told Arlo and Alfrid when they returned for the midday meal.

"Is she the woman who first became ill in the weaving shed?" Arlo asked.

"Aye, and her sister who shares the home. There are now nine others suffering with the fever. They are unable to rise from their beds, while some complain of headaches. Felice and Alfreda were weaving yesterday and they said the stench from one of the women was foul. She was at the point of collapse so had to be helped home."

"Felice's language is improving!" Alfrid commented, dunking his bread in the thick pottage.

"It was her expression that spoke for her, along with Alfreda's words!" his mother pointed out. "She will learn our tongue and, in time, we will accept her being here."

"Not yet though," Hilda said.

"Not yet," Eadlyn agreed, placing her arm around her daughter's shoulder and giving her a squeeze.

Despite the fact that no more stone could be hauled onto the site, work on the church began again. There was enough to give height to the wall by a couple of rows, and the thane ordered that another scaffold tower be built to raise the men so they could work on the upper part of the walls.

"We have the wood, and this will give our carpenters work," Cenric told Godwin. "Soon, nothing will be achieved from the ground, so work will proceed all the quicker if we have several towers."

"I agree," Godwin replied. "Spirits are low. This will give the men something to do. Once we have more stone, the walls must be completed as soon as possible."

"I hope to see the windows taking shape soon." Cenric seemed once more to be satisfied with life as they approached the church. He turned to Father Theodore who walked behind them. "What do you say, Father? Are you pleased to see the men at work again?"

"I am pleased," the priest responded. "I have prayed for the rain to cease and our good men to be working

198

for our cause again. Now I pray for their good health – this sickness brings another cloud to hang over us all."

The tower was taking shape and all three men paused to admire the sturdy uprights lashed together with rope. "We were thinking of raising the others," one of the men said. "These will take us up to the eaves, but to move the beams into place we must go higher."

"Do it now!" the thane answered with his usual enthusiasm. "I want nothing to slow us when the walls have been built." He strode on to the men who were picking through the stone, selecting the next pieces to be used, and followed them to a scaffold where another man was climbing to the top.

There was a light breeze, and the smell of stale body odour drifted towards the three men who had come to view the day's progress. The labourer had patches of sweat on his back and, when he turned, they saw his face was glistening.

"Are you unwell?" Godwin asked, his voice sharp.

"I'm well enough," the man insisted. "There is work to be done and I'm no use being idle at home." He took a further step, his fists tight around the supporting poles.

"He's not well," another said, beginning his climb upwards. Moving swiftly, he was soon lowering a rope to be tied around a piece of stone. "But as he said, well enough and his wife needs food for the young ones."

The first now crouched at the top, seemingly unaware of his surroundings, and unable to focus on the task in hand.

"Come down," Godwin ordered. "You will have food. We will make sure of it. If you fall, you will be of no use to your wife."

"Do as he says."

"Go on, John, take it easy. Get yourself down."

Shuffling into position, the sick man lowered himself over the side of the platform then began his descent. Almost seeming to slip to the ground, he managed to keep his balance and turned to Godwin. "I'll do some work on the ground. I thank you."

"Go home to your bed," Godwin replied. "Tell your wife she will have a basket of food and some logs for the fire before noon."

Another couple of days passed. There were now five deaths in the village: four adults and one child. Although the rain had ceased, the people still walked with their bodies stooped. Afraid for their own lives and those of their families, they whispered about the sweating, headaches and grey skin. Heads were bowed further as a sign of respect when the homes of the dead were passed.

One evening, as the sun dipped below the horizon and the sky was streaked with pale yellow and grey, Eadric stepped into his parents' home. "Felice is ill," he said.

Chapter Nineteen

The pan hanging above the fire was not the usual cauldron of pottage, added to over several days, but a small pot releasing a sweet aroma. "I pray the scent will lift Felice's spirits." Megan stirred rosemary, lavender and rose petals with a wooden spoon, then reached to remove the pot. "She is alone in our land, and this will show we care for her."

"We care that she lives, for she is young and carrying Eadric's child," Alfreda responded. "But I cannot say I care for *her*."

"I understand." Megan sighed, then turned to her daughter. "Felice tries to please us, but I cannot see a time when we will think of her as part of the family. It is not easy. I try to believe that she meant no harm in tempting Eadric." Changing the subject, she asked, "Do you have the squares of cloth?"

Alfreda passed a small pile of clean linen squares, and offered, "I hope she is no worse."

Megan stepped outside. Sitting on the bench by the doorway to his home, Eadric held his head in his hands. He looked up on hearing his mother approach. "She is asleep and seems to be at peace."

"Did you put a clean cover on the mattress?" Megan asked.

"Aye." He indicated with his hand that the soiled sheet was in a basket nearby. "Why does she sweat so? And how can it smell so foul? I would rather sleep beside a pig than my wife."

"It is the nature of the illness," Megan replied. "Pour a little of this into a bowl and soak the cloth in it, then use it to wash her body. The rest can keep warm over the fire, giving a scent of lavender and rosemary."

"I thank you." Eadric stood; he took the pot and cloths and stepped towards the open doorway.

"Would you like me to help you clean her?" Megan asked.

Eadric faltered and for a moment his mother saw him as a young child. However, he straightened himself and said, "Nay. It is my duty to care for Felice."

Megan smiled the best she could, then picked up the basket. "I'll wash the sheet and be grateful for the breeze today."

On the way to the stream, Megan saw the gravedigger at work. *It is a pitiful job in any weather, but he will battle with the sodden ground. I wonder if there have been more deaths, or is this grave being prepared for the next victim*? A wave of sickness rose in her throat to think of Felice lying in the ground with the child still in her womb.

At the water's edge Megan plunged the sheet amongst the rotting leaves and the murky water. No one would wash clothes at the moment with the intention of cleaning them, but she was not the first woman of the village to rinse the sweat and odour from nightclothes and bedding. *I fear we will be doing this for weeks to come*. She hauled the sheet from the stream, regretting that Alfreda was not there to help, and placed it on the ground to squeeze out some of the water. *It won't dry like this. It was foolish of me to try. I hope Eadlyn or Alfreda are there to help me once I have got it home.* Megan, a slim woman and, like the others, disheartened by the month of rain, used all her energy in taking the water-logged cloth back. By the time she and Alfreda were twisting and squeezing the cloth, her head was pounding and her body hot.

"Modor, you must rest," Alfreda insisted.

From her bed, Megan watched as her daughter prepared an infusion of sweet herbs and left it to brew over the fire. Then she slept.

When Megan woke, the home was almost dark. The curtain was half-pulled across her bed, but she could see a candle burning on the table. Wood crackled in the firepit. It seemed as if she were an outsider looking into her home. *Foolish thoughts,* she scolded herself. She closed her eyes and listened: the scrape of a stool, the movement of animals in the pen and the low murmur of a voice. Opening them again, Megan realised that the headache had passed, but her body felt weak. She allowed herself to drift off to sleep. On waking again, she had no idea how much time had passed. The candle still burned and there was the soft hiss of a damp log on the fire.

Soft footsteps approached and Alfreda pulled back the curtain. She was holding a dish and Megan recalled the soothing water with which she had been washed earlier.

"Modor? Are you awake?" Alfreda asked. Her voice was no more than a whisper.

"I'm awake." Megan's mouth was dry. It was almost painful to speak, and she wondered if the scented water might trickle into her mouth if her daughter were to wipe her face.

It seemed that Alfreda understood her mother's needs for she turned away, saying, "Faeder! She is awake and needs a noggin of wine. Nay, half a noggin or I will spill it."

Penton must have had the wine to hand for it was swiftly poured, then Alfreda sat on the edge of the bed, encouraging her mother to sit up a little and take the rich liquid. It trickled into her mouth and she swallowed, alleviating the painful dryness.

Megan drank some more, and asked, "How many days have I been here?"

"Just two days, Modor."

"It passed?" Megan queried. She put a hand to her chest – it felt cool, and the linen shift dry. There were strange dream-like memories of someone pulling the damp one from her body and washing her clammy skin with warm scented water.

"Aye, it passed."

"Felice?"

"Felice is very ill, Modor. She is no better, but Osric will go to tell Eadric that you are recovered, and the news will give him hope."

Word flew about the village, from one cowed figure to another: some people recovered in a day or two, yet others lay in their beds for longer, their bodies emitting a foul sweat and their minds not knowing where they were or who tended them. There was no acceptable pattern to who lived or died: Ann Ashtree, thought to be the oldest person in the village, rallied around and was nursing her grandson, while John Thatcher, young and strong, drifted from this life three days after his head began to pound. It had spread, they reported with certainty, from the northern side of the village and now it was everywhere. Even in the thane's hall.

Cenric stood beside the bed and watched as his baby daughter was put to his wife's breast. "There is no nourishment for the child," stated his cousin, who had just cleaned the soiled newborn. "Do I have your permission to place her with a woman who can feed her?"

"Aye," Cenric replied. The mewling of the baby was distressing, and he was sure Otha could hear it despite her being barely conscious. "Let this be the last time she suckles from her mother." But the child was tossing her head, unable to latch on, and the breast was no longer full. "Take her now," the thane decided. "When Otha wakes, it will ease her mind to know her daughter thrives."

The cousin lifted the baby away from her mother, ensured that she was well-swaddled, then left the thane's hall. Cenric followed and stood at the doorway, looking towards the village. For once his heart and mind were not full of the stone church, although he spotted Father Theodore walking through the village and wondered where the priest was heading.

Godwin approached. Cenric lifted his hand in a gesture of recognition.

"How is Otha?"

"It seems that she is barely with us," Cenric told him. "There is no milk left for the child; she is being taken to feed elsewhere. I thank God I will not have to suffer her crying and I am sure it must be the only sound her mother hears as she lies there."

205

"It is for the best."

"What news from the village?"

"There has been one death overnight," Godwin informed him, "and some people are showing signs of recovery. Spirits are low and people are scared."

"We are all scared," Cenric reflected. "This sweating sickness will take who it pleases, and all we can do is pray it soon passes. The Lord must have his reasons for bringing this to Aldington, but I struggle to understand them."

They stood for a moment, without speaking. As they did so the priest came into view again. This time he walked with his head slightly bowed. Behind him two men carried a shrouded body on a stretcher. A short trail of villagers followed, passing not far from the thane's hall and proceeding to the burial site. Cenric and Godwin shadowed them, then stood a little way from the others while the priest performed the rites of burial.

When they turned away from the grave and mourners, there was movement to the south. A cart trundled into sight, pulled by two heavy horses, with a couple of men walking beside them. "The first stone for the day," Godwin commented. "It will do the men good. Not all of them will fall ill and they need to work."

"We still have enough labourers. Edwin Woodman has returned to work, despite being ill. His recovery will lift the spirits of the others."

"Aye, he will give hope," Godwin reflected.

The church walls now encompassed the beginnings of three narrow windows on each long side, with their ledge being three layers of thin red Roman brick and their sides cut square by the masons. There would be one window above the altar to light the church with the golden beams of sunrise. The rounded tops were still to come, but it was hoped they would be completed not long after the shortest day of the year.

Nearby the great oak beams were stacked alongside slimmer roof trusses. The men were under orders to strengthen the scaffold towers, for the weight of the beams would be greater than any stone they currently withstood.

Cenric and Godwin walked up to the wagon as it came to a halt. They looked over the stone, running their hands over the angles cut by those masons of past centuries. The builders joined them, and the load was soon passed from one to another, joining the stacks on the ground. Once the wagon had been turned, then dispatched again to the hilltop above the fort, Cenric returned to his home, and Godwin turned to walk the village boundaries.

Despite there being a chill in the air, the doors to the thane's hall were flung wide open. Cenric knew why: the stench of the sweating sickness was not restricted to the poor, the elderly or weak. Inside a fire roared, fed by sweet applewood. His daughter, Edina, was breaking lavender and rosemary to add to the small pot of herbal infusions simmering above the fire. "How is your modor?" he asked her.

"She is sleeping."

"And where are your sisters?"

"They are with your cousin, Faeder. You asked her to look after us," she reminded him.

Cenric pulled back the bed curtain. With little natural light in the home, Otha's features were indistinct. Her breathing, however, told him that this was no healing

207

sleep. The breaths came sporadically, accompanied by a low rattle.

"I am going to fetch Father Theodore," Cenric told Edina. "His prayers will bring peace to us all."

Megan passed a cup of thin gravy, rich with chicken juices, to Eadric. It was the sixth day since Felice had fallen ill, and for the first time she was able to sit up in bed. Her skin was sallow, and cheeks hollow. The baby was merely a mound on a skeletal body. Yet the sweating sickness had passed, and Felice survived.

"Alfreda made this," Megan told her son. "There is pottage for you. Come and eat with us when Felice has sipped hers."

"Aye, I will," he replied.

"Do you know… has she said if the baby still moves?" Megan asked.

"Nothing has been said. I think it is too much effort." Eadric stepped forward, away from the doorway to his home. "What will be the point of all this if the baby dies?" he asked.

Megan heard the anguish in his voice. It was a question asked between her and Penton over the last couple of days. "I don't know," she responded. There was no point in offering platitudes, saying that Felice was pleasant enough, or that another child would come in time. If the child were to die, Eadric would suffer in a marriage filled with resentment. *And Felice?* Megan pondered the matter as she walked home. *Most likely she will remain quietly jubilant in securing a home and husband. But I am being cruel. She will have lost the child.*

208

In her home, Megan sat at the table, while Alfreda ladled their meal into wooden bowls. She had been to the bakehouse that morning, and later to the stream. That had been enough, leaving her exhausted. Within their small family, two had succumbed to the illness, and Megan feared for who might become ill next. From a distance, she had witnessed two burials that morning.

On her mattress of scented hay, covered by blankets of finely-woven wool, Otha drew her final breath. The women of the family were beside her, including Edina who was just ten years of age. Nearby, the baby slept in the home of her wet-nurse, her stomach rounded with milk. Thane Cenric was, at that very moment of death, kneeling in front of the wooden cross, and praying for his wife's peaceful departure into the next world. By the time he returned to the home, unscented candles had been lit and Otha lay on a bench, eyes closed, her expression peaceful. Her hands, feet and forehead had been anointed with holy oils by Father Theodore not long before she passed, giving her spiritual comfort during her last moments.

"She has passed," one of the cousins told him.

"May God bless her soul," he replied. "I must go for our priest."

"He was here, not long before she left this earth, but had to attend a burial," the cousin reminded him. "Your brother was with him."

"Aye," Cenric had a recollection of there being a burial taking place in the land reserved for this use just beyond the village boundary. "They will be here soon." He rubbed his knees, damp from kneeling on the ground, and said, "How sad she didn't see the church completed. There is no roof, but our treasured altar must be put in place and a candle lit for her soul. I will speak to Father Theodore about it."

At that moment, the priest and Godwin walked into the thane's hall. "She has gone," the priest spoke with regret. "I trust she passed peacefully from this life to the next?"

The women murmured that the moment had been calm, then gave one last glance towards the body. They bowed their heads and left, taking Edina with them.

Father Theodore approached the dead woman and stood, with Cenric and Godwin on either side. Bowing his head slightly, he began to pray: "Farewell Christian soul…"

Later that day, Otha's body was wrapped in linen, and she was lifted into a long oak box by the carpenters who crafted it. Cenric placed her favourite brooch of gold inlaid with garnets in the folds of the shroud and, close to Otha's right hand, there was the key used to lock the box of family treasures. Penton Smith had cut a matching key that morning, and for the moment it hung from the belt of one of the female cousins. A candle was placed on the bench near the dead woman's feet to burn through the night. The coffin remained unsealed, with female members of the family sitting beside it through the darkest hours.

"The men have returned to close the lid," Cenric was told, while slumbering in his bed the following morning.

"I'm coming," he replied, swinging his legs out of the bed, running his hands through his thick wavy hair and reaching for his cloak. It was in this dishevelled state that Cenric looked down upon his wife for the final time.

"I'll pray for your swift journey to heaven," he told her. "The good Lord will look kindly on us and remember we are building a church for him. You can be assured of a fine welcome." He made the sign of the cross on his body before turning away. "I am done," he said to the carpenter.

One of the women who served in the thane's hall placed a bowl of warm water on a stand and a clean tunic on the bed. Cenric splashed the water over his face, immediately feeling revived, then began to dress. As he fastened the leather straps around his calves, keeping the loose trousers in place, Father Theodore entered the home, going immediately to pray beside the coffin.

At first they ate breakfast in silence, but not much could stop the thane's mind from churning over ideas and schemes. Before the bowl had been scraped clean, he said, "I would like the Roman altar to be moved to the church. The stonemasons have completed the supports, and it will come to no harm while the roof is open. Better placed as it should be in an unfinished church than used as a door plinth for a fort!"

Father Theodore nodded his understanding but did not reply immediately. He must have been pondering on the matter because, as they rose from the table, he remarked: "The altar stone won't suffer for the rain, but it would be best to place the cross and candle holders there later. They will rust otherwise."

"I was thinking only of the altar," Cenric confirmed.

Not long after, Godwin and the cousins, with young Edina, gathered at the thane's hall. The priest led the way, followed by the four coffin bearers, then the other family members. Their pace was slow as they walked past the part-built church, towards the burial plots at the edge of the village. The gravedigger, busy preparing the ground for future use, paused in his work to bow his head. In the distance, villagers hovered, looking on at the scene.

Having spoken a few words about Otha's life and giving his condolences to the family, Father Theodore asked that the body be lowered into the ground. Clasping his hands around the golden cross recently bestowed on him by the thane, he lowered his head and prayed:

"Lord, our sister, Otha, has moved from this life to yours and gone to her rest in the peace of Christ. May you now welcome her to the home of God's children in heaven. Look with favour on those who mourn, and comfort them at this time of loss. Let them, with faith and hope in eternal life, assist her with their prayers. O God, by whose mercy the faithful departed find rest, bless this grave, and send your holy angel to watch over it. Through your mercy, O Lord, may Otha rest in everlasting peace. Amen."

"Amen," the words were echoed amongst those standing close by. Cenric leaned to take soft earth in his hands and threw it onto the coffin. The others followed, even Edina, who was pale and lost. Finally, they turned back to the thane's hall where warm wine, cheese and fruit would be served.

The gravedigger filled the hole swiftly. Before the sun had reached its highest point, there was to be another burial.

Chapter Twenty

In Lyminge, the same rainclouds had hung low for a whole cycle of the moon. By the time the rain passed, the golden leaves had fallen from the trees. Lanes were thick with mud, and homes suffered just as they did in Aldington. Yet the Nailbourne bubbled pure water, filtered through the chalk and, although it burst its banks in the village, the water remained clean.

When the skies cleared, the villagers continued the patterns of their daily lives, now wearing thicker shifts under their tunics, and cloaks wrapped tighter around their shoulders. There was a chill in the air, and they knew the days would only become colder as they shortened.

It took some time for word to pass from one village to the next, and on the day Thane Cenric buried his wife, Lyminge heard of the sweating sickness sweeping through Aldington. It came to Clover's ears as a piece of gossip exchanged between the women in the weaving shed, with no thought of the distress it could cause.

"Sickness in Aldington?" Clover repeated to the woman who sat beside her, working the wool into a thread.

"Aye, and it doesn't care who it takes. People are dying."

"What type of sickness?" Clover persisted.

"Terrible sweats. Stinking sweats. It's like the devil is with them, making them rage and talk nonsense," the woman continued. While the horror of the illness passed from person to person, village to village, the symptoms had been embellished, as if the reality were not bad enough. "Their skin is grey, not red with fever, and all they can do is lie in their beds until merciful death comes."

"Do any recover?" Clover asked, as her skin chilled and throat tightened.

"We can only pray they will," the woman replied.

"I must tell Janna, and my brother." Clover tossed the yarn back into the basket at her feet, then fled from the weaving shed.

She found Janna in the chickens' coop. Words poured out: "They are saying there is sickness in Aldington. A terrible sickness. I should go… They may need me."

"Where have you heard this?" Janna asked.

"In the weaving shed."

"There will be a truth in it, but you cannot trust words spread about the village. Only believe what comes by messenger, the nuns or monks."

"Aye," Clover's response was subdued. "But…"

"Find your brother, in case he has heard anything. But, Clover, the tracks to Aldington will be barely passable after all the rain. If your mind cannot rest, go to see Mildrithe and she will tell you if all is well."

The thought of the old woman in the woods immediately reassured Clover. Like her aunt, she felt only comfort in her presence and had visited Mildrithe several times, making special trips through the rain with nourishing food.

"I'll do that!" she announced. "I'll go to the minster for some honey before I go."

"And Cym?"

"Aye, I'll see him too."

Soon Clover was walking past the minster buildings, slowing her pace to show respect for the gentle routines of the monks and nuns. She passed silent figures, their heads bowed, and moved away from the central area to the less-orderly collection of stores and workplaces. Slipping into a small shed, Clover nodded to the nun. "Good morning, Sister."

There was a whispered response. Lips barely moved behind the gauze veil, and although the facial features were concealed, Clover could see this was an older woman with a rounded face.

"A jar of honey, please."

The nun turned and selected a clay pot, then poured thick golden honey into it before placing a stopper in the neck.

"I thank you," Clover said, her voice hushed. She left and, having no other business in the minster, returned to the courtyard lined with the church, dormitories, kitchen and refectory. There was a small, covered shelter near the kitchen where she left her offering to the holy people – some leather laces given to her by Cym days beforehand, so she might trade with the nuns and monks when needed.

The weak sun was moving towards its peak by the time Clover was picking her way along the narrow tracks towards Postling. They were thick mud, and in places

215

deep with fallen leaves turning to a rotting sludge, but she was young and able to move with ease from one dry patch to the next. Invigorated by the walk, the distress felt on hearing news of the sickness lessened. Clover was soon surrounded by open countryside and approaching the patch of woodland.

On entering the shadowed area, Clover breathed deeply, inhaling the scent of damp leaves mingling with the woodsmoke from the fire smouldering outside Mildrithe's humble home.

"I thought it was you!" the old woman exclaimed. Usually reserved, she had taken a liking to Clover, who had learned her mother had often visited in the past. With Janna, Mildrithe had told the story of the pendant cross and her prediction it would return to Eadlyn when it was lost many years before.

"I brought you some honey," Clover passed the jar into the gnarled hands.

"I'll enjoy that!" Mildrithe disappeared into her home, returning with clay cups, then busied herself ladling steaming herbal tea into them. "Your modor has been parted from the cross – I know that. But it is in safe hands and still has the power to protect her. She is wrapped in love."

"You knew I was worried!" Clover replied. "There is a sickness."

"There is a sickness casting fear over the village. Your modor is frightened, and it will touch those around her, but she is safe."

"But my sister… and brother and…"

"All will be well." Mildrithe sat on her bench. She gestured for Clover to do the same. "How is your brother Cym Leatherman?"

216

They spoke about other matters for a while, and as they did so the wildlife came closer. Birds flew to the woodland floor and tugged at insects. A mouse scurried about in the undergrowth.

As Clover rose to leave, Mildrithe had one final thing to say, "The man you sometimes think about - the one with the fiery hair. This sickness will not touch him, but I cannot speak for the dark woman. There is some confusion in my mind when I see her. It is not yet clear."

"Oh. I…"

"He is not your future," Mildrithe stated with confidence. "I see you coming here to see me – you have good news to tell – and I am rejoicing!"

"I thank you!" Clover reached out and clasped Mildrithe's hand. "I will return soon. I promise."

With her hand resting under her unborn child, Cate, sister of Cenric and Godwin, walked slowly into the village of Aldington. Her husband, along with a servant, led a pair of handsome mares. Pregnancy made her weary, so that neither walking nor riding was comfortable. "I pray we are not too late," she said to her husband. "I pray the reports are wrong and we will find Otha recovering."

"We'll know soon enough," Brice of Lympne replied, and not for the first time since they heard of the sickness.

They spotted Cenric standing by the church, gesturing to the stonework at the windows. "He is not at her bedside," Cate observed. "What does that mean? Perchance she is recovered?"

At that moment, Cenric turned and they noted the look of surprise flit over his face before he strode towards them.

"Brother, we heard the news of an illness. Is it as bad as they say?" the words gushed from Cate's lips.

"It is worse," Cenric answered.

"But Otha? She's recovering? Can we see her?"

"You are too late." Cenric nodded in the direction of the grave. "We buried her yesterday. People are dying and this sickness takes whom it pleases. Even those with a baby to feed."

"The child?" With her own baby growing fast in her womb, Cate could barely imagine being taken from it so soon after the birth.

"My daughter is with a nursing mother," Cenric replied. "The three older ones are staying with my cousins for a day or two, but they cannot care for the baby as well. She has been fretful, and no wonder when her mother's milk dried up, but has settled now her belly is full again."

"It's good to hear she thrives. I hope it continues," Cate responded.

"And that the older girls remain in good health," Brice added.

They walked side-by-side back to the thane's hall where Cenric called for the woman who cooked for him. He ensured that his sister was comfortable by the fire and soon the family from Lympne were holding cups of wine while listening with horror to the extent of the sickness.

Before they ate, Edina slipped in to sit quietly at her aunt's side. She was a docile child and, prior to leaving, Cate had a suggestion to make: "Cenric, why not send the girl to live with us? The marriage between her and Thane Selwyn's son is agreed. I can care for her until they marry."

"She is too young to marry," Cenric stated.

"I am not suggesting they marry yet. The child is only ten and I would prefer her to wait until she is fourteen, although they may press for a wedding beforehand. She can live with us and be a part of our family."

"The baby?" Cenric asked. "And the other girls?"

"I cannot feed a baby," Cate told him. "Besides, it would be wrong to take them all from you. We had already planned that Edina make Lympne her home in the future, and that is why I suggest we take her now. I am sure she will be happy with us."

"It would be too much to take them all," her husband swiftly added. "Besides there are women here to care for them. Edina is welcome in our home though."

"There are other women to care for my children until I marry again," Cenric agreed. "Here I am with four daughters and no son to continue my good work here. Otha was a fine woman but not built to breed boys. I must choose carefully next time."

"You could do worse than taking a widow who is happy to look after your children with her own," Brice suggested. "One who is proven to have the womb to produce a male child."

"You have a wise husband," Cenric said to his sister. "You chose well." He waved to the serving woman, indicating that there were noggins to be refilled, and continued, "Brice, I shall take heed of your advice while I cast my eye about. If you were to hear of anyone…"

219

"Are you looking for a dowry?" Brice enquired. "Land?"

"Nay," the thane replied. "Aldington is rich with land both on the hills and across Romney Marsh. If I could have more on the marsh it would be welcome, however someone to breed boys and care for my daughters is enough." He paused for a moment, reflecting on the opportunities awaiting him, then added, "But a pair of pert breasts would be appreciated!"

"Let us discuss your daughter," Cate's tone was sharp as they returned to the matter she had raised. "Do you have any objections to her making a home with us?"

"None at all," Cenric answered. "She is a sweet girl, as you know, but I have two others as well as the baby. I am sure she will be happy with you and I am grateful to know you are fond of her."

"I'll speak to her before we leave," Cate said. The child had slipped away when they were midway through the meal, no doubt returning to her sisters, or perhaps to visit her mother's grave. "I think she should have a few days to become used to the idea."

"Aye, you could return for her shortly," Cenric agreed.

"Nay, Cenric," Brice interjected. "You will bring your daughter to us. Our child is due in another cycle of the moon, so Cate will not make this journey again. Now it is time for us to return. I will call our man to fetch the horses. You can…" he turned to his wife, "…find Edina to tell her of our plans."

After the morning of Otha's burial, no others died in Aldington for two days, then an elderly man slipped

220

away in a restless sleep. Three more days passed, and a young woman died, leaving two children and a husband to mourn her. Tragic as these losses were, the rate of death was slowing, and fear began to leave the faces of the villagers. The weather turned colder, while the people who had bent their backs against the month of rains and cowed before the sweating sickness, began to straighten themselves. The air they breathed was icy and there was the prospect of snow to come, but for now the days were bright and they found themselves cheered by this.

Two weeks passed between it being decided that Edina was to live with his sister, and Thane Cenric setting off to her home in Lympne. His subdued daughter rode her grey pony beside him. A servant led a packhorse, with a huge leather bag strapped to its back. It contained the girl's dresses and her best cloak, as well as her linen shifts and her second pair of shoes. Nestled amongst these was a decorative box crafted by Penton Smith, containing ornamental brooches used for fastening her cloak, a gold necklace, and some amber beads chosen from her mother's box of treasures. There was a bale of red linen and another in a deep blue – luxurious gifts for the wife of Thane Selwyn, as well as Cenric's sister, Cate.

    Edina was not unhappy about the move to Lympne. As the eldest sibling she was fast becoming mother to the young ones and felt exasperated by this. Already whispers carried amongst the cousins: the thane would be taking a second wife as soon as the right woman could be found. The girl was not ready to have her mother replaced. To be with Cate would offer the comfort Edina needed, without having to accept a stranger into her life. Standing at the grave not long before sunset, when the colours of the land were enriched by the low sun in the sky, she had asked her mother to offer her blessing for the new life ahead. Edina felt certain that Otha approved of her leaving. Despite her resolution that to live amongst family in Lympne would be preferable, the girl was a gentle soul and her heart and mind were by no means settled.

They took the old Roman road to the escarpment, then turned towards Lympne. The ground was hard and more often than not there was a frost in the morning, making the journey easier than it had been in the past months.

"Ah, look at this, Edina!" her father exclaimed, as a heavy horse and wagon approached. "Those are my men – see how dedicated they are to building the church. I saw them leave our village before dawn and already they are here with the new stone."

As the wagon approached, it slowed. Cenric encouraged his daughter to follow him so they rode alongside and viewed the selection of ragstone blocks. "Very good! When I have been to Lympne, I will go to see the fort for myself again. How do the oxen manage on the hillside?"

"It is easy in the morning, my lord, when the ground is hard," one of the men answered. "Not so good later in the day after it softens."

"You do right to get there early then!" Cenric beamed. "Our Lord in heaven will thank those who laboured so faithfully for the church."

Murmuring their thanks, the men moved on. Cenric and Edina continued on their way. The road they took was not far from the steep hillside leading to Romney Marsh, and they glimpsed the flat lands stretching all the way to Sussex. In the early morning, it appeared as a place of mystery, with low-lying mists gently swirling to blanket the view of salt pans, creeks and patches of dry land.

"Is that where the spirits go, Faeder?" the girl spoke for the first time since leaving Aldington.

"The spirits?" he questioned. "The souls of good people like your modor are in heaven with the Lord."

"And the bad ones?" her voice was fearful and blue eyes round.

"They burn in the eternal flames of hell."

"But the ones that are not that bad, and not that good. They are waiting in the mists down there?" She glanced quickly towards the marsh. To her young imagination it seemed as if the land were becoming increasingly shrouded. A flock of birds took fright and flew from a cluster of stunted trees squawking madly. The grey pony side-stepped, and Edina struggled to maintain her balance.

"Where do you hear such things?" Cenric asked, with a hint of humour in his voice. "I hope my sister teaches you some sense."

"It's what the women say. They say it to the children, so we know to behave. No one wants to be there on Romney Marsh with the biting insects, and the water rotting in the ditches."

"They want to be there to gather the salt!"

"Aye, but they don't stay for long."

"They want to be there to trade at the Sandtun."

"I shouldn't want to be on the Sandtun. It is too close." As the road took them into a wooded area, Edina admitted her fears, "I worry that Lympne is too close."

"Edina…" showing a rare understanding, her father let a softness to creep into his voice, "my sister Cate will keep you safe, and when the winter passes, or before if you wish, you will come to see me and your sisters in Aldington." He gave his horse a nudge in the flank and it broke into a trot. Soon the homes of Lympne were in view, and Edina was smiling to see her aunt waiting.

At the table of Thane Selwyn, Cenric and Edina were welcomed to Lympne with wine and a platter of nuts and fruit. While the men spoke of village matters and news from further afield, the women were gentle with Edina, understanding her quiet manner was due to being taken from her home, but hoping she would soon settle. Cate's belly appeared as if it could hold the child no longer. It was clear the birth was imminent – an event to take the girl's mind off her recent loss. "You will be able to help me so much," the expectant mother cajoled. "With three sisters, you are more used to babies than I. My brothers were older than me, so I had no young ones to care for. It was they who looked after me!" Edina smiled, hardly able to imagine her father or Godwin as young boys.

They did not idle at the table for long as Cenric's thoughts were all about viewing the ruins of the fort. Brice met them at the doorway and, after greeting Edina, he turned his attention to her father. "Cenric, I will walk with you to the hillside, if it is no trouble. There is a matter of a widow who I believe will interest you."

Chapter Twenty-One

Had he expected to see the Roman fort changed, Cenric would have been disappointed. The walls, as tall as his church, had been twice as thick, and the area which they covered had been extensive. His relentless inroads into the prized source of worked stone made barely any difference. It was easier for the men to take the blocks which had tumbled, so perhaps the site was a little tidier. But to build a church from a fort was nothing. It was little more than taking a few buckets of pebbles from a beach.

The Thane of Aldington thought only of his own project; there was no need to see the fort diminished in size so as to make his church more worthy. From the hilltop, he stood for a moment, satisfied with the scene before him. There must have been a dozen men pulling stone blocks from the rubble, and several more heaving them into position so the oxen could pull the cart up the escarpment. The second pair of stocky beasts were halfway on their journey up, and a larger wagon awaited them at the top.

"This is just what I wanted to see!" Cenric exclaimed. "Look how well my men are working. I foresee we'll have all the stone we need within days.

The church walls are almost complete and would have been so by now if it were not for those cursed rains."

"It often rains as the temperature cools," Brice pointed out.

"Aye, but it is done now. It is forgotten!"

They picked their way down the hill, avoiding fast-running streams which burst from the ground in times of wet weather, the grassy hillocks and rabbit burrows. Once amongst the stones, Cenric made a thorough nuisance of himself by calling the men away from their labours and insisting they remove the stones picked out by himself. "This must be the finest. Look at how well cut it is," he would exclaim over and over.

Cenric would have happily stayed amongst the ruins all day, but Brice reminded him of the other matter to be considered. "We must return, for Udela is to join us at our midday meal."

"Udela?"

"Aye. A comely woman – married to a cousin of mine, and widowed last summer," Brice told him. "She is keen to meet you."

"Does she have sons?" Cenric's interest was sparked.

"Two of them born in as many years of marriage!" Brice knew he had chosen well, and continued, "She is only 23 years of age, so it should be no trouble to provide you with a son."

"And…" Cenric considered the pleasure to be found in this bride, "… pleasing to the eye?"

"Of course! I said she was comely."

By the time Cenric had eaten his fill of fried fish and a tasty stew of leeks and root vegetables, then wiped his

226

wooden platter with bread, he was assured by Brice's choice in Udela. Her figure was slim, yet womanly, and he had an urge to clasp her to his chest, to nestle his face in her fair hair, and to tilt her chin upwards allowing him to place his lips on hers. Blue eyes met his every so often and held his gaze for long enough to show that the young widow was interested in furthering their relationship.

While her smooth complexion and tempting curves would please him greatly, it was Udela's interest in his church which satisfied him the most. Cenric was encouraged to describe his plans in detail. The Roman altar, taken from the fort at night before Thane Selwyn had permitted the removal of stone, remained a secret for now. To imagine sharing the story of it with Udela gave him great joy.

Thoughts of the church jostled with his desire for this woman. It seemed as if she would please him both in his bed and in their shared talk of the new church, so Cenric hatched a plan as they were about to part. "Brice, I should very much like to show Udela my church. I understand my sister is heavy with child and cannot journey to Aldington, but you brother…"

"Aye, if she would like to?"

They looked towards the woman who stood waiting, gazing downwards to her slim hands clasped across her stomach. She raised her face a little and looked to Brice. "I would be honoured to see this church. What a task, to haul the stone up the hillside and on to Aldington. I would love to examine each stone and wonder at its previous life!"

"The days are short, and I cannot spare the time for that!" Brice replied with a grin.

227

"But if circumstances were to change…" Thane Cenric hinted at his future plans, "then perhaps that would be possible. Now I must leave, while looking forward to our meeting again soon, Udela." She murmured her pleasure, and he turned to Brice, "If I lead my horse, will you accompany me to the edge of the village?"

Barely remembering to say goodbye to Edina and Cate, his mind overfilled with glorious plans, Cenric took the track towards Aldington with Brice walking beside him. Once they were out of earshot he pleaded, "Make plans to bring her as soon as possible, and I trust you to tell Udela that I am making an offer of marriage. She and her sons would be made welcome by my family. There is no reason to delay."

"I will tell her, and it seems likely she will accept."

Cenric mounted his horse and they parted company. Spurring his mount into a trot, Thane Cenric had soon left Lympne behind. Before long, the views over Romney Marsh were spread in front of him, then he turned the horse, riding inland to his home village.

Returning from the stream, laden with a pail of water, Eadric saw the thane and followed his progress with narrowed eyes. There was talk in the village about the Roman altar and it disturbed him. *Before the earth shook… before he went sneaking around the fort everything was good. We were happy, Clover and I. Now she is gone. I hear no news of her and have Felice in the home built for Clover. It wouldn't have happened had I not been so unsettled by the movement of that holy stone. It was wrong, but no one else can see it. I*

228

shouldn't have been tempted if... The thoughts ran through his head until he forced himself to stop.

Eadric considered Felice, at home preparing the pottage and flatbreads. Learning his language seemed to elude her, so their talk was limited to what could be exchanged in gestures and two or three words strung together. They could not discuss the news spreading from other parts of the kingdom, or even tell each other about their day.

The one thing Felice seemed able to express was her passion for the new church. Whenever they went to hear Mass at the wooden cross, she seemed eager to point out the progress. In the metalworking shelter, on the occasions when she visited, the candle holders and the crosses held a fascination. Felice appeared to be drawn to these objects, running her fingertips over every feature, murmuring words unknown to those who watched.

Whilst pondering his wife's interest, Eadric passed near the church and the thane's hall. He saw Felice approaching, and her face light up as she spotted him. He grinned. *Does she notice that my smile does not reach my heart?*

As they met, Eadric noticed Felice walked more slowly now. The pregnancy appeared to be running smoothly, and the bloom to her skin, lost during the sweating sickness and the days of slow recovery, had returned. Her body was slimmer than it had been before the illness, making the baby's growth more pronounced. Sometimes he tried to ask her if the child moved as much as previously, but she shrugged and showed that it was now so large. Did she mean that movement was now more awkward for it?

229

When the leaves start to appear on the trees and the crops begin to shoot upwards in the fields, then the child will come. My life will change, and as my child learns my tongue so will its modor. He smiled at Felice, again attempting to feel hope for the future.

Felice soon turned her attention from Eadric, taking his hand and pulling him towards the church, with no thought of the pail of water now placed on the ground. He could understand her excitement: that day the end walls had been completed and each one rose to a point far higher than any other building in the village. In Eadric's limited experience, only the minster at Lyminge rivalled this church in height. He pushed the memories of Lyminge aside to focus on the mixture of English and an unknown language pouring from Felice's lips.

Since they had last viewed the church together, the oak beams were now in place, linking the north and south walls. Eadric could not deny they made an impressive sight, and now he realised Felice was wanting to practise counting in his tongue. *She is trying to learn,* he told himself.

As they turned away, the thane approached. Eadric felt his stomach tense. *The man is a fool and it is he who brought a pagan altar to our village. Nothing has been the same since his meddling.* Yet, he had no choice but to give a cheery greeting when Cenric neared.

"Look at this," the thane called. "I've been out of the village and missed the final pieces of stone being put into place."

Felice was full of smiles, but it was Eadric who was forced to respond. "It looks fine, my lord. Soon we will see the roof taking shape."

"But before then, the Roman altar is to be moved here. There is nothing to stop it taking its place."

"Before the roof is complete?" Eadric questioned.

"Aye, as soon as it can be moved."

What a foolish plan. Our thane becomes more ridiculous by the day. Why set up an altar when the roof has not been covered?

"I wish you well with that," Eadric replied.

Winter was upon the Kingdom of Kent. On the ridge of hills known as the North Downs, there had already been a thin scattering of snow. Elsewhere the frost was thick in the mornings, offering a beauty to the land as it accentuated slender branches, evergreen leaves and full red berries.

The woodpiles were healthy but men still roamed about looking for fallen trees, and all day long the sound of the axe could be heard. These were the first weeks of winter and there would be many months of hardship before the sun warmed their skin again. It was best to be prepared and, without wood for the fire, life would be intolerable.

"How many eggs today?" Eadlyn asked Hilda when her daughter returned with the basket.

"Three," the girl answered.

Fresh food was now sparse. In the summer, each hen laid an egg daily, but in the winter the supply was sporadic.

"I got two jugs of milk from the goats." Eadlyn gestured towards the clay vessels on the table. Reaching for the sack of oats she scooped some into the pot.

"Can we have apple on our porridge?" Hilda asked.

231

"Nay, sweet. We must save them. This is enough." The apples were stored high in the rafters above the goats' pen. They were inspected weekly for rot – not the easiest task in the dusky light, but an enjoyable task as the air was sweet with their aroma.

"I'll put some bacon in the pot though." Eadlyn was thinking ahead to their midday meal.

Hilda smiled – to taste the salty-smokiness of the meat would give satisfaction. In the past few days, there had been nothing but beans, turnips and leeks in the cauldron hanging over the fire. She reached for the barley flour, then the rye, pouring some of each into a large wooden bowl, and added yeast from a small clay pot. Balancing the bowl on her hip, Hilda turned towards the open doorway. "I'll be back soon."

Eadlyn smiled, and watched her youngest child walk away with a spring in her step. *Clover would be pleased to see how her sister is taking on some of her tasks, but I wish she were here so they could work together.*

As she poured milk onto oats and set the pan above the fire, Eadlyn reflected on the latest news to be passed from one villager to the next. *Can our thane be marrying again already? It's what they are saying from the weaving shed to the bread ovens. Some of them saw her – a woman with fair hair and short in stature. She came accompanied by his sister's husband, so most likely is from Lympne. If her cloak was lined with fur, as they swear it was, she must be of good birth. But not a cycle of the moon has passed since his wife left this world. Not half a cycle…*

In the church, the stone masons had worked on the best pieces of ragstone and now they stood back, studying the results.

"These will hold the altar slab," one said.

"It would take twice the weight! I swear it!" the second responded.

"Aye, it will! I think I hear them coming."

They turned from the eastern end of the church and left the building by a narrow doorway. While they had been in the church, the sacred stone had been manoeuvred out of Father Theodore's humble home, and now four men were shuffling along with the cumbersome load.

Thane Cenric looked on, with the priest at his side. His expression was eager as he called out encouraging remarks: "That's it. Small steps. Watch the mud. Take care."

The stonemasons stood back, allowing the men to move awkwardly through the doorway, then they followed, with the thane at their heels. There was nothing for them to do now, for the thane allowed no one but himself to decide on the exact position of the altar, although he made a show of consulting the priest. After fussing over moving it a hair's breadth here and there, Cenric finally announced, "That is it. Do you not think so? Or do you think a little more to the…? Nay, it is perfect."

The men who had made that awkward journey from the low shelter which was the priest's home, and through the narrow doorway, stood back. When the thane asked no more of them, they left in haste.

Now it was left to the stonemasons to ensure the slab was bedded upon their upright supports and to add

233

the thinnest slivers of stone where needed. They had a few pieces to hand and used them sparingly. Nothing should detract from the subtle beauty of their worked stone and the ancient altar.

"These letters…" Cenric traced the angular shapes which told the history of the stone "…they could be cleaned up a little so if anyone were to study them, there would be no mistaking the symbols."

The lines meant nothing to the stonemasons. It made no difference to them if the script was in English or Latin, but they appreciated the work which had gone into carving such neat, evenly-spaced letters. One of them eased a blade under one of the ancient barnacles encrusting a small patch of the stone. It lifted away, leaving a tiny, raised ring where it had once suckered on.

"Not the barnacles! These crustaceans are part of the unknown story of our stone. How can it be that an altar found on a hillside has sea creatures upon it? They tell us about its former life when it must have served a Roman fort on the shore. Leave the barnacles!"

The mason stood back, confused by the outburst. "You want us to clean these markings, but leave these… these growths?"

"Exactly. It is just what Father Theodore and I wish for. The history of the altar will not be lost."

The priest who had merely watched from his position a step or two behind the thane, now spoke for the first time. "I trust that our Lord is leading you to follow His wishes, and the barnacles are His creatures, as we all are."

The masons exchanged a glance, communicating their confusion.

234

"Clean the letters as best you can," the priest continued, "but then we shall dedicate this altar to our Christian God. It must have five small crosses engraved on it, reminding us of Christ's five wounds on the cross. When the time comes for our first Mass, they will be anointed with holy oils."

"Where do you want the crosses?" one of the masons asked.

Father Theodore considered it and pointed to his chosen spots. The masons nodded their agreement.

"This must be done in haste," Thane Cenric ordered. "There will be no great ceremony to consecrate this church. I want it done within two days."

"Before the roof is finished?" the mason could not hide his surprise.

"Aye, I am to marry before the snows fall. A quiet affair." The thane paused, oblivious to the surprise caused by his words, then he continued, "I will order that a pig is killed. Every household will have a piece of fresh meat, so they may celebrate with me and my wife."

The stonemasons became the first to hear it from Thane Cenric himself and so the rumour became the truth, albeit much altered as it travelled from one home of wood and thatch to the next. The men and women of Aldington, who huddled by their fires and wrapped themselves in thick woollen cloaks, waited in anticipation of filling their stomachs with the gift of pork.

Chapter Twenty-Two

Those people of Aldington, whose stomachs craved more than a stew of beans and vegetables, soon heard that a pig had been killed. Some even claimed two of the beasts had been butchered. Their mouths watered at the thought of being presented with their portion of meat.

"The thane told Arlo it will be a simple wedding ceremony," Eadlyn told Megan when they walked together from the bread oven to their homes. "There must be a show of respect to his dead wife."

"I thank God that sickness has passed," Megan responded. "It came too close to our family, but we were spared."

"I should like to see her." Eadlyn's thoughts returned to Udela, who had arrived the day before and was now ensconced in the thane's hall with her sons, while Cenric was staying in Godwin's home.

"We'll see her soon enough. He'll want to show her the village and if, as they say, she has children they will be eager to roam about."

"Two boys," Eadlyn informed her.

"Perhaps they will deliver the meat together?" Megan suggested. "It will be the thane's way of introducing her and bringing pleasure to everyone."

"Aye, a piece of meat in the pot will bring nothing but goodwill to our thane!" Eadlyn grinned at the thought of it.

A tub, half-filled with hot water, was placed close to the fire in Godwin's home. Cenric threw aside his fur-lined cape and placed one foot, then another, in the water. Rosemary-scented steam rose up as he squatted and reached for the jug Godwin was handing him.

"If it were not part of the wedding ritual, I should never bathe in the winter," he claimed. "And your tub is too small."

"We can be pleased in knowing that Udela has yours and will cleanse herself in comfort!"

"That gives me some joy." The thane took the soft lye soap from a nearby stool and began to lather it in his hands before washing his hair and beard. The process was repeated over his body, and jugs of warm water were offered to wash away the soap. Cenric did not linger in the water for long, complaining that it had chilled. He was soon rubbing himself dry.

Godwin handed his brother a woollen shift and long socks, then the linen tunic with deep bands of embroidery at the hem and cuffs. Cenric fastened his belt and slipped his feet into shoes. They each drank a noggin of rich wine while putting on their best winter cloaks. The pins fastening the material at the shoulders were elaborate with garnets inlaid and reminiscent of the circular shields used in battle.

"Come, brother, I have a woman to marry and a son to sire," Cenric bragged, as he led the way to the door.

The church was no distance from the homes of the thane and his closest family. Cenric and Godwin were soon stepping through the opening which, as yet, had no door and into the cavernous space. Father Theodore was standing at the altar cupping his hands around the weak flame emitted from a candle. The ornate holders crafted by the metalworkers were being used for the first time but would then be set aside. Decorative features such as these would wait until the roof was complete.

As he turned to acknowledge the arrival of the two men, the cross at his neck moved a little amongst the priestly vestments. Godwin scowled to note the elaborate pendant with the dome of a ruby at its centre. He glanced at his brother expecting to see joy. The prized golden cross was adorning his priest just as desired. Instead, a look of confusion flashed across Cenric's face and he urged Godwin to accompany him to the rear of the church.

"I fear I was too hasty," Cenric whispered, flashing a glance towards the priest.

"Too hasty?"

"In honouring Father Theodore with the golden cross."

"Honouring the priest is all you think of," Godwin snapped. "How can you regret it?" He thought of Arlo Smith and his family – good, hardworking people – and the injustice of their having a cherished possession taken from them on the whim of the thane.

"Brice has done a fine job of seeking a new bride for me. Now I wish to give her a gift worthy of her beauty." Cenric raised his eyes past the part-built roof to the heavens, as if thanking the Lord for his blessings.

238

"I hoped you had finally realised the wrong you had done to a family in your village," Godwin remarked. "If that cross is to go anywhere, it should be returned to Eadlyn and the children of her first husband. It has a story, there is no doubt of it, and is theirs to treasure."

"I cannot take it from the priest," Cenric replied.

"It would be difficult," Godwin admitted.

"Udela will have something new created for her," the thane continued. "I shall give it some thought and, when she presents me with a son, my wife will receive a gift worthy of my appreciation."

Godwin, unwilling to pander to his brother's impulses for another moment, looked up to study the craftsmanship displayed in the rafters. Cenric wandered back towards the altar.

Movement outside, coupled with the sound of voices, heralded the arrival of Udela, escorted by Brice and a handful of Cenric's cousins, one carrying the baby in her arms. A trail of silent children followed, each as confused and uncertain as the next. Only Edina was absent from this gathering of Cenric's and Udela's children, it being decided that it would be disruptive to bring her back to visit Aldington so soon after her departure. Cenric rushed to the doorway to welcome his bride, with Godwin and the priest at his heels.

No sooner had he cast his eyes on Udela and appreciated her figure in the long blue dress, partly covered with a fur-lined cloak, than Cenric's attention turned to another matter. "There is no porch!" he wailed. "At least not yet. We were to build it afterwards."

Everyone turned their attention to him, their faces expectant.

"Where are we to marry if there is no porch for the exchanging of vows? I hadn't thought…" He looked from the priest to Udela. "Where is best? In the place where the porch is to be, or just here inside the church?"

There was silence as they considered the matter, until Udela responded, "Outside, then we will still step through the doorway to Mass."

"She is right," Godwin approved.

"The porch will be here sometime in the future," Father Theodore stated. "It will be as if it covers us, if we imagine it here."

"Of course!" Cenric was eager to agree.

Clearly used to the offers made between the families as the ceremony approached, the priest asked. "Are there any exchanges to be made before you take vows?"

"Nay, I only seek a fair woman to look after my daughters and provide me with a son," Cenric beamed. "I want nothing else from her or her family."

Udela smiled and bowed her head a little. As a widow her hair was covered, but blonde tendrils showed at her neck and rested on her cheeks.

She is an attractive woman, Godwin admitted. *I have spent too much time watching over my foolish brother and doing the jobs of the thane, with no thanks. I should have made more effort to find myself a wife. If I had asked Brice, perchance Udela could have been my wife. He considered this for a moment. Nay, I am wrong. The villagers thank me and see how hard I labour for their good.*

The children – Cenric's daughters and Udela's sons – were so young and not fully understanding the effect on their lives. They watched as pledges were exchanged, then plain gold rings given, and gave each other furtive looks although as yet no words had been exchanged between those who were now to be as brothers and sisters. The baby cried a little and fretted for the woman who fed her.

A commitment had been made, and Cenric was placing his lips on his new wife's. They lingered there, and his hand roamed to her firm bottom, giving it a squeeze. Once released, Udela giggled – a short chirp of appreciation. She tucked her arm through Cenric's as they prepared to enter the church for the Holy Sacrifice of Mass.

Attractive, but as foolish as he is, Godwin surmised.

The family group shuffled about, discreetly attempting to maintain some warmth in their limbs while observing Father Theodore perform the ceremony. Godwin noted Udela's gaze falling upon the elaborate gold cross settled on the priest's neck. She gestured to it, her surprise at seeing such a glorious piece was evident. Cenric beamed and whispered to her, no doubt promising of a story to tell, and perhaps hinting of the jewels he meant to endow upon her.

Outside the church some of the villagers had crept close, having kept their distance during the exchange of vows. They loitered against the high walls, hoping to snatch a line or two of the Mass. Not that they could understand the words spoken in Latin, but the priest's voice was melodic and drew them to him. As well as the word of the Lord, there was another reason to bring people to the church. Word was spreading: a few had glimpsed the fair Udela and spoken of her gentle beauty. The people of Aldington were keen to catch a glimpse.

241

Father Theodore gave his final prayer and raised his voice with the words, "*Ite, missa est.* Go forth, the Mass has ended." It soared to the rafters and those outside knew the time had come to retreat. If their thane had wanted them to celebrate alongside him, he would have called upon every family in the village to invite them, and a hog would be roasting over a fire. They were grateful to view his new wife from a distance and would await their portion of the slaughtered pigs.

Yet as the men and women backed away, another passed the village boundary in haste. Caedmon Messenger carried a flagon of honey mead brewed by the monks in Lyminge. Striding towards the church and thane's hall, he noted Godwin and raised an arm in greeting. "Am I too late?" he asked. "I made the journey as quickly as I could. Thank the Lord it was mostly downhill on the return."

"They are just married!" Godwin gave a wide smile. "I thank you. My brother will be eager for this."

The mead was passed into Godwin's hands and the messenger stepped away but, like the others, he lingered nearby. There was much merriment from the thane and laughter from his wife. Had she shown any modesty before vows were exchanged, it was all but forgotten.

"Your mead." Godwin gave the clay flagon to his brother.

"Excellent!" Cenric gave a knowing grin. He placed his arm around Udela's waist and guided her towards the privacy of his hall.

"The mead came," one of the cousins remarked.

"Aye, and he'll make sure she sups it for a cycle of the moon," another replied. "Then her womb is sure to be ready for the son they desire."

"They alone will be wishing for a son," the first said, his voice low. "For as long as he sires daughters, we can remain in hope that his brother will follow him as thane."

A month passed and the Kingdom of Kent was cloaked in snow. Those villagers who had straightened their backs when the rains ended and the weather became frosty, were once again cowed by dark days and a lack of variety in their food. Hour after hour was spent in gloomy smoke-filled homes until it became an effort to tell a story or sing at the fireside. It was too dark to whittle wood, to sew or darn. The people crawled into bed early, trying their best to sleep the winter away.

The building of the church still caused some interest, giving the people a sense of awe to see it standing high. Before the weather stopped work, they had watched the progress of the sycamore shingles being laid until the roof was almost covered. Now the roof tiles were coated in a sparkling layer of snow, and a great dark hole to the west end was a clear reminder that the work had not been completed as quickly as the thane had hoped.

In Eadlyn's home, she recalled the pleasure given by stories passed on in the form of songs. In Lyminge when Clover and Cym were young, they had shared a home with Todd's mother, known as Elder-Modor. The old woman had enthralled Clover with her stories of the royal family in that village and the building of the Christian church. Eadlyn tried to create the same love of a story told by song in Hilda. Together they began to form a tale about the building of the church in Aldington.

Whereas the holy building still inspired a sense of admiration in most villagers, in the home of Eadric and Felice it caused resentment and a small knot of anger. The young man, always so content with life before the earth quaked and the fort toppled, still allowed feelings of bitterness to ferment in him. Felice, now in the final stages of her pregnancy, ceased to tempt him in their shared bed. She appeared to be brooding on something, and communication between them was no better.

Penton suffered for the cold as he did every winter when the old injury to his leg caused an almost unbearable pain. The ache travelled upwards to his lower back and he shifted his position constantly when sitting or lying. Megan warmed poultices of dried leaves from wild berry plants and placed them on his skin, giving a blessed soothing heat.

The men were finally taken away from the building of the church as snow settled on the roof. On sunny days, it melted a little and water eased its way into the gaps between the stones. A small section of the wall began to suffer for having been hurriedly constructed during the month of rain, at a time when Cenric had pushed the men to work in difficult conditions. No one noticed how the lines of stonework began to bow. They no longer looked at every detail of the building but admired it as a whole. More snow came. The oak beams, huge and heavy, shifted a little under the extra weight.

Cenric could not help but feel a little disappointment when yet again he noted how few of the villagers came for the early morning Mass. "I pray their lack of commitment does not cause offence to our good priest," he said to Udela, as they approached the church and saw the motley collection of men and women huddled under their thickest cloaks. The building was not large enough to hold a quarter of the village, so those who wished to attend would hold back until the thane and his family had taken their places. Most would stand outside while Mass was said.

"In many ways they were more involved when we stood at our wooden cross," Godwin suggested.

"Aye, but a wooden cross does not tell our Lord how we honour him."

"It is so early," Udela pacified her husband. "The people will come to a later Mass, when the sun has risen fully, and they are able to feel a little of its heat."

"Of course, they will!" Cenric was always ready to agree with the comely woman who was fascinated by his church and loving in their bed.

Only three of the cousins braved the cold, so it was just the six of them from the thane's family. The villagers crept in, standing at the back where the melting snow dripped from the open rafters. Cenric and family gathered under the shelter of the roof and imagined themselves to be warmed by the candles on the altar.

Before the service began, Udela looked back at the men and women standing in silence. She took the opportunity to speak with them, knowing it increased the popularity of the thane if his wife were to offer a word of comfort. There might be some small gesture of kindness she could give – some food or herbal medicine that would be welcomed. Godwin went with her, knowing the people well and having a genuine interest in them.

Just as Father Theodore was about to give his opening blessing to the congregation, and Godwin was suggesting the villagers come closer to the altar, there came a sound of movement above them – a great whoosh of sliding snow. As the roof unleashed its load, the top layers of stone in a portion of the wall gave way. The main beam leaning on this wall creaked and fell heavily, smashing down upon a lower part of the stonework. The rest of the wall stood firm, taking the weight of the beam. Godwin pushed Udela back towards the roofless portion of the church and, as he did so, lesser beams fell, bringing with them a shower of sycamore shingles. A scream of pure agony ripped through the building, so chilling that afterwards no one ever remembered the gasps, the cries and the shrieks.

It seemed as if time moved slowly. It was now brighter in the church, highlighting the dust motes, dazzling the congregation. More shingles fell, not all at once, but causing an irregular smashing sound upon the floor. Bodies tentatively moved in the area where the priest had been about to say the Mass, and Father Theodore emerged from beneath the altar. Then it seemed as if, all at once, gasps of shock and horror escaped from the throats of those who saw that, pinioned under an oak beam, was the body of their thane.

Chapter Twenty-Three

The Thane of Aldington was pinned between a roof beam and the sacred altar. The church and the altar – his two great passions. He was alive. Twisting his head a little, Cenric's gaze fell on another of his obsessions: Father Theodore. He closed his eyes. The weight of the beam lying across him was immense, and tiredness overcame him. Perhaps he slept a little. He wasn't sure. The next thing he was aware of was Godwin bellowing to someone that strong men were needed. Udela was there stroking his hair, while whispering words of affection.

Cenric opened his eyes. Prone upon the holy altar slab, it was too much effort to move his head. His view was limited to the end wall of the church, Father Theodore's robes and the blue of Udela's dress. He flexed a hand, then tried to wiggle his feet – there was no feeling in them. *I am a tall man and my feet are a long way away. No wonder I cannot feel them. This beam is heavy. It was the best oak in my woodlands.* He closed his eyes again.

"Your men are here, my lord. Strong men who can lift this beam." There was a sense of joy in Udela's voice, but anguish too. Some shingles fell from the roof and one smacked him on the shoulder. "Can someone come to stop this from happening?" Udela screamed out. "Catch them as they fall! Do anything! They must not land upon the thane."

There was a scuffle of feet, and whispers. Cenric sensed others standing by, ready to stop a sharp stab from a sycamore tile. In the distance, there were deeper voices and above them all was Godwin – his brother, who led the workers in the fields. Now he was instructing them on how to lift the beam. Another voice came: it was the carpenter who had been in charge of building the roof. *He will know how best to shift the oak without causing more damage*, Cenric approved.

"We are going to move the beam." Godwin was standing next to Cenric, but it seemed as if his voice came from far away. "There are six strong men here. Do you understand?"

Cenric gave the slightest of nods. It would take too much effort to speak. He closed his eyes and opened them again. *There is something I must say.* Godwin saw his brother move his lips a little and stood closer.

"What is it, brother?"

"Udela… she… she carries the next thane."

"That is fine news." Godwin forced his voice to sound bright.

"If I die, you must marry her."

Godwin felt his body chill. "You will live to see your son born and your church completed," he told Cenric.

The men shuffled into position and began to take the weight of the beam. Udela stood back, murmuring words to soothe her thane. Godwin also moved away from his brother and watched as the length of oak was eased from his body, then placed on the floor. The men who lifted it stood at a respectful distance, while family members stepped forward.

248

"My lord, the beam has been lifted. Where is the pain? A stretcher will be brought for you." Udela was once more at her husband's side. She reached to touch his cheek.

Cenric heard her words, but they meant nothing to him. They were the sweet sounds of summer birdsong or the movement of a warm breeze through the treetops. He opened his eyes: the light before him was pure white, like the sun shining on snow-capped shingles or thatch. The roof beams had gone. The jagged opening had gone. Above him there was nothing but luminous gold, and he was compelled to move towards it.

Cenric did not hear Udela's wails, or Godwin announcing that the thane had passed to the next world. Perhaps the priest's words flowed with his soul and eased its journey to heaven? The onlookers would never know.

"Is it true you are carrying Cenric's child?" Godwin asked Udela, a week after his brother had been buried in the frozen soil. He stood in the thane's hall while Udela sat holding some sewing on her lap.

"Aye. We hoped for a son." A flash of satisfaction crossed her face before she composed herself.

"You hoped for the future thane," he stated. "Cenric's desires were well known. But he planned to rule the village himself until the child was fully grown. For now, it is I who will act as thane on behalf of your child, or I will take on the role as Cenric's heir. It will make little difference."

"It will make little difference," Udela confirmed. "But if you are to act on behalf of my son then I hope we can be good friends. Would you care for some wine?"

"Nay." Godwin remained standing. "I have to speak with the villagers. They are unsettled. But one other matter is the care of Cenric's daughters. Between us, we must give them some thought."

"I'll remain here in the thane's hall," Udela stated. Or was it a question? Godwin was unsure. He did know that this woman was determined not be pushed aside now she was widow rather than wife.

He was at the door when Udela spoke again. "Will you follow Cenric's dying wish?"

Godwin paused, knowing full well what his brother had asked of him. It haunted him every morning on waking and was the last thing on his mind at night. His first impressions of Udela had been favourable. For a moment, when they first met, he had gazed at her fair hair and slim figure, wishing she had been chosen to be his bride. But in the short time he had known her, Godwin had found Udela to be a foolish woman, pandering to Cenric's needs rather than guiding him down a more sensible path. The attraction to her had been shortlived.

"I'll give it some thought," he replied. "My brother has only been dead for a few days. It is too soon."

Having planned to visit some of the families in the village and assure them that there would be few changes, Godwin was now compelled to take a break from his responsibilities. The covering of snow was light on the ground, so he took the track to the knoll.

Godwin knew this land as well or better than anyone. His strides were long, and he barely noticed how cold it was. He paused on reaching the knoll and looked up, admiring the steep slope created by those men who had laboured to construct a burial site here. Then, feeling for the burrows and areas of loose chalk or flint, he picked his way up the incline. At the top, he stopped and breathed deeply. The air was sharp in his chest. For that moment, the burdens slipped away.

With no snow settling on the saltwater wetlands, Romney Marsh was a patchwork of waterways, sodden marshland and tracts of dry land. Godwin gazed across it, fixing his eyes on the point where land met sky in a grey haze. This was the place to stand and consider his future.

In many ways, it would be easier to run the village without Cenric's influence. *In all ways it will be easier,* the voice in his head screamed, and he slumped a little, knowing it to be true. The men responded well to his leadership. They respected him for being steady, whereas Cenric had been creating erratic plans for as long as Godwin could remember. With the support of his cousins, there was no reason why the land could not be farmed better than ever before. When the baby came, he would pose no threat and there was no one else likely to come forward to claim the settlement as their own to rule. *And if the newborn is a girl, I shall be thane!* Godwin felt no particular pleasure in this. *I only want stability in Aldington.*

He considered the most recent cause of unrest in the village – the removal of the stone from the fort and the building of the church. Had he, Godwin, not stepped in then the crops may well have rotted in the fields. *The*

251

villagers show a pride in the new church, at least they did until it fell. But they would have preferred progress to be slower and that they had not been pressed to toil during the rains and fever. There is conflict here. Godwin frowned thinking of the difficulties suffered: *the wooden church burned down; Eadric Smith married a stranger to Aldington; villagers died, and others left; the rains caused a sinking of spirits.*

While he pondered over the past months, another man joined Godwin on the knoll. He turned to see Eadric and gave a nod of welcome. *You are part of the story of the sorrows Aldington has suffered since the summer. How could you be taken from a good and beautiful woman?*

"I expected to be here alone," Eadric voiced his surprise. "It is a good place to come and think."

"It is," Godwin replied. "I'll happily leave you to have time here alone."

"I wish you well as thane," Eadric said.

"I may not be thane," Godwin told him. "We must await the birth of Cenric's child."

Eadric pondered on the words. It had been suggested amongst the villagers that this must be the case. Had the widow not been carrying a child, Godwin would have been declared thane without hesitation. "Whether you are thane or doing the role on behalf of the child, you will do a good job," he concluded.

"I thank you." Godwin turned his back on the view of the marsh and prepared to descend the knoll. He felt uncomfortable in Eadric's presence, torn between a long-standing respect for the family and contempt for this man's weakness.

252

However, Eadric's next words stopped him. "Your brother died on the Roman altar, and it isn't for me to say, but it seems no good has come to Aldington since it came here. I was involved with stealing, and it *was* stealing, the stone at night." He paused to reflect on his next words. Godwin waited, compelled to hear the other man's thoughts. "It seemed wrong to move a holy stone, and to be involved made me feel as if black clouds were pressing on my shoulders. I shouldn't blame the stone for my wrong-doings but for some reason I do. We had a good wooden church, but it burned to the ground the night the altar was placed there. Then a woman lured me to her, and I was foolish..."

Godwin, who had been waiting for his admission, could not help snapping back with, "There is no excuse for the planting of your seed in a stranger when you had a woman as fine as Clover."

Eadric's eyes met Godwin's for the first time, and he answered, "You are right. I cannot blame the stone for my weakness, yet I do."

"I am glad to hear you admit that."

Eadric heard the disgust in Godwin's voice, and for a moment he wondered why it mattered so much. He continued, "We had the rain and the sickness, and finally the thane died on the stone. This is what I want to ask of you, Godwin of Aldington, please remove this stone from our village and, when you do, I beg you to allow me to be one of the men chosen to help you."

An image of his brother lying on the altar slab flashed before Godwin's eyes. It was a picture which rarely left him. "My brother's church and his wife are foremost in my thoughts," he told Eadric. "Do I pull the church down, or rebuild it in his memory? How do I care

253

for his new wife, her children and his, when I wanted to find a wife of my own?" Having voiced his thoughts to an unlikely confidant, Godwin felt some of the tension ease from his body.

"The church only needs repairing," Eadric replied. "Take the stone back to the fort, then have your masons replace the altar with one of your own design. It will be a truly Christian altar – what made the thane and his priest covet one from pagan times? The church can remain, but that cursed altar is best laid to rest where it was found."

"Why was it not so clear to me?" Godwin asked. "I thank you and apologise for the disgust I felt when I learned you had chosen Felice over Clover. None of us are perfect."

Eadric looked across the marsh and considered this admission. That his family were disappointed in him he had been left in no doubt, but when his actions led him to become noticed by those who ruled the village there was renewed shame. "I preferred Felice for a moment," he admitted. "If I could go back and change things, I would. Felice is gentle and works hard, but she could never replace Clover. It may appear that way, but you don't see the pain in my heart."

"Perhaps I do now," Godwin said. "I hope you find happiness with your wife and child. Now I will leave you to find the peace you sought in coming to the knoll, and I will return to order the immediate removal of the stone from the church. My cousins will give their full support. Unless she gives birth to a son, Udela has little to say in the running of our village." He took his first step down the steep knoll, then continued, "Expect me to seek you

254

out tomorrow, as you will move the stone with me, and I want it done as soon as weather conditions allow."

"I thank you and thank our good Lord that we met here today," Eadric responded. He gazed along the line of the hillside towards the Roman fort and the Sandtun, feeling a peace which had eluded him for so long. Then he recalled Godwin's comment about caring for his brother's wife and felt compelled to say something before their time alone together passed.

"It is nothing to do with me, and wrong to advise you," Eadric called to Godwin's retreating back. He waited until the other man paused and turned to look at him. "You spoke of your brother's widow – I wonder if you feel you have no choice but to offer her marriage?"

Godwin did not respond, but Eadric saw the recognition in his eyes.

"I had to marry the woman who carries my child and forgo the woman I love. This woman, Udela, carries another man's child. Allow her to live in the thane's hall, and offer her your support, but if you have the chance of marrying a woman you love and respect, do not sacrifice yourself to care for a widow alongside the children born to her and your brother."

"I hear your words and I thank you," came the reply. "I shall think carefully about the way ahead."

Godwin returned to the village, his heart feeling lighter than it had done since Cenric's death. Eadric's words had gone right to his heart, and he began to ponder on a matter which he had never dared to consider before.

"…And I want to move the altar stone back to the fort," Godwin concluded.

Father Theodore nodded his acceptance, knowing there was no point in prolonging the matter. His stomach, used to the fine fare previously enjoyed at Thane Cenric's table, grumbled a little. Udela was welcoming enough but absorbed with the children, and he could no longer be sure of a hearty meal in the hall. His thoughts returned to the altar. No doubt the stonemasons would create something far better than the barnacle-encrusted stone, but he felt a bond with the ancient piece of Roman history. After all, it was he who had found it in the humble position of being used as a doorstep.

"Where will you put it in the fort?" the priest asked. "Perhaps in the remains of the chapel?"

"Nay, it will be returned to exactly where it was taken from and it will be as if it were never removed."

"Do you want me to come with you?"

"There is no need," Godwin replied. *The less time spent with the priest, the better. Am I being unfair? My brother chose to dote on him, to feed him as if he were close family and endow him with gifts. Father Theodore asked for nothing. Mayhap he will settle into a humble way of living, as befits his vocation.*

The priest had been in no way neglected. Godwin had spoken to Udela and they had agreed that a woman in the village would be paid to provide him with a pot of vegetables and beans, as well as a small loaf of bread every day apart from Sunday. On that day he would be invited to eat with Udela, Godwin or one of the cousins. Anything else, such as cloth, wood for the fire, herbal medicines and ale, would be given as needed.

256

"Are you happy that the church is safe?" Godwin asked out of courtesy. He had been assured by the carpenters and builders that all was well.

"Aye." The priest's eyes lit up. "The church is safe. All I can do is pray for warmer weather so repairs can take place."

"It will be a fitting memorial to Thane Cenric," Godwin said. "He will be remembered as the man who had the vision for our church."

"He will indeed. God rest his soul."

Two days later, the Roman altar left Aldington without fanfare or sorrow. No one spoke much of its going, although word spread that it was to be replaced with a piece of worked stone. Once admired for its glorious history, it became forever remembered as the place where Thane Cenric met his untimely death. A new altar would mark a fresh beginning, where Aldington would be ruled under the steady hand of Thane Godwin. And if he were not yet truly their thane, that was how the villagers saw him.

Chapter Twenty-Four

Snow lay heavy over the Kingdom of Kent for two cycles of the moon. When it began to thaw, the signs of a new season were to be found in the form of plump buds on fruit trees and tightly furled leaves on ancient oak, beech and ash. The ground was at first hard, then slippery; streams ran full and fast.

Under her swathes of fine woollen clothing, the curve indicating that Cenric's child thrived in Udela's womb were not yet visible. Yet where the metalworkers lived and toiled, Felice's child could wait no longer. It pressed down, sending spasms of pain across her stomach and to her thighs, all through a long night. In the morning, when the sun cast a soft glow in the sky, Eadric went for his mother.

"The baby is coming," was all he said.

"It's too early," Megan replied. "I will go to see Felice later, but it is normal to have some tightening and discomfort in the weeks before birth."

"Nay, Modor. Felice has been in pain all night and when she stood to walk about a little, the waters poured from her."

"I'll be there soon."

Soon Alfreda had been instructed to warm a pot of water and to ask Eadlyn to make their bread for the day. With a bundle of old cloth under her arm, and some herbal remedies in a basket, Megan set off to be at Felice's side throughout the birth. Eadric retreated to his work.

Seeming to be comforted by Megan's presence, Felice bore the pain without fuss. She crouched, paced and clutched at the other woman as her body prepared for the birth. It was late that morning when a baby boy pushed free of his mother's body and into the hands of Megan, while Alfreda supported Felice at the shoulders. At first the child was silent, but a firm slap on his bottom resulted in him gasping for his first breath. Then he cried.

He is large for an early baby. Megan pushed the thought from her mind as she swiftly wiped the child and wrapped him in a piece of clean linen. *Dark too… but we would expect that.* She placed him in his mother's arms, took a knife from her belt, and cut the cord. "Alfreda, can you tie this?" Megan asked. "Then go and tell your brother that he has a son!"

She set about preparing a hot drink of rosemary tea for them all but, before it had cooled, Felice cried out, placing a hand on her stomach.

"It's just the afterbirth," Megan tried to reassure her, but knowing the words meant nothing. *Felice must know of this – she must have a family somewhere and have seen new life come into the world.* The placenta was soon expelled, and Megan was relieved to see it looked complete.

Over the coming weeks, Eadric watched in wonder as Felice strapped their son to her body, then went about her usual tasks. She murmured to the child in words unknown to her husband and fed him from breasts swollen with milk. They named him Chad and

259

together they admired his dark eyes, strong limbs, smooth skin and button nose. Eadric felt a sense of peace and acceptance of his life.

From a distance, Godwin looked on, wondering how Eadric felt to be a father. The two men had shared no more confidences since the time they had met on the knoll, and it was unlikely they would ever speak of personal matters again. They shared a mutual respect for the work each one of them did for the good of the village, and although Godwin could not approve of the hurt Eadric had caused Clover, he came to accept that even the best of men can make mistakes.

Udela was to remain Cenric's widow. Despite his brother's dying wish, Godwin could not bring himself to offer her marriage. To be father to her children and Cenric's was more than could be imagined. "I will be uncle to them all and will you have a comfortable life," he had told Udela. "But I cannot marry you."

She had flirted with him at first, but Godwin's attraction to her had passed within a day of their meeting, and Udela gained nothing from her efforts. "What shall I do?" she had asked him. "How will I spend my days?"

"You will care for the children and visit people in the village to ensure all is well. You have women to prepare your meals and to do the washing, but I am sure you are able to make your own clothes and those for the children."

"And if I seek a new husband?" she asked, her expression coy.

"I suggest you think about that after giving birth to Cenric's child," Godwin said, his tone cool.

Those scenes had taken place some time ago, and now the pair of them lived side by side in an uneasy truce. Until the child was born the following autumn, Udela held a certain power, and Godwin was forced to consult her about village matters of which she knew little but enjoyed giving her opinion.

With the signs of spring evident, Godwin began to plan the work to be undertaken in the fields over the next few weeks. Yet while he spoke of seeds, ploughing and the welfare of the animals, there was something else on his mind. All the time he hoped for dry weather and for the roads to become passable. When conditions were right, Godwin set off for the northern edge of the village to seek Caedmon Messenger. He scanned the area, looking for a familiar shock of white hair and short beard, then spotted a man working on a repair to the thatch roof of his home.

"Hey!" Godwin called, as he neared.

Caedmon raised his hand in recognition and a broad smile passed over his craggy face. He lowered himself to the ground, stepping from a wooden ladder.

"Good morning! I have a message needing to be sent to Lyminge," Godwin told him. "But first, I hope all is well with you and your family?"

"Aye, we are in fine health and thankful to feel a little warmth from the sun. I'd be happy to take a message. I've been a long time in Aldington." Caedmon was a slim man with stocky thighs made for riding long miles delivering messages, occasionally in the form of writing, but more often passed on verbally. Sometimes he carried small packages with a sense of pride to know he was trusted. The messenger had a smile that warmed everyone to him, and if his nose was rather

261

large due to an old injury, it was only he who was bothered by it.

"We have all been confined to our homes for too long," Godwin remarked. "The winter seemed long this year."

"You want me to go to Lyminge again?" Caedmon queried. "For mead?"

"Nay! The last flagon served Cenric well, but this time I want you to go to the village with a message for Clover, daughter of Eadlyn. It must only be heard by her ears."

"You can trust me," Caedmon stated. His eyes, a curious mixture of grey and brown showed no curiosity. Yet there was a story to be told if Godwin, acting Thane of Aldington, wanted a message sent to Clover, the daughter from a family of village craftsmen. When the tale unfolded, as no doubt it would, Caedmon would hold his part of it close to him and say nothing of it.

"I know that."

"Can you go tomorrow, and set off at first light?"

"Aye, I'll do that."

"The message is to ask Clover to meet me by the church in Lyminge at midday on the following day."

"That's easy enough to remember!"

Godwin grinned. "Let me know when you have delivered it."

Always happy to give work to Caedmon Messenger Godwin left, knowing his words to Clover would be delivered both in haste and without causing her undue concern. His next task would not be so easy, and he would do it knowing it was going beyond his role as acting thane.

262

Back in the area of the church and dwellings belonging to the thane's family, Father Theodore was spotted gazing at a pile of wooden shingles on the ground. The priest, believed to be of about forty years, had aged visibly since Cenric's death. Where once he moved about with his back straight and a sense of purpose, now his eyes were wary and skin drawn. As confidant and favourite of the thane, his time had been spent pandering to Cenric's whims while enjoying the luxuries associated in being close to the leading family in the village. Udela, cast in the same mould as her late husband, gave the priest a fair amount of attention but she had her children to care for, so Father Theodore suffered from neglect and a sense of uncertainty for the future. Like Udela, he prayed for her child to be a son, limiting the influence of Godwin and his cousins.

As he came closer, Godwin noticed that the priest's hair had thinned to mere wisps under his hood, and his eyes watered in the weak spring sunlight. *It is not his fault that he has been spoiled by my brother,* Godwin told himself, and not for the first time. *I must think of him as a man of God and not associate him too much with Cenric's foolish plans. He shows a dedication to his prayers and the welfare of our people. I shall insist that the roof of his home is rethatched this summer and ensure he has thick undergarments next winter. And I couldn't help noticing he enjoyed a noggin of good wine at Cenric's table...*

"Good morning, Father Theodore," Godwin said, raising his voice a little. "I trust you are well?"

The priest nodded and, as his cloak moved, Godwin noticed that the cross hanging against his chest was wooden, not the plain gold one bestowed on him by

263

Cenric, nor the prized pendant with the ruby. *He wears a cross more befitting of his place here in Aldington.*

"Father, I want to express how I appreciate all you do for us and to say that you are in my prayers," Godwin began. "Our thane lost his life in the church, and I know you suffer for this as I do. The snow has gone. It gives me hope to see the wall is now repaired, and the roof nearly complete."

"I thank you," Father Theodore responded. "It is God's will, and I will strive to understand his wishes."

"The foundations for a porch are to be dug this week," Godwin announced. "We cannot have another wedding with no porch. My brother didn't know whether to marry outside or inside the church!" He smiled to recall the confusion moments before vows were exchanged.

"We have enough stone," the priest observed.

"Aye, I can't have the men moving stone when there is work to be done on the land. We must be thankful they laboured so well before the snow came." Godwin paused, then turned to the true reason for seeking the priest. "I am not thane, but I act as one, and although I respect my brother's desires in most matters, there is one that lies heavy in my heart. The gold cross with the ruby – it was not his to give. No one knows the history of it, but it belonged to Eadlyn and the children of her first marriage. I would like to return it to them."

Father Theodore stood, his attention seeming to be on the church roof. It appeared that he had heard nothing of Godwin's request, as his eyes roamed the lines of wooden tiles, and the straight ridge where a cross would soon be fixed to the eastern gable end. Finally, he spoke, without turning to face Godwin. "The cross belongs to a bishop or abbot, not a village priest. I am not worthy of it and to have it pressed upon me was wrong. I will gladly give it to you, but you will face the wrath of the widow, Udela. I believe she wants it as her own."

"My request is beyond what I am entitled to ask of you as we wait to learn the sex of her child, but I will face her fury for I believe so deeply that the pendant is not in its rightful place."

Even as Godwin spoke, Father Theodore had moved away and was walking to his humble home. Bending down, he pushed the curtain aside, then stepped through the doorway, returning a moment later with a small leather pouch. "I thank you," he said, offering the package. "I will rest better for being parted from this excessive gift."

Godwin was about to express his thanks and leave, but he now saw Father Theodore as a man who had not been totally spoiled by Cenric's attentions. Preferring this humbled character, he suggested, "Come and eat with me at sundown. I believe there is bacon in the pot."

"I would like that," the priest replied.

In Lyminge, Clover was preparing turnip and onions for the pot. Although it was chilly, she chose to work on the bench outside, rather than in the dark confines of the home. Her days followed much the same pattern as they had in Aldington, albeit with Janna at her side rather than Eadlyn. The long winter meant that she had rarely ventured further than the minster to the west and the leather-making area to the north-east of the settlement. The weather had kept villagers close to home. However, in recent weeks they had been able to roam further afield. Clover had checked on Mildrithe at the first opportunity and reassured herself that all was well. Now spring was here and, if Clover were to be honest with herself, the only pain in her life was the knowledge that Eadric would soon be a father and his life no longer linked with hers in any way.

The turnip was diced, and Clover was about to tip it into the pot, when something caught her attention: a man was walking past the Nailbourne Spring and appeared to be asking for directions. She saw one of the women point, then he raised his arm in thanks before striding away. Clover frowned, now recognising the man as Caedmon Messenger. Her chest tightened. It had been months since she had seen her family, the only news being that they had all survived the sickness. Now the messenger from Aldington was bearing down upon her and she feared the news he brought with him.

The turnip remained on the bench, while Clover stepped forward looking about for Janna, certain she would need her comfort.

"Caedmon! Have you come for me?" Clover's voice sounded small.

"Aye," he flashed a wonderful smile that gave some reassurance. "I don't bring bad news, Clover. Your family are well."

"I thank the Lord for that!" Relief flooded through her body. "It's wonderful to see a face from Aldington, and I will pour you some ale, but if your message is for me and Cym, we must walk together to the leather-making area over there on the hillside." She indicated towards homes and sheds on the cusp of the village.

"Nay, the message does not come from your family. It is for you alone," Caedmon replied. "But I can tell you that I passed Eadlyn in the village two days ago and she looked to be well. Also, I saw Arlo and your younger brother at work recently."

"Come and sit by the fire," Clover offered, gesturing to the open doorway of the home. She picked up the turnip and tipped it in to the pot before reaching for ale. Puzzled, she was both eager to hear whatever Caedmon had to say and nervous of it too.

Caedmon picked up the clay beaker and took a gulp. "The message comes from Godwin of Aldington…"

"Godwin?" The word came out as a squeak. Clover felt herself begin to flush.

"He is asking you to meet him by the church here in Lyminge at midday tomorrow."

"Meet him? But why?"

"There was no more to the message, and it is not for me to pry nor try to make sense of it," Caedmon pointed out. "But your modor's sister is a sensible woman I am sure, and you can speak to her."

"The Thane of Aldington wants to meet me by the church tomorrow!" News of Cenric's death had reached Lyminge, although the details were unclear.

"Nay, Godwin of Aldington wishes to meet you. He is not thane, but we pray that will soon be the case."

"Not thane?"

"Udela is carrying a child."

Clover considered this, understanding Godwin's position. He would be working for the good of the village as always, and willing to do so, but without the authority of thane. What could he want with her?

"Tell me the message again," she asked. "The exact words."

267

"Ask Clover to meet me by the church in Lyminge at midday on the following day."

"That's all?"

Caedmon shrugged his shoulders and grinned. "He asked me to let him know you had received it."

Clover considered this. She looked towards the church, picturing herself standing and waiting, then seeing Godwin approaching. Caedmon then Godwin – two men from Aldington. Reminders of her other life. "I'll meet him," she told the messenger. "Will you eat with us before you return? My family here will be glad to see you."

"Nay, I'll make haste to Aldington," he replied. "My horse is tied up near the minster and will have eaten her fill of fresh grass."

"It's been good to see you," Clover responded. "When you see my family please tell them that all is well with Cym and myself."

"I will do that." Caedmon turned away, lifting his arm in a gesture of farewell.

Chapter Twenty-Five

Godwin dismounted and led his chestnut mare around the minster boundary before tying her to a tree not far from the church. He had timed his journey well for the sun looked to be at its highest point in the sky. His path took him to a promontory in the land and, on reaching the rounded eastern end of the stone church, the whole of Lyminge was spread before him. However, the view went almost unnoticed, for the person so frequently on his mind was walking up the steep slope towards him.

She looked a little slimmer… a little older than he remembered, yet it had only been half a year since they had last met. Her hair was exactly as Godwin remembered: the colour of ripe corn, rippling in waves down her back. Her dress was plain, but fitted well, and he saw the leather belt at her waist had pretty detailing on it. She wore a thick cloak around her shoulders, fastened with a decorative clip, no doubt the work of Arlo Smith. The smile on her face was tentative, and the expression in her eyes wary. *No wonder, she must have no idea what brings me here today*. Godwin – who led the men of Aldington with such confidence – suddenly didn't know what to say… where to begin.

"Good day." Clover spoke first. "Welcome to Lyminge."

"I thank you. My brother would have been envious of this church!" Godwin gestured towards the high stone walls, the round-topped windows high up beneath the eaves, and the curved chancel wall.

"I am sorry to hear about his death," she replied. "It takes some time for news to travel in the winter, but I thought of you and prayed for his soul."

Godwin, who had planned over and over how to greet Clover and express his admiration for her, said nothing in return. He listened to her voice, soft and gentle, wanting her to say more, but she stood waiting for his response. With no words coming to mind, he reached into the small bag hanging from his belt. His fingers wrapped around an object in a piece of cloth and taking it out, he mumbled, "I brought you this."

Clover took the package, then pulled back the covering with her fingertips, her heart pounding. She had never imagined it could be … yet there it was … the precious golden cross. Holding it up, she gazed at the beauty of the craftmanship.

"How?"

"I hope you knew how angry I was when my brother took this from your family? I begged him not to, but he was obsessed with endowing gifts upon Father Theodore."

"I saw you that day." Clover recalled how she had seen Godwin storming away from the village and barely able to exchange a pleasant greeting when he passed her. "I know you tried to help us." She looked at the cross again, running her finger over the dome of the ruby, then frowned and asked, "But why didn't you give it to my modor? It is hers more than mine."

"Because I hoped you would wear it when you are my wife," Godwin blurted out. This was not how the words were meant to be said. Surprise flashed across Clover's face – just for a moment – before she paled. "I'm sorry," he babbled. "This is not how I meant to ask... I planned it differently."

"You are thane, or as good as..." Clover attempted to compose herself while all the time her heart pounded. He was a fine man – she could not deny that Godwin's good looks and friendly manner had not gone unnoticed. Most of the women in the village had expressed their appreciation of him as they worked alongside each other, whether it was foraging for food, washing clothes in the stream or working with yarn in the weaving shed.

"And you are from a family of well-respected craftsmen." His tone was gentle, and he smiled, albeit tentatively. "I've put it badly, Clover, but now you know my wishes. I've got it all wrong because I came without speaking to your modor and bringing the cross as an excuse to see you. The pendant is yours to keep, or return to Eadlyn, and in no way binds you to me."

"I thank you." She paused and allowed herself to gaze into his brown eyes. There was no doubting the sincerity in his words. Godwin of Aldington was a man who could be trusted without doubt. But for her, Clover, to marry into the thane's family, and for him possibly to become thane... it was... it was the stuff of girlish whispers rather than true life. "You cannot marry someone like me. You must marry someone of your own kind."

"But I should. Aldington doesn't need land or money. I need a sensible woman. My brother married

271

well with Otha, but his second wife is as foolish as he was."

Clover said nothing, as his words ran through her mind.

"I don't know how else to express my feelings, other than to say I have admired you for a long time and whenever Cenric said I should take a wife, I was looking for someone like you. I could not find her. When I heard that you weren't marrying Eadric, I could not believe he had been so foolish. It seemed as if I felt a part of your pain, but it also made me wonder if…" Godwin paused. A fresh anguish assaulted him: a new thought – something not considered earlier. "You must have someone else? I'm sorry… What a fool to think you could be here all winter and not meet a man worthy of you. Keep the cross – you will, won't you? And forgive me…"

"There is no one!" Now Clover smiled, almost laughed, as she reassured him. "I needed time to heal, and my life here has been good, but I have no husband in mind."

"Then let us go and see your brother. Let's show him the cross, and I will give you time to think about this. Caedmon Messenger longs to ride about the countryside, so I will ask him to return in a week and ask if I am welcome to come to see you again?"

"Aye, any face from Aldington is welcome. I'll be glad to see Caedmon knowing that he doesn't bring bad news. Let us go to find Cym," she gestured towards the leather-making area across the shallow valley. "Afterwards, will you eat with us? It will be simple food though. Otherwise, I am sure our thane would be pleased to have you at his table…"

"I will gladly eat with you!" Godwin declared. "I would not ask you to be my wife, then insult you by refusing your food. It would be an honour to meet your mother's sister and her family!"

"We'll show them the cross, but not mention the other matter?" Clover questioned.

"Aye, you can tell them when you are ready," he agreed.

They walked through the village, feeling comfortable in each other's company. There was plenty to speak about, and Clover learned that Felice's son had been born. The news did not bring the pain she expected. Time and distance had been a great healer.

Cym was pleased to see Godwin. He pored over the pendant cross, grateful to have it returned and eager for news of Aldington. Bertana looked on, concerned that the visitor may be intent on luring Cym away from her. She was none the wiser when Godwin left, but felt a relief in watching him depart. Back in the heart of the village, the meal served by Janna was appreciated, and talk flowed easily around the table. Not a word was uttered about Godwin's intentions towards Clover, yet Janna sensed his reasons for being there and approved.

While walking Godwin back to his horse, Clover tried to picture herself being back in Aldington, *if* she were to return. "Before we marry – if we were to marry – I would be with my family and she would be there – Felice and her child. Their child."

"Nay, before we marry, you would stay with Udela or my cousins. Or in my home and I will be elsewhere. It will be your choice," Godwin replied. "Unless you prefer to be with your family?"

273

"I don't know. It's hard to see how it would be," she admitted.

"I understand." Godwin's admiration of Clover had been growing long before she left for Lyminge. She needed time to consider his offer and her feelings for him.

As they parted, he moved to offer his open arms. They found themselves clinging to each other, drawing strength and warmth. This unexpected show of affection and comfort in each other was reassuring to them both. Godwin mounted his horse and left Lyminge with his heart a great deal lighter than it had been on his arrival.

Clover held her secret close all through the afternoon. She moved about her usual tasks while her mind flitted from the wonder of marrying a man admired throughout Aldington and beyond, to confusion as to how she would fit in amongst his family. In the weaving shed, she picked up the wrong yarn, gazed out of the open doorway, and the gossip from other women went unheard.

"Godwin of Aldington must think a great deal of you to bring the cross all this way," Janna began, as they returned to their home not far from the Nailbourne.

"Aye, our family are well thought of," Clover answered.

"I am thinking of you, not the family."

"I don't know what he can be thinking..." Clover could hold back no longer. "Godwin has asked me to marry him. Why me when I have no land or wealth of any kind? He could choose any woman of good birth."

"Why you?" Janna repeated, not as surprised by the news as Clover might have expected. "You said it yourself, Arlo and Penton are respected craftsmen. Men to be relied upon. And you… you are both good-natured and beautiful. We have heard many tales of his foolish brother over the years, and now Godwin waits to see if he is to be thane or is to continue to rule the village on behalf of his brother's son. As thane, life will be easier: he will finally be able to make decisions without answering to anyone. If the child is a boy, its modor will have a certain power. Godwin's future is uncertain."

"But what does this have to do with me?"

"Godwin needs a wife who is respected by him and the villagers. Now more than ever he must choose carefully."

"The villagers will not want me as wife of the thane, or whatever he may be," Clover objected.

"There is only one person who will have difficulty with it," Janna observed. "Ask yourself these questions: do you want to marry Godwin, and can you return to live near Eadric?"

"I can answer neither of them!" Clover replied, despair in her voice. "How could I have known this was to happen?"

They had reached the home now, but Janna turned to retrace their steps. "This is not the place to think about it. There is no quiet to be found amongst the people and animals here. Fetch the cross and let's go to sit by your faeder's grave. I believe there you will find the answers you seek."

"I have it here." Clover patted the pouch hanging from her belt. She turned with Janna and together they followed a winding path past homes, workplaces and animal pens. They crossed the Nailbourne by one of the many wooden plank bridges and ascended the rise in the land leading to the church. Todd's grave was to the south of the place of worship, not far from where the woodland began. From the depths of the woods, there were the muffled sounds of men sawing and chopping wood. These brought comfort without intruding on Clover's thoughts. They mingled with the distant calls from one person to another in the village centre, but the short distance from all this gave her mind a chance to settle and reflect.

Janna merely stood but said nothing more. She had already voiced her thoughts and would wait until her niece was ready to speak. The pendant cross was withdrawn from the pouch and lay in the palm of Clover's hand. The mystery of how Todd Leatherman had come to have this valuable piece of jewellery with him when he died had been explored fully by Eadlyn and shared with her children over the years. Arlo and Cousin Fremund had told of them and Todd seeing monks roaming Romney Marsh at night when the men visited the Sandtun as traders with their families. It seemed likely that the monks had something to hide and that Todd had discovered a treasure mislaid by the holy men. Were there more treasures secreted on the marsh, Eadlyn, Arlo and Fremund had wondered? They could do no more than conclude that the golden cross had once belonged to a holy man, while being thankful it had come to them.

Having deliberated in silence for a short time, Clover questioned, "How can I know? I can think of no man better than Godwin. He is fair, hardworking and admired by everyone, but he is of good birth and I am not." In her mind, she saw the collection of larger homes, including the thane's hall and Godwin's home, set apart from the rest of the village. There were women cooking for the members of the family, men bringing in the wood for their fires and girls washing their clothes at the stream. She visualised the colourful clothes the thane's family wore, with embroidered hems, and cloaks held in place by ornate pins or brooches.

"Do you trust him?" Janna asked, cutting into Clover's thoughts.

"Of course."

"Then trust that he makes the right choice in knowing you can be his wife."

There was a moment of silence in which Clover considered this, before realising that Janna had not been told of the other news: "Eadric's child has been born. A boy."

"Earlier than expected?"

"Aye, an early baby." Clover pondered on this, wondering if the child was weak or sickly, but Godwin had said all was well.

"How do you feel when you think of Eadric with his child?"

"I feel nothing!" Clover replied and, as these words flew from her, she felt released from all attachment to Eadric. "I wish them well and can only be thankful that his weakness showed before we married." Now Clover looked down on her father's grave and murmured a few words to him, then stepped away. "I must go to see Mildrithe!" she announced.

Janna followed. She had thought only of Clover since Godwin's unexpected arrival earlier, and now reflected on her own loss. Her sister's daughter was particularly dear to her and to have her return to Lyminge brought great happiness. It would not be long before she lost her to marriage, but Janna had assumed Clover would remain nearby. Yet reflecting on this, she knew that no other man had sparked any interest from her niece. Godwin's arrival brought a glow alongside the confusion – this could only lead to aunt and niece being separated. *But she will not be far from me, and I could not imagine a finer man for her. He ate at our table as if he were no better than us, and that is to be admired.*

Bringing herself back to the present, Janna responded, "Aye, go to see Mildrithe. She'll advise you, and when Caedmon Messenger returns you will be sure of your answer. It is too late to walk there and back today. Tomorrow is soon enough."

Mildrithe took the golden cross in her twisted hand and stepped into a place where a beam of sunlight had found a path through the canopy of newly unfurled leaves. She moved her hand to and fro, taking in the details of the cross, from its outstretched arms to the decorative scrolls and the smooth red ruby at the centre. "I've seen this many times," she murmured.

"Seen it?" Clover queried.

"In my mind." Mildrithe was mesmerised by the pendant and spoke as if in a dreamlike trance. "Eadlyn had lost it. It wasn't her fault: it was hidden in the bedding and the old woman, Elder-Modor, emptied the mattresses then put the hay in the goats' pen for bedding. She searched but it couldn't be found."

"She told me," Clover whispered.

"But there was something else on your modor's mind – she had been offered marriage and was unsure."

"Unsure of Arlo?" Clover queried.

"Nay! Not Arlo. There was another showing an interest in her, and she wanted to do the best for you and Cym. I told her there were two paths open to her, and neither was wrong. But I saw this cross…" Mildrithe paused, holding it a little higher towards the light. "…I saw this cross and I told her when she claimed it again, her future would be clear."

"Arlo found the cross!" Clover exclaimed.

"Arlo was her future," Mildrithe confirmed. "Now you have the cross… There is no choice for you. Your path is clear. Just as Arlo found the cross for Eadlyn, it has now been gifted to you by someone. He is important and his interest in you comes as a surprise. But his love is true, and you can trust him."

"I can trust him."

"Wait…" Mildrithe closed her eyes for a moment before speaking again. "You will wear this cross and it will not be hidden! You wore it, but under your dress. Now it will be there for all to see if you wish it to be."

"I thank you," Clover said. "You have put my mind at ease. I will be leaving Lyminge soon, but when I visit, I will always remember you and come to spend time here."

"I knew you wouldn't stay," Mildrithe stated, while leading Clover towards the fire where the infusion of rosemary and camomile brewed. "Take a drink with me, before you leave."

Chapter Twenty-Six

I should have gone with him… I should have waited outside the village for Caedmon to give me her answer. Godwin could settle to nothing on the day when the messenger returned to Lyminge to seek Clover's response. He strode about the fields, talking to the men but recalling nothing. Outside his home, he chopped logs in an attempt to quash his frustrations, and, seated alone, drank broth without tasting it. Finally, Godwin could wait no longer; he mounted his horse, then set off in the direction of Sellindge. It was on passing through that village and heading uphill along narrow lanes that Caedmon was seen approaching. The men both raised their arms in joyful recognition.

It wasn't the messenger's business to ask the meaning of the communication between the lovely young woman he had known for many years and the well-respected man who worked as thane for their village. However, it was not hard to surmise from the blush on Clover's cheeks, or the eagerness of Godwin to learn of her answer, that somehow a tenderness was forming between them.

"You are welcome at Lyminge tomorrow!" Caedmon announced, flashing a grin. "And if you want an opinion, my lord, I would say you are very welcome!"

"I thank you!" Godwin replied. "Did she look well?"

"Very well!" Caedmon responded.

They returned to Aldington together, riding in single file along the tracks. As they parted, Caedmon ventured to ask: "Will I be returning to Lyminge for some mead from the monks soon?"

Godwin, knowing full well the meaning behind the words, lost his usual confidence and found himself stammering, "I hope so, my friend."

A week later, and the talk of Clover's return flew about the village from one home to another, from the workplace to the stream, to those who tended the animals in their pens or worked in the fields. Eadlyn and Arlo knew of it of course, but they held the news close to them, both delighted and bemused. Nothing had been said of Clover coming home to anyone other than the family circle. When she was sighted walking down the gentle hillside into the village, leading a pretty bay mare, and with Godwin walking beside her, word spread swiftly.

"If she's just visiting, why come with the thane and his horseman?"

"He's not the thane…"

"As good as."

"She was riding a horse, you know."

"Not riding it exactly, but she had been. I'm sure of it."

"And I'd say she was here to stay, because there were bags and all-sorts."

"Did she look well?"

"Aye, and *he* looked as proud as anything."

"She's not with her family."

"Nay, he's taken her to where *they* live – the homes of Godwin, his cousins and the widow."

Clover stood with Godwin at the entrance to his home. He had opened the double doors, despite there being a chill in the air, so it could be seen at its best. It was much larger than those of her family here in Aldington or in Lyminge. The plank walls were straight and tall; the floor was wooden, and no doubt insulated with straw. A curtain of thick cloth separated the sleeping area, and a fire blazed on a hearth of stone in the centre of the main room. Clover's eyes smarted a little as the woodsmoke wafted towards her, but she noted a hole in the roof and a raised cover to protect the opening from the wind.

There was a long table, with benches running on either side. Sturdy shelves held jars, baskets and sacks of grain, as well as plates and cooking pans. Clover became aware of a woman working at a side table; she turned, nodded to them both, muttered something about needing to fetch water and sidled out.

Now they were alone for the first time and Godwin turned to face Clover. He took her hands in his and, leaning forward, kissed her gently on the lips. Her response was encouraging, and they wrapped their arms around each other's waists, kissing deeply. Then, with one hand in hers, Godwin pulled back the curtains to the sleeping area, revealing two beds behind further drapes of material, as well as trunks and pegs for storing clothes.

"I'll stay with my cousin," he said. "This trunk is empty and..." he indicated another, "...that one has wool and linen in it. You can choose what you want, and have new dresses made whenever you like. It is still so cold in the evenings. The fur-lined cape on the peg over there is yours – a gift from me."

Clover stepped forward to feel the thickness of the wool and fur. This was a luxury previously only dreamt of. "I'll wear it every day!" she exclaimed. "Although I wouldn't want to spoil it."

"I'm glad you like it. And here…" Godwin pushed aside a panel on the chest. "… is a secret compartment. Put your cross in there if you're not wearing it." He pulled out a small box and placed it in her open palm. "Your modor gave me this!"

Clover smiled to see the special container where they had always placed the pendant. It had been kept by the family when Cenric had taken the cross. "Modor said it would come back to us," she reflected, thinking of Eadlyn's words when they lost the pendant to Father Theodore.

"I am so glad it did."

They moved back into the main living area, leaving the curtains open to allow the warmth from the fire to seep through.

"I have a cousin who would happily stay here with you," Godwin suggested. "But I wondered about your sister, or Alfreda?"

"Or both?" Clover pictured them sitting by the fire, sharing confidences. "There's a week until the wedding, so I can spend time with one and then the other?"

"Is there anything else you need?" he asked, looking around the home. "It suits me well, but if you want to change anything…" Godwin thought of Udela whose pregnancy was pronounced. "Of course, if the child… Cenric's child… is a girl, we will move to the thane's hall."

"I can't imagine living in the thane's hall, or that there could be anything else I should need," Clover replied. She reached over to run her fingers across a tapestry hanging from one of the walls. "I would like to make one of these after we marry." She considered it for a moment, then continued, "With pictures of the barley you grow, and the berries in the hedgerows? Or the new church? I am not sure I would be skilled at it, but I could try?"

Godwin was at the fire, stirring the broth which was rich with chicken. "I like that idea," he answered. "Speak to my cousin Alodie. She would guide you." He ladled the thick liquid into bowls. "Usually, Aedre would be here to serve our meals, but she has left us to be alone, which suits me well. Shall we eat, and then you can go to visit your family?"

Soon they were seated at the table, at ease in each other's company, despite this being the first meal they had shared. Clover insisted that she washed the wooden dishes in the tub of water before they parted, with her leaving the area where the lords of the village lived to seek out her family, and he to speak with Father Theodore about the forthcoming wedding.

Clover took the carefully folded material and allowed it to unfurl in front of her. It was soft beneath her hands, but it was the colour which filled her with wonder. She saw her feelings echoed on the faces of her mother, Hilda and Alfreda. The linen was a muted red, a shade worn only by those who could afford such a luxury.

"It's beautiful," Alfreda whispered.

284

"Someone made it for you?" Hilda questioned.

"Aye, it was Godwin's cousin and her daughter," Clover replied, turning the dress so they could see the shape. It would fall to above her knees, while a plain underdress of a natural colour would show beneath, its hem reaching her ankles. "Now we must embroider the hem and cuffs. There are only four days until the wedding."

"Sweeting, we will rush at it, then each part of the pattern will be different from the next," Eadlyn worried.

"I know, but we must do some of it together, as we always do. I have the thread." Clover handed the dress to Eadlyn, then reached for a basket. "Dark red, and blue. Gold!"

Alfreda and Hilda pored over the basket: picking up the balls of yarn, moving to the open doorway and turning them about in the light.

"We could choose a pattern, and if there is a woman who could…" Alfreda began to suggest, then wavered at the thought of asking someone to do their stitching for them.

"I find it strange too," Clover said, understanding her cousin's confusion. "But we need deep bands of embroidery and the four of us would struggle to work on the same piece of clothing at once. This dress must look impressive. Modor is right – we cannot finish it without help."

"When you marry, you must look as if you are worthy of him," Eadlyn observed. "The villagers will expect it."

"They should also know that there was little time to create a dress," Alfreda suggested. "And Godwin will see only your beauty, not the pattern on the hem."

285

"There will be some people who will be looking at the detail," Eadlyn reminded them. "If we were to make a design, each of us will be a part of Clover's dress, but the work can be done by a woman who can work both swiftly and with a neat hand."

They took a scrap of linen and Alfreda, who they decided could stitch the neatest line, created a straight hem. Then the four of them worked to design a pattern of loops and lines, using the red, blue and gold coloured threads.

Over the next couple of days, this was recreated by the woman who usually sewed for the thane and his family. It was inspected several times a day with Hilda often asking to be allowed to sew a simple line or loop using the beautiful threads, which were as enthralling as jewels to her young mind. Finally, the dress was once again held up to be admired, then placed on a hook beside the fur-lined cloak, ready to be worn on the day of the wedding.

Those days of preparation for the wedding passed swiftly. On a warm spring day, Godwin and Clover of Aldington married in the porch of the completed church, with all the villagers forming a semi-circle around them. As man and wife, they entered the holy building, then stood before Father Theodore while he celebrated Nuptial Mass. The new altar was cut from Kentish ragstone and placed square on supports of the same stone. Its lines were clean, without a trace of seawater crustaceans. The only items to adorn it were candle holders and a cross crafted by Penton and Arlo Smith. Light from the chancel window offered a soft glow to the grey stone. Over time, stories of the completed church

286

and freshly-hewn altar would include those 7th-century Saxons who gathered that day. Father Theodore took quiet pleasure in the church over which he now presided.

An intricate brooch of bronze fastened Clover's soft woollen scarf at the shoulder. She could have worn gold and garnets, or a pin inlaid with black and white glass, both items which had belonged to Godwin's mother. Her choice of ornament showed her affection for Arlo who had been as a father to her, and now stood behind her with Eadlyn at his side. The pendant cross rested on the bodice of her dress, keeping the memory of Todd close.

No service in the church had ever been so well attended. Inside it was crammed beyond a comfortable capacity. Clover could not allow Janna and her family to remain outside, and Bertana had forced her way in with Alwin at her heels. Cym stood close to his sister, and somehow all five of the quiet girl cousins from Lyminge squeezed in. Of the close family, only Eadric remained outside, his excuse being that the baby Chad might cause a disturbance. Godwin's family of cousins filled the last of the space, and Udela watched from the side with a simmering resentment that Cenric's wish she should marry Godwin had been disregarded.

From his position by the altar, Father Theodore said Mass. Much as she tried to focus on the words flowing in Latin, it seemed as if they poured past Clover. All thoughts were of the implausible happenings of the last few weeks. Looking down at the embroidered cuffs on her dress, she recalled the hours spent planning and watching the stitching progress. Then she turned and her gaze met Alfreda's. Clover smiled to think of the

287

evenings when they had sat by the fireside sharing memories. Godwin's hand sought hers and she looked up at him, her eyes alight with joy. He too followed none of the priest's holy offerings, thinking only of his future happiness with his wife.

"*Ite, missa est*, Go, the Mass is ended." The priest indicated it was time for the congregation to leave. They murmured their thanks, first shifting towards the church walls, allowing Godwin and Clover to pass through, before following.

Outside, villagers remained gathered by the church, each one of them fond of Clover and admiring of the man they hoped would continue to lead their village for many years to come. The air was still, with the aroma of roasting hogs drifting from the fires near the thane's hall and Godwin's home. Both family and villagers breathed deeply, their mouths watering in anticipation of the feast to come.

Pausing at the doorway, even Godwin was overwhelmed to see such a crowd gathered. "Come my good people, there will be wine and meat." This was followed by a great cheer. Like those in the church, these onlookers moved aside to allow him and his new wife a clear path.

While the meat was cut from the roasting hogs, and the people of Aldington held out their cups to be filled with the good wine, Godwin and Clover moved amongst them, lingering to speak to each person, whether poor and ragged or a skilled craftsperson of some standing. Villagers ate from shared platters, licking the meat juices from fingers. Sweet offerings of honey, apples and nuts were consumed with relish, as the last of the winter food stores were used. When their hunger was

288

satisfied, they sang and danced, only leaving the celebrations when the sun moved behind the clouds gathered to the west, the sky darkened and the air chilled.

"I thank you all. May God bless you, each and every one of you!" Godwin bellowed. Clover stood at his side, happy but exhausted. The last of the revellers took this as a sign that it was time for them to leave, and the close family members retreated to the fireside in the home of the newlyweds. Now they relaxed and spoke with ease, resting on cushioned benches.

On the table there was a slim clay bottle and two drinking horns. The contents had not yet been sipped, but Clover eyed it every so often, knowing that this special mead from the monks at Lyminge would play a significant part in their day. One by one, those who joined them in their celebrations retreated to their own homes. It was only when Godwin stood to reach for the mead that the three cousins remaining glanced at one another realising it was time to leave, their stomachs full of food and heads befuddled by copious amounts of wine. They were now alone as Clover accepted her honeyed drink, tasting it and allowing its rich flavours to fill her senses. She watched Godwin sip his, then they kissed, sharing the flavour, before moving to the bedchamber.

Chapter Twenty-Seven
Midsummer 694 AD

Udela basked in the certainty that the future thane thrived in her womb. Her body was now cumbersome, and the heat of the summer did not suit her. Yet she was determined all would be well after the birth. As the summer advanced, and food became more varied, Udela ate for both herself and the growing child; her limbs became soft with an excess of white flesh. She usually made little effort to take herself or the children beyond the comforts of their home or the church, but suddenly there came a longing to paddle in the stream and cool her aching feet. The baby shifted within her, pressing outwards, giving the widow an excuse to sit for a little longer before hauling herself to a standing position.

Settled on a bench, with her back against the planks of the thane's hall, Udela could watch the lives of those who lived nearby. Cenric's cousins were friendly enough, continuing to care for his daughters – an arrangement which was welcomed. Her sons enjoyed the company of other children and roamed the nearby countryside, only returning for food. Sometimes she sat with Cenric's little girls, teaching them how to sew or weave, but mostly the exertion was too great for her.

While she rested, Udela watched Godwin and Clover leave their home. She scowled to see him place a hand on Clover's arm. It was a small gesture but showed the obvious affection between them. Hoping to snare Godwin for herself, she had been furious when the announcement came that he was to take a bride and secretly sneered at his choice. *All I was due is now showered on her – the daughter of a leathermaker!* There was a superiority in Udela's manner towards Clover, but in time, and to her confusion, it became noticeable that it was only she who scoffed at Godwin's choice of wife. The cousins, those of good birth from local settlements, and the villagers, all accepted her.

The baby would be born in the early autumn. Until then Udela had to endure the position of being widow of the thane. Having lived in Aldington for such a short time before Cenric's death, she had not gained the respect or devotion she would have liked to achieve. Once she was mother to the child-thane, Godwin would have to step back a little and defer to her wishes. Perhaps then he would regret his rejection of her as his wife?

Pregnancy had made her lazy, so Udela was still resting when Godwin and Clover returned, he leading a pair of horses. *Now she shows her humble birth. The daughter of a village craftsman will never be a natural horsewoman.* They collected a small sack of provisions from their home, and Godwin helped his wife mount her bay mare. She swung herself up with ease and sat, her back straight, further infuriating the bitter woman observing the scene. The couple, now on horseback, turned their mounts towards the Roman road and left with a wave to Udela.

Looking down at her swollen ankles, Udela again felt the need to bathe them in the chilly waters of the stream. She heaved herself up, then set off at a slow pace, leaving the homes and church behind her. There were women collecting water and washing clothes at the stream. They perched on stony banks or amongst the grass, looking towards the pregnant woman as she approached. There were tentative smiles offered, but no one felt as if they knew Udela well enough to strike up a conversation.

Preferring to be alone, she decided to walk a little further to where the stream was a mere trickle. *The women will not gather here, but it is perfect for my needs.* So Udela lumbered on, past the copse, to the narrow ribbon of fast-flowing water. Perched on a grassy hillock, she eased her feet from leather shoes and dipped her toes in, giving a small gasp. Time passed; with the warm sun on her body and the cool water flowing past her feet, Udela relaxed, allowing her thoughts to drift to happier and easier times.

There was no need to consider cooking a meal for the children, or if the fire needed replenishing with logs. There were women to do these tasks, so Udela's time was her own. She lifted her feet from the stream and stretched out on the grass. The sounds of a gentle breeze in the trees and the water trickling over rocks were soothing. In time, her eyes closed.

When she woke, there was an immediate sensation of danger. Disorientated and feeling slightly queasy, Udela pulled herself up into a sitting position. Then she noticed the cause of her unease – a man was standing just a short distance away. He stepped back, turned, and walked in the direction of the knoll. Udela's heart tightened and the baby pressed outwards. She had seen his features only for a moment but knew the man to be a stranger to the area, and possibly from foreign lands. His skin was a little darker and his eyes almost black, topped with thick brows. As he strode away, she watched, and her heart began to settle. The stranger was gone, but Udela was left feeling confused. Something told her that his presence in Aldington was not welcome, but she could not begin to know of the troubles that would be created in his wake.

Godwin of Aldington and his wife, Clover, drew their horses to a halt on the edge of the escarpment. There was a backdrop of trees behind them and one of their horsemen waited in the shade, giving them the privacy they needed. The day was warm, and the darkest times of winter almost forgotten. Clover's dress was a finely-woven linen of mid-blue, with subtle embroidery at the hem and cuffs. Her hair, much admired by her husband, was caught back at the nape of her neck in a ribbon of material, and lightly covered in a linen to match her dress. The pendant cross rested on the gentle swell of her breasts.

"This is where it began," she said.

Below them the toppled Roman fort basked in the full sun. The stone it offered to local people would be used to build their churches, and later homes, for many centuries to come. A couple of men roamed about the walls, while sheep huddled in the cool shadows.

"We'll walk down." Godwin dismounted, then reached out to steady Clover as she dropped to the ground. He looked towards the man waiting nearby and gave a nod to indicate that he should take the horses.

Hand in hand, they navigated the steep hillside track, taking small steps and pausing to gaze at the view across Romney Marsh. The colours of the reed-lined creeks, the patches of dry grassland and water-logged bogs were muted by the midday sun. Feathery reed-tops were turning brown and seedheads were ripe. To their left, the *Oceanus Britannicus* shimmered a pale blue, while the horizon melded into sky. Straight ahead, the distant shingle banks at a place called Dungeness were nothing but an indistinct grey haze.

"Our salt pans," Godwin said, pointing to water-filled squares dotted about the marsh.

Clover squeezed his hand. Over the past months she had learned more about how his family – her family – managed the land and understood his quiet pride in it. The week before, they had ridden past the knoll and down the track to the marsh, then followed the paths on top of embankments until they reached a set of nine salt pans grouped around a slight rise in the land. They stayed for a short time, sitting on a bank as the tide crept in and filled the ponds.

Now they neared the ruins and Clover recalled that night a year ago when the ground had shuddered. "We were sitting over there." She waved her hand in the direction of the upper walls of the fort.

"I thank God you were above the walls." Godwin's voice was thick with emotion. The thought of not having Clover in his life was already unbearable.

The track was dusty, bearing the marks of much traffic since the fort had toppled. They took their time, cautious of potholes and taking care not to slip on the patches of loose stone. It led directly to the fort but, once within the walls, they stepped over long ragged grass and rubble before approaching the main gateway.

"There!" Godwin pointed to a slab of stone with weeds growing in the cracks between it and the adjoining stonework. "It looks as if it has been there for centuries."

294

Clover fell to her knees, running her fingertips over the Roman altar. She explored the lines of the ancient letters cut in the stone and crusty barnacles clustered around the edges. "It seems right that it should be here. Is it wrong to say that about a holy stone?"

"Nay. When it came to Aldington we had nothing but trouble. Now it is returned, blessings come to us and those in the village."

Turning from the stone and rising to her feet, Clover grinned and asked, "What blessings?"

Pulling her close, Godwin replied, "I found myself a wife!" He kissed her soundly, loving the way she responded. "My brother was always telling me I should."

"Thane Cenric was right!" Clover entwined her fingers through his and pulled him with her as she stepped away from the Roman altar. "Let's go to find my family and look at the goods for sale on the beach."

They continued down the escarpment, taking small steps over the rough ground which appeared to have buckled in places since the earth had trembled the previous year. A spring broke through the hillside tempting them to its chilled waters. With cupped hands, Godwin and Clover drank deeply before stepping into the shadows of ancient trees lining the edge of Romney Marsh. Here they turned direction and took a narrow track.

As they walked, the sounds of activity filtered through the trees. They were approaching the Sandtun where a temporary camp was set up on an area of raised land. The sandy area was surrounded on one side by the hills, on the other by marshland and on the third by a sheltered tidal lagoon. Here on the beach, men from Francia would meet and trade with those from the Kingdom of Kent.

The track ended as it reached a wider stony road coming straight down the hillside. Known as the Shipway, this was the route taken by traders who made the annual trek to the Sandtun. Both steep and, at times, treacherous, it had been the only road available when the families had been forced to flee their deluged camp.

Still partly concealed by the trees, Godwin and Clover watched as a man scurried past on the Shipway. His head was bowed, and his back slightly hunched as if wanting to pass by unnoticed. "One of the men from Francia," Clover commented. His features were darker than most of the local men, and he looked to neither side, seeming not to have seen them.

"There is something I find strange about him," Godwin remarked.

Clover frowned, trusting his instincts. "Perchance they are all nervous, remembering what happened last year?" she suggested.

"I don't know, but I will look out for him on the beach."

The Shipway ended no sooner than they reached it, and a wide plank bridge crossed a creek along which the incoming tide rushed. Then the view opened out and the Sandtun was before them. The day's trading had started: carts were on the shallow beach offering displays of items crafted by local men from leather, wood, metal and clay; in return the men from Francia gave coins or their own goods. The atmosphere was light-hearted, with banter flowing in the form of gestures, as well as words foreign to men from both countries. Amongst the carts, and on the shoreline, children roamed. Women gathered shellfish or bartered with local fishermen; they tended fires where beach met rough ground on which tents were pitched, and cradled jugs of water collected from hillside streams.

Clover grinned to see it all. "It is just as it always was!" she exclaimed. "Nothing has changed!"

"Where first?" asked Godwin, loving the expression of enthusiasm on her face.

"I can see Arlo over there," Clover waved in the direction of the beach, "and Eadric." The young man was nothing but a cousin to her now, and slowly an easy affection was returning. "But we must find Modor."

"And see what she has planned for our midday meal?" Godwin suggested.

"It has to be fish!" Clover pulled at his hand, then bounded onto the rough sandy ground across which a rough track trailed.

"Where does this track go?" Godwin asked.

"Here and there across the marsh," Clover told him. "To the sea, I think, and other paths will lead off it. No doubt we could reach your salt pans if we tried."

"I shouldn't want to try!" he responded. Then he spotted Eadlyn. "There she is!"

An hour later, having explored the camp, Godwin's mind was filled with stories of Clover's childhood. They had visited every craftsman selling his wares on the beach and bought several items. Finally, they were relaxing at the fireside eating fried fish and flatbreads.

"Look what I've missed out on every year!" Godwin remarked.

297

"It is as if nothing has changed at all," Eadlyn replied. "We didn't know if the tidal wave would have changed the Sandtun."

"Or even if the men from Francia would come," Hilda added. "But it is the same as always."

When they had eaten and washed their wooden plates in the shallow waters of the lagoon, it was time for Godwin and Clover to leave. They crossed the bridge, under which the tidal waters were retreating, and stepped into the shadows of the tree-lined Shipway.

The road was steep and, before reaching the crossroads at the top, Clover urged Godwin to slip through a gap in the trees in search of a spring on the open hillside. Once refreshed by the water, they turned to look at the view of the beach and Sandtun. Both fascinated by the tiny figures below, and the boats moving away from the shore, they scanned the area for those they knew.

"Look!" Clover pulled at Godwin's arm, and pointed to an area away from the main body of activity. "Down there, a figure..."

A woman scurried along by the edge of the lagoon, following a track which would eventually lead to the sea. Her headscarf had fallen back, revealing long dark hair. There was something familiar about her, something that Clover could not yet make sense of. While they watched, a man approached from the opposite direction. He held his arms out to the woman and they embraced. They continued along the shoreline of the lagoon, moving swiftly side by side.

"It's the man we saw earlier, and... and *Felice*?" Godwin exclaimed. "But I didn't see her here?"

"She stayed at home." Clover felt her body chill despite the heat of the sun. "You are right. It is Felice. Does she have the baby?"

"I don't know. I don't think so."

They watched in silence as one of the boats moved away from the Sandtun beach and headed towards the narrow opening between the open sea and the tidal inlet. It veered towards the shore and an anchor was lowered.

"They're going in the water!" Clover whispered. "There is no child. She's left him behind."

Hand in hand, Godwin and Clover looked on as the figures waded through the shallows, then swam to the waiting boat. There was nothing more to say. Over the past year, Felice had taken shelter and food for herself and the baby. Now she was leaving for her homeland. The man, presumably Thomasse, who had been with her in the copse, had taken his chances and found another way to survive. Yet he had returned for her. Whether this had been planned between the pair of them from the moment Felice pressed herself on Eadric, those left behind in Aldington would never understand. Even her husband, as yet none the wiser, would not learn the truth. Neither would Eadric know if the child, born early, carried any Saxon blood in his veins.

"She has gone." Godwin's voice was low, as if filled with emotion. "Eadric has been freed but cannot be with you to whom he belonged."

"Nay," Clover turned to face her husband, taking both his hands in hers. "Life does not follow the patterns we believe it will. My faeder died up there by the Shipway Crossroads, and so our lives followed a

299

different path. Felice came and caused great harm, but in turn I found you. I cannot regret her coming and the hurt she caused. We can feel sad – sad for Eadric, and for the child left behind – but never sorry that events since the earth tremor led to our happiness." She raised her face and kissed Godwin briefly, "Eadric is nothing more than my cousin. You are my husband." She moved one of his hands and placed it on her flat stomach. "I believe I am with child. Our child."

"That's wonderful!" A grin spilled over his face, and his brown eyes danced. "Will our child be the future thane? We cannot know until Udela's son or daughter is born. God will choose our paths, and I will trust we are wise enough to listen to Him."

Turning their backs to the coast, they retraced their steps up the hillside, pausing at the top of the Shipway. Here Clover's father had met his death and, in doing so, a chain of events had been set in motion. They led to her being back on the hilltop that day, with Godwin of Aldington at her side, and the pendant cross nestled amongst the folds of her dress.

The End

Many Centuries Later...

In 1850, Mr C. Roach Smith led a team who excavated the ruins of the Roman fort *Portus Lemanis*, also known as Stutfall Castle. A 2nd-century limestone altar was found, covered in barnacles and reused as a gate platform. The inscription on it shows a dedication to Neptune, Roman God of the Sea, by high-ranking officer, Aufidius Pantera, a commander of the British fleet in circa 33 AD. The presence of barnacles suggests the altar was once placed in a previous fort closer to the shore and had been in the sea for some time. Other evidence to indicate there was an earlier fort nearby includes tiles bearing the stamp of the British Fleet *Classis Britannica*. This stamp was no longer used at the time the current fort was constructed. It appears the altar, tiles, and most likely other stone, was reused in a later fort built further up the hill.

Portus Lemanis was built in about 270 AD and abandoned by the 4th-century. The ruins can still be seen on the hillside today but have slipped from their original positions. Could this be due to an earthquake, as suggested in the book *Hythe Haven* by Duncan Forbes, or merely due to the fort being sited on an escarpment? The altar is now in The British Museum.

About the Author

Romney Marsh writer, Emma Batten, loves to combine her interest in local history with creative writing. It is important to her that historical details are accurate in order to give readers an authentic insight into life on Romney Marsh. She enjoys giving author talks about her journey as a writer, planning unique writing workshops and meeting her local readers.

The Sacred Stone is Emma's ninth novel.

Her first, *A Place Called Hope*, is set in the 16th century and tells the story of the lives of two young women living through the decline of the remote settlement of Hope on Romney Marsh.

Her second novel, *Secrets of the Shingle* is a mystery set on the wild, windswept wastes of the Dungeness peninsula in the 19ᵗʰ century and seen through the eyes of a naive young teacher.

Her third, *What the Monk Didn't See,* is the story of New Romney and the 1287 storm which changed the fortunes of the town forever.

But First Maintain the Wall is set in Georgian Dymchurch. Harry is passing through the village when the seawall breaches and events force him to stay. As an outsider, he struggles to be accepted and a tentative friendship is forged with a young woman who seeks answers to her past.

Stranger on the Point, a sequel to *Secrets of the Shingle,* is the story of a young woman's quest to fulfil her worth as the shadows of WW1 live on. Set in Dungeness and Ashford. This is followed by *The Artist's Gift set* during WW2.

Inspired by the pub sign for Botolphs Bridge Inn, *The Pendant Cross* introduces West Hythe and Lyminge in Anglo-Saxon times.

Still Shining Bright, a prequel to *Secrets of the Shingle*, again features Dungeness and Ashford. Cora and her daughter are brought ashore by lifeboat. With no home or possessions, they rely on the kindness of strangers and Cora must use her wit to survive.

For more details take a look at Emma's website:
www.emmabattenauthor.com